# The
# *Young Widow*

## HOLLI IRVINE

H I BOOKS

TORONTO

## Dedication

*For Michael, my best friend, and my daughters, Amanda and Lauren,*
*who encourage me to be my very best and entrust me with their hearts.*

# ACKNOWLEDGEMENTS

I owe a debt of gratitude to the Markham Village Writers, group coordinator, Donna Marrin  who encouraged me to write and believe in myself. I want to also credit my proofreaders: Denis Farbstein and my husband Michael Irvine who read this final draft multiple times. And to Sheila Horne, the quintessential beta reader who critiqued this manuscript  through its many growth spurts. Thank you from the bottom of my heart.  And to Joanne Rusnell, what would I have done without you?

Special thanks to Bryan Irvine, always on call to help me out of a computer jam, and to my editor, Caroline Kaiser, whose insightful suggestions have enriched my writing and inspired me to continue to hone my craft.

Book design by: Scarlett Rugers Design, 2016, scarlettrugers.com

Lastly, I want to acknowledge the love and support of  family and friends.

# TABLE OF CONTENTS

# Friday, February 19, 2002
## Toronto, Canada

Dry-eyed, slumped against the railing, I stared up the staircase. Men in dark suits carried Joe toward me. If I hadn't known better, I'd have thought they were ambulance attendants carrying a patient on a stretcher. But the black plastic bag, zipped to the neck . . . well, that was a sure giveaway. They paused at the bottom, waiting to see if I wanted another look. I turned my eyes to the star pattern of frost etched onto the window.

On one of the kitchen island stools I reminisced staring out at the frozen white backyard. On my wedding day, Sylvia, the optimist, had shared her dire predictions: "You're making the biggest mistake of your life, marrying an old man." But to me, Joe wasn't an old man. He was an irresistible, athletic, well-groomed, successful man of culture and fine taste. I jumped into the role of princess and revelled in it. How was I to know that terminal brain cancer waited in the wings? Joe's age was unimportant. Sylvia couldn't get that into her fucking head.

I laid my cheek on the cool granite counter. The tray was there, with Joe's blood pressure cuff, his thermometer, and prescribed medications. The only ones missing were the new bottles, which he'd acquired on a return trip to Norway. I'd left them where I'd found them, on the counter of the upstairs bathroom.

"Mrs. Sax?" the attendant said. "Are you all right?" He rushed over to me, found a glass, and ran the tap until he had a cold cup of water to offer me.

"I'm fine, I'm fine," I said, my hand up in the air to ward off more coddling.

I had epilepsy but hadn't had a full-blown convulsion since around the time of Joe's diagnosis. Sure, I was woozy, but waking up next to a dead man would make anyone woozy.

# CHAPTER 1

## JOAN

### Tuesday, March 19, 2002

### Toronto, Ontario

Ian and Rebecca thought they'd convinced me to go for counselling, but it was actually the appeal of getting sleeping pills. I wanted to escape, to be alone and cry. I sat in the comfortable waiting room and scanned an article written by Dr. Martin. The magazine's picture of her showed a young woman, but not so young that I distrusted her experience.

"Why don't you tell me why you're here, Joan," she said.

"Well," I began. I fidgeted with my bag, not wanting to put it on the floor but not wanting to flaunt the Chanel logo either. So I held it on my lap, my hands covering the label. "That's the referral in front of you, isn't it? My husband died of brain cancer." I paused. "What do the kids say today? Life sucks." I sounded angry and stopped myself from saying more. I thought I was far beyond the "denial" and "anger" stages and my tone surprised even me.

Dr. Martin's lips moved as she read over her notes. "This happened, what, a month ago?"

"I'm sorry?" I said. "This sofa is pretty comfortable for a very modern one, isn't it?"

"Nonsense," she said, "that sofa's hard as a rock." More relaxed, both of us laughed.

I moved my bag onto the carpet and rubbed my hand over the quilted black leather. "You probably know this." I twirled my loose wedding band. "Joe passed in February, last month. Important events in my life always seem to happen in the month of February." I moved my bangs out of my eyes and shifted forward to the edge of the seat. "I have two step-kids, Ian and Rebecca, who go to university in London. London Ontario, that is."

"And?" she asked.

"And lucky for me, they're good kids. It could be a lot worse. They seem to be adjusting well."

"Do any kids adjust well to losing their father too soon?"

I nodded, thinking I'd said a stupid thing. What was I doing here? The soft rain pinged against the window pane, distracting me. "I'm sorry, did you say something?"

"I asked if you'd mentioned everyone?"

"Everyone but Sylvia," I answered. "Sylvia Sax is my bitter, vitriolic mother who's only happy when everyone else is miserable. Of course there was a father—very briefly. He was gone before I was born, leaving my mother with two daughters to care for." I paused, realizing I'd provided more information than intended. I glanced at her and placed my hands on my knees. My elbows were so straight, I thought they might break.

Her eyes lifted as if there were something fascinating on the stuccoed ceiling.

I focused on relaxing my posture. "It feels like I'm handling it fine, but I know it'd be natural to be depressed."

"You just mentioned two daughters. Is your sister older or younger?" Dr. Martin said, ignoring my last statement.

I picked at invisible lint on my sweater. Outside, the slanting sheets of rain obliterated the other side of the street. I couldn't find anything to focus on.

"Esther's my twin, but she was diagnosed with early-onset Alzheimer's. She lived with me for a while but has been institutionalized for many years now. She doesn't recognize me anymore, so she's not a big part of my life." I pulled my open black cardigan closer together in the centre. I stared at my hands and hid my bitten fingernails.

Dr. Martin took her pencil and began to write. While she faced her desk, I looked around the room. There were no family photos, although I'd noticed she wore a wedding band. Her own signed paintings and her credentials were the only things that reflected her interests. She had rights to privacy that her patients didn't. "I like your art," I said to her back.

"Thank you," she said, turning around. "I did them at OCA, the Ontario College of Art as it was called then, here in the city. I was passionate about watercolours when I was very young."

I smiled. "You're still very young."

"Well, of course." Dr. Martin blushed like a young girl. "Another time we'll talk about your interests, but it's important we address your worries now—what keeps you awake at night."

I tried to relax back into the sofa, its hardness thwarting me. It felt cold to the touch. "Humph. I don't know where to begin." I placed an elbow against the sofa's high arm and held my chin in my hand. My head felt heavy.

"Describe your feelings."

"Helpless and powerless. When I have trouble sleeping, I get up and pace the house, looking at photographs." The rain had reduced the snow to grey slush. "I've lost my appetite, can't concentrate on my reading, and prefer being alone to anything else." My eyes welled up. My chin quivered, and I took the tissues she offered as my nose ran, mucous mixing with the tears. I squeezed my eyes shut. Dr. Martin moved the tissue box across the coffee table. I blew my nose and drew the tissue along the underside of each eye.

"What are you thinking?" she said.

"It's funny." I took a big breath. "A year ago I would've said my great loves are Joe, food, reading, and lastly, being with friends. None of that matters to me anymore."

In the silence I bit the rough part of my index finger cuticle with my teeth. Then I continued explaining. "I refuse invitations to go out, and I feel guilty about it. Thank God for call display." I laughed and knew it didn't sound like me.

"Guilty? Why?"

I had to think. "I guess it's because it's hard to be rude to people who are trying to be kind. Why can't they let me be sad?" I pushed my bangs away.

"Ah, I see." She jotted a few notes down. Facing me again, she took the water jug from the coffee table between us and poured herself a glass. She motioned to it to ask if I wanted one. I shook my head. "My main role is to be a sounding board for you, not to give you ideas or solutions to your problems. Your friends may not allow you to do this, but you know it's okay to embrace the grief, the sadness." Her pencil beat rhythmically against her armrest. She swivelled, placed the pencil alongside her notebook on her desk, and turned back to give me her full attention. "Now tell me about Joe," she said, leaning forward.

I sighed. I'd realized it wasn't Joe per se that I wanted to talk about. I wanted to talk about me. I confided that I was somewhat afraid of being single and growing old alone.

"You know, I was single unti I was forty, so I can handle the finances and the household maintenance. And if I find myself out of my league, I know where to get help." I clasped my hands together and leaned forward. "But Dr. Martin, I don't think I'm the confident woman I was before my identity got so wrapped up in being Joe's wife. I think that's why I'm here."

"Ah." She tapped her fingertips together. "I can see you're a well-educated woman. Tell me Joan, where did you go to university?"

"I attended University of Toronto for my bachelor of arts degree, a long time ago, it seems."

"That means you've studied the humanities. You know what a social being man is. You've got friends and interests. Don't worry, the boat will right itself, Joan."

I didn't come to be pacified like a child. My face reddened. "Really? 'Don't worry'" I knew my voice lacked respect and conveyed condescension. I began rolling my hands over one another and paced a well worn circle in her carpet. What had happened to being my sounding board?

"Your interests will take you somewhere, and it won't involve loneliness," Dr. Martin said.

How dare she trivialize my concerns! Without bothering to hide it, I glanced at my watch. Almost fifteen minutes to go. I sat down on her low, awful couch. The rain had stopped, leaving behind dark angry patches on a canvas of flat grey, which reflected my mood perfectly.

"I'm going to give you some homework, all right? Before I see you next week, I want you to invite a friend out to have dinner. Will you do that?" Dr. Martin asked.

I nodded, having no intention of doing any such thing. She hadn't even come close to discovering that I'd known Joe was suicidal, had supported his idea to end his life before the cancer took him, and was, in fact, complicit in his plan. I poured myself some water and wondered if there were limits to doctor-patient privilege.

"Joan, describe your nightmares. That was a point stressed on the referral." Looking at me as I spoke, she swivelled her chair, making me dizzy.

I'd invented nightmares to obtain a prescription for sleeping pills. Dr. Martin questioned me, digging with a toothbrush like an archaeologist scraping away the surface to get at what was buried below. We watched one another as I led her to unearth the truth. Her expression of joyful discovery was comical.

"Truth is, I don't sleep well, and I don't remember my dreams. I just know I can't get back to sleep," I said. I rubbed my eyes and wondered if my mascara was now streaked down my cheek. I blurted out the truth. "Joe had a plan—and I knew about it."

"What?" She drew her brows together, leaned forward and said, "What are you talking about?"

I sat up taller. "I can't share any details, but I want you to understand I wasn't traumatized by any protracted period of suffering. I knew his end would come long before the average five-year survival rate that doctors quote, but the timing was Joe's decision. If anything, I felt bad to have been left out at the last minute."

Dr. Martin shook her head. "I'm lost. I'm having trouble wrapping my head around this new information." She exhaled loudly and poured herself some water. "How were you left out if you knew of his plan?"

"I knew Joe had medication to end his life, but I'd thought he'd tell me the night he decided to take them. Only it didn't happen that way." It was my turn to pour some water. I held the glass with both hands to still my trembling. "I also feel somewhat guilty."

"Just somewhat guilty?" she asked, clasping her hands together and resting them on her knees.

I kept my face expressionless. I'd shared enough.

"All right then." Dr. Marin looked at the pocket watch clock that sat on a miniature easel on her desk. "I have one more question, well two actually."

I inhaled deeply, practising the three-part ujjayi breathing I'd mastered in yoga. In through the nose, out through the teeth.

"Who helped care for Esther when she lived in a private home? And who was there to arrange her move to residential care when that became necessary—you or Sylvia?"

I paused, inhaling and sucking in my cheeks. "Esther had me to rely on. If, God forbid, that's my fate also, I'll have no one." I quietly closed the door behind me while that sunk in for both of us.

# CHAPTER 2

## RACHEL

### *Wednesday, January 1, 2003*

### *New York, New York*

Times Square, the day after New Year's, was a deserted mess. The view out the condo window was usually awesome, but not today. It wasn't just bad, like seeing dirty slush on a mid-winter day, but there were tumbleweeds of littered garbage: chip bags, pop cans, crumpled cigarette packages, and other stuff lining the gutter and swirling across the plaza. By comparison, my place looked tidy.

I leaned against the arm of the sofa while pulling on my runners. The gym would be operating on holiday hours, so I'd better get my ass in gear. I began throwing everything I saw off the shag rug in search of my cell. It took forever to find it, hidden as it was under my crumpled sequined red dress.

"Frieda, hi." I waited while she cleared the frog in her throat. "No, no classes today, but we could still do an hour or so on the machines and then have a light bite. I'm dressed and nearly ready." I put the phone on speaker, laid it on the sofa, and chose a light winter coat from the closet.

"Tell me what the holiday hours are again," she said.

"Ten to two, so, like, chop-chop. Get those lazy bones out of bed."

I heard her yawn and imagined her stretching like a cat. "I'm your closest friend, right? Your weight is perfect—you know that, right? So I don't understand your obsession with exercising every day." Frieda had begun with a compliment but went on to criticize— so social worker-like and so Frieda.

"As a matter of fact, Rach . . . people ask me all the time if you're anorexic." There was a long pause. I could hear her breathing, waiting for me to say something.

"Well, how do you answer them?" I paused. "Do you tell them I actually love to exercise, to show off my discipline and strength? You of all people should know that. And . . ." I grabbed the phone, carried it into the washroom, and rested it on the edge of the sink. "And I function best with regular routines." I flushed after a quick pee and rinsed my hands under the running water. "I wanna get going. You coming or not?"

I found a hair elastic in the vanity drawer and tied my hair into a loose ponytail. Finally, I picked up the phone, switched speaker mode off, and grabbed my keys. I held the cell under my chin while I locked my door.

"Rach?" I heard her say. "Why don't you skip the gym and we'll see a movie this afternoon."

"I'm in the elevator, already en route, and not dressed nicely enough for a movie." I pulled out a lipstick and applied it carefully in the elevator mirror. "I could meet you in two hours if you want, or will Bob be expecting you by then?"

"Good news," Frieda said. "Bob's gone to help his parents this weekend."

By the time the elevator arrived at the parking level, we'd agreed to meet at my favourite pizzeria, Queen Margherita's. I dug in my purse and pulled out my wallet.

Frieda said, "There's a good chick flick playing at the theatre beside Queen Margherita's. I'll find out the time, and we'll make a whole night of it." Her enthusiasm told me she was more awake, more alert now. I knew Frieda loved popcorn and a movie on the big screen as much as I loved a good sweat and exercise in a smelly gym. Sadly, the cash in my wallet wouldn't quite do it. Oh well, she would spot me the movie cash if I paid for my own dinner. *Comme toujours.*

When the elevator arrived at the parking level, I knew I had to go back up. I flew back into my unit, found the colourful brochure, and got back into the elevator before anyone had pushed the button and caused the elevator to move from my floor. I wanted to share the Royal Caribbean brochure with Frieda. Avoiding that single supplement would sure be a help, financially.

# CHAPTER 3

## *JOAN*

## *Friday, January 31, 2003*

## *Toronto, Canada*

The snow returned. Sylvia paced the room.

"Look, I'm going on this cruise whether you like it or not," I said. "It's been almost a year." I tucked a shawl into the suitcase.

"You're not ready. The headstone was just laid. It's too soon to take a holiday." Sylvia shook her head, underscoring her disapproval. "You can't escape this," she went on. "You're a widow here, and you'll be a widow in Cozumel or wherever it is you're going. And what about your sister? Who will visit Esther?"

"You could visit Esther, that's who. I think you've taken the easy way out and have abandoned her."

Sylvia's nostrils flared as she recoiled from the accusation. "You know, it's your voice that calms her. It's because you're a twin. And she panics when she sees me. She gets this frightened look and moves high on her bed, hugging her knees and burying her head." Sylvia sat down on the blanket box at the end of my bed. "I just upset her. Sorry, but that's a fact." She smoothed her hair and finger-combed her bangs. "You and I are very similar. We've both been abandoned, but we're survivors with obligations to other people."

"Stop right there," I said. "No, our situations are not the same." I threw the shoe I'd been holding against the wall. "Your spouse left of his own accord, on his schedule, and without discussion."

Sylvia's hands moved to her hips. She narrowed her gaze. "My point exactly," she said. "Joe left by choice too. And he didn't even confide in you. The cancer didn't actually kill him—he died by his own hand." She moved to sit at the side of my bed, next to the open suitcase.

I bit my lip. It wasn't fair. I didn't trust her.

"Joe abandoned you, just like your father abandoned us." She smiled smugly.

I wanted to hit her. "My father didn't abandon us—he abandoned you!" I shouted. "I wasn't even born yet." I breathed through my nose. My heart pounded. I walked over to the chest of drawers and picked up my wedding portrait. I'd had nothing to do with my father's leaving, but I was involved with Joe's premature departure. I knew what I'd done; my complicity in the planning stage was illegal. At least in Canada. But who would charge me? Besides, although I'd known of Joe's intention, I hadn't assisted him—he had gone alone to his end.

I sat on the bed and sobbed. Sylvia came over, placed an arm cautiously around my shoulder, and told me to get hold of myself.

"Joan, you had a seizure just a month ago," she said. "You know what happens when you're stressed." I shrugged her arm off, got up, and wrapped the picture in a T-shirt before putting it into the bag on the bed. "Joan, listen to me. I'm your mother. Subconsciously, something's bothering you. It's a bad time to be taking a trip." Sylvia walked to where I stood. I kneeled on the carpet runner and stretched my hand along the closet floor, searching for but finding only one white summer sandal. My fingers curled around a forgotten but unmistakably familiar item, my favourite lens. I pulled out my long lens, the Canon 70-200mm IS. There were grey dust bunnies clinging to it. I sat back on my heels, running my hand over it.

"Taking up your photography again might give you a new purpose," Sylvia said.

That was my thought exactly, but I wouldn't give her the pleasure of thinking we agreed on something for once. I searched until I found the match for my shoe and took it, my beloved lens, and my favourite camera and placed everything on the bed. I added all my finds to my suitcase and zipped it up.

"My neurologist upped my meds after that last episode, and I'm stable. When I stopped working I stopped taking pictures, which was wrong. I can change that now."

"No, no, no," she said. "You can't go back to work. It's too soon. You're a big shot among your social circle now, and—"

"Oh Sylvia, stop. Can't you see I've stopped caring about what other people think anymore?" I said.

Sylvia moaned. Her hand rose to the side of her head as if she were warding off a headache.

"It's all right. I don't expect you to understand." I kept my eyes on my feet as I lugged the heavy suitcase off the bed and down the stairs.

# CHAPTER 4

## JOAN

### Saturday, February 1, 2003
### Day 1, aboard the Liberty

It was a three-hour flight from Toronto to Miami. The expected temperature change was welcome, except it was a little hotter and more humid than I liked. I pressed up against a column of marble inside the Miami Cruise Terminal. If only I could trade my internal heat for its coolness. In our travels, Joe used to make fun of me every time I took up a position pressing some body part of mine against cold stone.

The weather and the dysfunctional air conditioning seemed to be conspiring against me. I was starting off my holiday not sure it was such a great idea. My empty stomach growled. The disorganized long line in front of the registration desk did nothing to improve my mood. I scanned the crowd. I saw many well-dressed older couples, a handful of single men, and a few clusters of women travelling in twos or fours.

I felt self-conscious travelling without Joe. Considering he'd been twenty years older than me, I should have been the one telling him to rest while I did things like stand in long lines; instead it was the other way around. I'd waited my whole life to meet someone as perfect as Joe was. I blinked away the tears and dug in my bag until I found something to blow my nose with. This often made a honking noise that Joe and I had laughed about. I sneaked a peek around to see if anyone had noticed.

A heavy hand shoved me and I stumbled forward. I dropped the crumpled tissue. "Oh." Surprised, I faced the big man behind me who stood towering over me.

"Your turn," he said, waving me on with a shooing motion. He kicked the tissue I'd dropped on the floor.

At the registration desk, I handed my Set Sail Pass to a clerk named Jorge.

"Welcome, Mrs. Sax. Is this your first time sailing with us?" he asked. My voice cracked. I didn't even get to answer before Jorge continued, working on autopilot. He searched as fast as his fingers could pedal through his box of alphabetized envelopes. "Here's your package: your stateroom key card, a map of the ship, and a Cruise Control program." He waved this last item and explained the obvious. "This lists the scheduled activities and entertainment all over the ship and it changes daily. Every evening a new one will be delivered to your stateroom." As if he were sharing a secret, he leaned over the counter and whispered, "It'll be on your pillow with a little chocolate." The face he made suggested I should be excited.

I felt like being a bitch. I had to stop myself from telling him I was allergic to chocolate. I pursed my lips but tried to smile pleasantly. I was so predictably polite, so typically Canadian.

"Before you go, I need to see your Visa and passport to double-check the information we have on file," Jorge said. "Is this the credit card you want to use for extra charges to your account?"

I nodded. Satisfied that all was in order, he tapped the bundle of papers on the counter and passed them over. "I hope this will be the first of many happy voyages aboard the *Liberty*," he said.

A man about my age, around fifty, was holding the elevator door. My smile turned genuine before I averted my eyes and stared at the blue carpet. Slim and attractive, he reminded me of a famous actor who played an American POW-turned-CIA agent in a television series. I chanced another look to see if I was right. His red hair was military short, and he dressed in khakis like a man in uniform. Look-alike or movie star?

"Excuse me. Excuse us," a pear-shaped older man said as he and his wife moved between the red-headed man and me. I pulled my carry-on in and rolled it into the corner behind me.

The red-headed man continued holding the door while an Asian couple squished inside. His green eyes, flecked with gold, latched onto mine. He smiled. Embarrassed, I realized he'd caught me staring at him. I shifted my gaze back to the carpet. Out of the corner of my eye, I caught the toothy smile of the petite Asian woman. Her long dark hair, streaked with grey, fell over one shoulder in a thick braid. Her husband was unusually tall for an Asian man. Like the handsome redhead, the Asian man had compelling eyes. I decided right then to meet him and ask if I could take a few shots of him. An idea for a new series of mature multi cultural head shots jumped into my head, and I felt excited about where I could go with this week's opportunity. The Asian man stared straight ahead as he wound his mechanical watch.

I felt overdressed in my linen suit, LV scarf draped around my neck, and Chanel handbag. If I'd still been working as a photographer at the magazine, I'd have dressed differently. Maybe I'd go back to work, get a new wardrobe, and explore new things. No. I wasn't ready for any big changes.

The redhead cleared his throat. I wanted to talk but felt speechless. Standing behind a camera was easier than talking over it or without it. I sighed loudly and looked down. Today's date had been slipped into a special slot in the carpet of the elevator flooring.

As the tenth-floor indicator lit up, I stepped forward and reached back to grab my hand luggage. Instead, I found myself groping a muscled thigh. I heard a man's laugh. Red-faced, I took off at a fast clip, dragging my bag behind me. My cheeks felt flushed. The bell continued to ring in the elevator. Six, maybe seven, doors down the hall, I came to stateroom 1010. As I swiped my key card, I noticed the handsome redhead had followed me but was stopping two doors away, on the side closer to the elevator. The elevator bell continued dinging. Confused, I looked back to see a small foot stubbornly blocking the elevator door. The Asian woman was watching, grinning.

Once inside my cabin, I leaned against the door and took several deep breaths before I moved to look around my accommodations.

The tiny bathroom was a disappointment. Joe would have had to turn sideways to close the folding door of the tiny fibreglass shower stall. I flopped down on a really comfortable queen-sized bed, pleased to find the feather pillows were perfect.

There were two envelopes on the bedside table. One, a formal welcome letter, bore the stamped signature of Royal Caribbean's president. I relaxed and punched the pillow to provide more support under my head. I took my time opening the other letter, postmarked a week ago from Toronto. I braced myself, anticipating the ill will it carried. Holding it above my head, I read it.

> *"My dearest Joan,*
> *What did you expect, marrying a man twenty years your senior? Clearly he was unstable as well as cowardly. Sadly, you're worse off now. When you foolishly decided to marry Joe, you had just turned forty; you were trim, had no visible wrinkles, and were considered beautiful. You could have had anyone. Now you're past your prime, as the saying goes. Hate to say I told you so.*
> *Your mother, xo, Sylvia"*

I sat up, swung my legs over the side of the bed, and began ripping her note into as many tiny pieces as I could. I could barely hold all the little bits in my hands. I let them fall into the plastic bag inside the waste basket. Then I carried it out to the balcony.

I pushed aside the overcrowded arrangement of furniture on the balcony and leaned over the railing, turning the bag inside out. Little fragments of paper floated in the air and fluttered down into the ocean. I swung the inverted bag and let all reminders of Sylvia scatter like confetti. It filled like a wind sock about to be carried far way.

"Stop! What the hell do you think you're doing?"

The shout scared me. I knew instinctively where and who it was coming from. My head jerked over to the right, where I met blazing green eyes. The man's head was surrounded by a halo of red.

The wind blew his hair and muffled his voice. "Plastic! Do you know what plastic does to sea life?" he yelled.

Almost separate from myself, I saw my body, my thin frame, normally fluid and graceful, begin to contort. It started with jerky movements from my extended right arm. My Gumby legs lost strength and strained to support my weight. I know from the descriptions of onlookers on previous occasions what happens next: my upper torso sways, and my legs collapse under me. Once down, one or both arms thrash on the hard surface. While I've often awoken on the ground with bruises on my hips shoulders and elbows, the only movement I recall actually seeing is the first one, when the fingers of my right hand cramp and point spasmodically overhead.

# CHAPTER 5

## JOAN

### Sunday, February 2, 2003

### Day 2, aboard the Liberty

One swollen tongue. A few blood blisters inside my mouth. A little piece of skin hanging from the inside my right cheek. Lower lip puffy, bitten in the corner.

There were two people outside on my balcony. The female must have been the ship's nurse, although she didn't look like any nurse I'd ever seen before. In spite of the white lab coat, she wore exceptionally high-heeled shoes, white platform sneakers to be specific. Her short platinum hair lent a sophisticated Parisian glamour to her elongated frame. As we said in the business, she was all legs.

"Ah, you're up," she said, coming into the room. "Open your mouth." She stuck a digital thermometer under my tongue. She picked up my arm and turned it to look at the bruising on the underside. She neglected to introduce herself or ask how I was feeling. I noticed the name tag on the gaping pocket her stethoscope hung from. The name was Ellen.

The man, my red-headed neighbour, moved closer. "I think the bruising's the worst of it— nothing's broken."

"Open the balcony door, will you? I want to smell the sea air," I said. The white cotton drapes blew inward, and I realized it was cool out. I hugged the coverlet to my chest and stole a peek underneath to confirm I was still fully dressed. I asked the redhead how long I'd been asleep.

The nurse answered for him. "About fifteen hours, according to Sam, your neighbour here," she said. "Your temperature is fine. You've had a seizure." So officious. This wasn't my first rodeo. Hadn't they seen it?

My back was to her. I held up the wrist with the MedicAlert bracelet.

"Yes, we saw that." She gazed at her clipboard notes. "Sam reported the accident around three thirty yesterday afternoon. Said he'd seen you smack your forehead on the railing during your seizure." Her voice lacked emotion. "Head wounds tend to bleed a lot, so it's lucky he noticed you." Her fingers slowly grazed my forehead. "Funny, seizure victims usually hit the back of their heads, risking skull fractures or concussions." Her touch was so soft, lingering, like she'd momentarily forgotten what she was doing.

Automatically, I reached up to feel the size of the bandage at my hairline. A clump of matted blood stuck to my hair beside the gauze. It covered the forehead and hairline above my right eye.

"Sorry about that big gauze bandage. We had to shave a good amount of your hair for an effective adhesive butterfly to hold. You should be able to remove the gauze the day after tomorrow. And don't try to wash your hair before then."

I thanked them both and rolled over, hoping they'd get the message. My voice sounded garbled. I pictured Marlon Brando with a mouth fill of cotton. I wondered if it was my tongue or my face that was swollen.

Where was Joe? I needed him. He'd have taken control and said, "Joanie's had a hard time of things. Let's leave her alone to rest now. I'll take care of her from now on." But I was on my own, for the first time.

"Tell me how you're feeling," the nurse said. "What's the frequency of your seizures?" She picked up a chart and began adding a few details.

"Is this necessary now? I'm fine."

I soon realized I'd get them out sooner if I answered their questions. It was a liability issue for the ship. "Okay, I get it," I said, "but before I answer any more questions, tell me why *you're* here?" I said, looking directly at the neighbour who'd played Good Samaritan.

The nurse sat at the edge of my bed and used her knuckles to touch my forehead. Her fingertips then swept my bangs aside, and she placed her hand on my forehead as if she wanted to know if I had a fever.

"I'm Sam Hoffman." He stepped around the bed to stand beside Ellen, who continued to stroke my forehead. I wanted to tell her I didn't have a fever, but more pressing than that, I wanted to know about the strange man who'd been allowed in my room.

"It wasn't your name I wanted. Who are you, and why are you here?" I asked.

"Well, first I want to apologize for scaring you like that. I feel somewhat responsible for all this." He pulled at his chin as if he were stroking a little goatee but his chin was smooth as a baby's bottom. "I know you're tired, but you've been sleeping a really long time. I think it'd be a good idea if we got you up and made sure you weren't hurt anywhere else."

"That's enough." I slapped the sheets on either side of me. "You, particularly, should leave—now." I pointed to the door.

"Wait," Sam said.

He looked for Ellen to say something. Her hand gesture said, "By all means, you go straight ahead."

"I'm an MD," Sam said, "and since I was the one who reported the accident—"

I fell back into the cushions and closed my eyes, wishing them gone, hoping they'd give up and leave me alone.

"Can I give you a guided tour of our beautiful floating hotel?" Sam said. "It's a little early for sunshine, but we could have breakfast together and then go for a walk."

Out of the corner of my eye, I spied Ellen with one arm stuck inside my closet door.

"What the hell are you doing, going through my things?"

"Just seeing if you'd unpacked yet. I'd suggest you get a little fresh air and then return to unpack and have a rest this afternoon." She paused to look around the room. "I'll leave you to it." Ellen said, a little flippantly. Her officious nature had disappeared rather suddenly. She raised a limp hand as she left the room.

Sam smiled. "I'd like to be sure there's no after-effect from the bang you took on the head. Please say yes," he said.

"If I do, will you leave me alone then?"

He seemed to know he could count on his red hair, freckles and deep green eyes to add to his persuasiveness. "I really do feel badly about lacing into you like that yesterday. I can be quite charming if you give me a chance."

I had no doubt of that.

Sam moved toward the door. "I'm going to let you get up and get washed now. How about we meet at the entrance to the main dining room on deck three in an hour?"

# CHAPTER 6

# JOAN

While waiting for the elevator to go down to breakfast, I studied the wall map to locate the gym, restaurants, pools, and theatres. The formal dining room, my destination, was on deck three.

Inside the elevator I noticed the new date had been place in the slot in the carpeted flooring. It read "Sunday." If departure day counted as day one, I had indeed missed my first day at sea.

When I got off the elevator, Sam was standing in what would become familiar; his lazy cowboy pose, wearing narrow jeans, one leg bent against the wall, chin down under a wide hat. "What are you smiling at?" he asked.

Although he'd been dressed casually earlier Sam looked more relaxed now than previously. Seeing him in tan cowboy boots, remembering how much Joe and I had loved our annual visits to Arizona and Tennessee, envisioning my own multiple pairs of boots, my smile broadened. Country music had been on an equal footing with classical in our house.

We stood outside the Rembrandt Dining Room with a large crowd waiting for the main dining room doors to open. It was a little before eight o'clock. Sam's hand rubbed the polished wood wall. "Although some people find it stuffy, I love its grandeur and try to eat every meal here. I only go to the cafeteria for a late night tea or second dessert."

"So this isn't your first cruise on the *Liberty*?" I said.

He shook his head and moved away from the wall. "It was in this very spot, about five and a half years ago, that I met my ex-wife, Carla. She was a Brazilian model."

I wondered if I'd ever been on a shoot with her, since I'd done many layouts with South American models over the course of my career. Unlikely, since that was a long time ago. I'd left work to stay home and make lunches for the kids when they were in high school and later stayed home because I enjoyed the social activities of Mah-jong that first year and in short order, I'd joined Hadassah, the art gallery, and the girls' book club. Although I'd worried about being a bored, stay-at-home mother, I was so busy, I didn't know how I'd found time to work before. I pulled my index finger out of my mouth, embarrassed to have been chomping on it in public.

"Where are you? Have I lost your attention already?" Sam smiled, his green eyes twinkling.

I promised myself to concentrate when conversing with someone and try to break the nail biting habit a goal for this week; like the AA member who aims for one day at a time, I'd break my bad habits.

Sam took hold of my elbow and guided me to the ladies' room. "I wash my hands a million times a day. Call me a germaphobe." He laughed out loud. "I'll meet you here," he said before ducking into the men's.

There was a short line in the women's washroom. I took a big breath and leaned close to the mirror. There was a small bruise over my eyebrow and a blue-yellow streak running from my under arm to the crook of my arm. I applied some fresh lip gloss. Someone stared at the gauze at my hairline. I pulled a crumpled Tilley hat out of my bag and arranged it to fall over my right eye. Very sexy, I thought. Wouldn't the camera just love this look?

At the entrance to the dining room, the maître d' said, "Mr. Hoffman. So nice to see you. Window, port side?"

"Andre, you've got an amazing memory."

"Certainly, sir," Andre said.

Sam beamed. I saw him slip a bill into Andre's hand . Money and memory went together like coffee and a cigarette I heard someone once say.

As we were shown to our table, I stopped in front of the three-storey tapestry depicting an immense passenger ship. The colourful tapestry was truly a work of art. We sat in silence for a short while. I hadn't wanted to come, so I had no intention of working at making conversation. Eventually, I caved and asked Sam about himself.

"I'm from Boston, but I uprooted my life for my Brazilian bride. Because of Carla, who I should clarify is my almost ex-wife, I moved to sunny California. She lived with me for five years before she took off." He smirked and threw back his water as if it were something stronger. We read our menus, closed them, and looked around for a waiter to take our breakfast orders.

I recognized the taste of warm blood and slid the napkin off my plate onto my lap. After applying a little pressure to the side of my index finger, I held it where I could look down and see the torn skin at the side of my nail. I hadn't even realized it had been in my mouth. It had stopped bleeding, but it stung.  I hid my hands under the table, disgusted with myself.

"So . . . have you relocated . . . since the breakup of your marriage?" Oh my God. Why had I asked such a personal question? I had no right. Sam was only concerned with my health. I looked down and twirled my watch around my wrist. But he was the one who'd made it personal, talking about his wife.

"No, I haven't moved back east." Sam explained how tough it'd been to establish a practice in California: "I'll be damned if I let her force me into another move." He looked around the huge room, trying to catch the eye of a server. There were many bustling around, only none were near our table in the corner.

"I think I keep coming back to the *Liberty* because that trip when Carla and I met was a game changer for me. But enough of my sad story. Tell me about you."

My finger had found its way back up to my face. My eyes teared up when I tore a sliver of skin from under the nail bed of my thumb. I blinked several times and tried to look calm.

"What's wrong?" Sam said.

I shook my head while blinking back the tears that threatened to start a conversation I had no interest in having.

He rambled on, talking about himself, his eyes on the expanse of blue outside our large circular window. Ripples appeared right next to the side of the ship. Farther out, the sea was as close to a sheet of pebbled glass as could be imagined. "Carla waited just long enough—the five years required not to bring accusations of fraud. Just long enough to get her permanent residency status in the United States." He swung his head, searching for the waiter who hadn't returned to take our orders. "Left me after maxing out every credit card I owned and landing me in serious debt," he added. His voice was anything but quiet or embarrassed.

"Ouch," I said. His humiliation and pain sounded like a familiar Hollywood script about someone being played for a green card— Gerard Depardieu? Only in that movie, I thought the couple fell in love for real. I wasn't sure; it could have been a green card scam like Sam's story.

"The irony of it," Sam went on, "is that our immigration system favours the new immigrant. The American who vouches for a foreigner gets screwed over." He ran a hand straight back from his forehead through his thick red hair. "Because I sponsored her as my wife, I became fully responsible for all her debts for the next ten years." He repeated this last phrase, staring at me and spitting as he spoke. "For ten fucking years!"

My eyes widened, and I looked around at the tables near us. "But if there's a change in your marital—"

He shook his head. "No, the government doesn't care. It would end up costing me more money. If she wants a divorce, she'll be the one paying for it." He gazed at the buffet, where bowls and deep containers of hot and cold cereals were laid out. Trays of sweet rolls, fruit, cheeses, cold meats, and yogurts also filled platters. "Unless you're planning to order eggs bennie or something from the menu, let's go help ourselves."

Sam picked up his napkin and carried it to the buffet spread. With the napkin inside his palm, he gripped the soup ladle next to the hot oatmeal and filled a bowl. Then he used the napkin to hold the milk jug. He repeated this as he moved on to the fruit tray, picked up the tongs and carried his two plates to our table. He wasn't kidding when he said he was a germaphobe. When I returned to the table, I wasn't at all surprised to see him generously dousing his hands in hand sanitizer.

We were both hungry and spoke little as we ate. No sooner had he finished his cereal than he began telling me more about this Carla person.

"Well, when you found out you couldn't use your own credit card to buy a new television that must have been the final straw for you." I said. "Understandably you were disappointed to find she'd married you for your money and not your good looks." I laughed. It was a cliché, but if the shoe fit . . . He clearly found no humour in the situation. I looked around for a waiter to refill my coffee.

"The system stinks," Sam continued.

Before he was able to continue his tale of woe, I interrupted. "Sam, I can't figure out how you handle being angry all the time."

"I get my revenge by hardly ever working. I live life to the fullest, which is a healthy attitude, and it doesn't include earning a lot of money. I love excelling at work, enjoying the respect my abilities earn me, and all that. But it's satisfying that Carla can't get her hands on credit cards I no longer keep or on bank accounts that are overdrawn more often than not."

This wasn't a cheap cruise. His life seemed more depressing than mine, but at least I knew to keep my sad story to myself. I tried to find the sparkle in those green eyes to remind myself why I had found him so attractive in the elevator yesterday. We sat in silence while an Australian waiter refilled our mugs and apologized for being so busy.

"After the first day, travellers start sleeping in. Try the barbie around the pool at lunchtime; people say it's very nice." The poor waiter was sweating, and it was only 8:00 a.m. "You'll see, the service won't be like this every day, she'll be right."

Hmm, I thought, the day better pick up.

Sam walked around the table to pull out my chair. I discreetly dropped my bloodied napkin on the floor and kicked it under the table.

# CHAPTER 7

## *JOAN*

After breakfast, the elevator was crammed with people talking loudly. Sam bent close to my ear. "Are you thinking I need a therapist?"

What a coincidence he'd raised the topic of therapy. Sam's sarcasm made his opinion clear. Unlike Sam, Ian was very receptive to the idea. I laughed to myself, thinking Sam didn't need encouragement to talk about his issues. But maybe he'd benefit from a more active listener.

"Why are you laughing?"

I answered tactfully. "Because I have family members who think I need counselling. In particular, my stepson Ian. He trusts the research he's read that supports grief counselling, but I'm not sure I do. I've read other studies which suggest therapy is of no help at all. Ian feels an obligation to me since his dad is gone, which is actually kind of sweet." I became quiet, reluctant to go down this path with a near stranger. I turned my watch around on my wrist. Since I'd lost weight, it was loose and hung like a bracelet. "Oh, I get it," I said under my breath. Ian was the one who still had grieving to do. Not only for his dad but for his mother who died when he was very young. I pulled my hat out of my bag and put it back on my head.

"You say something?" Sam said.

"Uh, no, sorry." I stared straight at the numbers on the elevator panel. Ian was elated when I finally agreed to meet Dr. Martin. I was ashamed to admit I had trouble with the stigma of going to a psychiatrist.

Sam took my hand in the elevator and patted it as if I'd been sending signals that I needed comforting.

"What are you thinking about? You look so serious," Sam said as we exited the elevator.

It occurred to me that Sam too was dealing with grief and loss, but I'd had enough of talking about Carla for one day. "Nothing special," I answered.

The doctor who'd held my wrist to take my pulse a couple of hours ago now moved his hand to the small of my back, and we began walking around the top deck. I relaxed as our strides matched one another's and the strain dissipated. I was glad I was here, where no one I knew would look at me and judge me for the signs of intimacy our physical closeness suggested.

During our second time around the track, the breeze picked up. I had to hold onto my hat, but it blew out of my hand in spite on my best efforts. It rolled over and over in front of us until it got caught under a chaise. Sam kneeled and stretched out on the wooden deck to reach it for me. I laughed as he hammed it up for anyone looking our way. He was quite the actor, making sounds as if this really strained his muscles. We plopped down on the wooden recliner chairs where my hat had come to rest.

Sam was breathing heavily, exaggerating the results of his exertion. I racked my brain trying to think of the television series that involved the POW-turned-CIA agent. I looked at his face closely, but with his silly antics, he didn't resemble any actor I could think of.

I ignored his noises. "This is so beautiful. I can see the energy in the waves, the ripples, the power of the tide. I love the way the light dances over the top edges of each and every wave." For the millionth time, I wished I had an ounce of creativity in my blood so I could paint and capture the water's myriad of blues and its churning movement.

"If you don't mind my saying, you look a whole lot better than you did when you woke up this morning."

I smiled at him and relaxed with my head against the wood recliner. "You look better when you look less serious too."

We were too far from land to see any bird life, but every once in a while a group of nature lovers pointed over the rail and shouted, "dolphins on starboard" or "whales on the port side." Neither Sam nor I joined the group that moved en masse back and forth from one side to the other in search of the marine life. We snickered, feeling a common bond of superiority. The group was leaning over the railing on the port side.

I called out, "flying mantas on starboard," and pointed opposite where we sat.

Six or seven of them ran over to our side and asked, "Where? Where?"

Sam stood up next to me at the rail. "Funny, they were here a minute ago. Must've gone deeper," he said. I hunched forward and covered my smile with my hand. Sam got the giggles just then, and I hit his back, hard. The crowd dispersed. Then we saw a turtle.

I bent my hands around my mouth and called to the others, "Turtle, right here." No one came over. We looked at one another and held our stomachs, laughing. "Oh well, their loss." I lay back down on the wooden chaise. "That's enough excitement for me." I placed my hat across my face.

"Is this a hint? Do you want to sleep?" Sam asked.

"No, I can talk—I just don't want sun on my face." The sun was higher than before and I had no sunscreen with me. "So what kind of doctor are you?"

"Uh, no. I already gave you an hour of my Sad Sam life story. Now it's your turn. There'll be time for more of my bio later."

That seemed presumptuous. I raised the brim of my hat. "You think?" I said, teasing him. "In answer to your question, I'm just your ordinary young divorcee."

He grabbed my hat and hit my leg with it. "Joan, there's nothing ordinary about you. So give me the scoop."

I squinted up at him. "I'd like to hear your guesses. What was my job when I worked?"

"No guessing games, not even of the Jeopardy variety," Sam said. "How many kids in the picture?"

"Okay, I have two; Ian and Rebecca. They were in nursery and kindergarten respectively when my ex and I separated." I sat up and tried to locate the sunscreen in my bag before I remembered I didn't have any. I scanned Sam's face to see if he bought my story. Well, why wouldn't he? Did I look like a young widow who was grieving? I didn't want anyone feeling sorry for me. I lifted the damp hair off my neck and prayed this wasn't going to be something worse than another hot flash. Once, on a vacation in Mexico, I had an ordinary menopausal hot flash that became a full-blown seizure. Don't let that happen again with Sam. The hot sensation passed.

"I thought . . ." he began and then rephrased, "but you mentioned grief counselling. I'm confused."

My fiction had been taking shape and flowing off the tip of my tongue as if I'd rehearsed it a million times. Sticking close to the truth was supposed to keep me in safe waters, but Sam knew I was lying.

I paused and pretended not to have heard him. "The kids are in their early twenties, both going to university away from home."

Sam squinted as he faced upward. I couldn't read his expression. "I need a drink," he said. "What can I get you?" When he returned with two Diet Cokes, he asked about the line of work my husband had been in.

I couldn't think. If I mentioned Joe's chain of hotels, I could just hear Sam saying he thought the owner of that hotel chain had recently died. "He was working for a company, but it's not around anymore." I coughed. I sounded so dumb. "He worked in sales, but the business went under just before the divorce. Umm, it was a long time ago." I had been picking at the polish on my nails, which made them look worse than usual. I wanted to go back to my cabin. Had I previously mentioned Ian and called him my stepson? I stood and took a step, tripping over my shoelace which had come undone. Sam caught me before I fell. I leaned on him and thanked him saying I felt ready to go back to my stateroom and lie down.

"Sure, sure," he said. He adjusted his glasses, which had green plastic frames. He looked very fashionable and young. With his red hair, freckles, green eyes, and slim blue jeans, Sam looked handsome, and he knew it. I wondered if he had any interest in me beyond the professional, or if his flirtatious manner was just part of his personality.

"I love them but aren't you hot in those?" I said, pointing to his cowboy boots.

"In case you don't remember, we were up early today. Actually, I was up even earlier than you. And at 4:00 a.m., it's cold out."

"Oh, I'm so sorry." I felt hot in the face.

"No need. My feet are hot now. It's time I changed into a swim suit and flip-flops. If you're ready to go, I'll walk you back to your cabin."

"No, not necessary," I said.

"My room is almost next to yours, remember?"

We rejoined the group walking the circular track.

Sam stopped walking. He took off his sunglasses and dug in his pocket for a cloth. "If there's one thing I hate, it's having filthy glasses," he said. The caramel colour of his boots shone in the light, and I guessed he'd buffed them right before we met for breakfast. I used to insist on cleaning Joe's glasses all the time. It was amazing that they could get impossibly dirty and Joe wouldn't notice.

"You know, my late husband always wanted to try cruising, but we never got around to it. You remind me of him in some ways. But then in other ways, you're the polar opposite." I twirled my hat in my hands, avoiding his eyes.

Sam drew his fair, almost invisible eyebrows together. Shit. I did it again. He released my elbow from the crook of his arm.

# CHAPTER 8

## *SAM*

We walked in silence to the other end of the ship. Joan had contradicted herself. Why the discrepancies? What was she: divorcee or widow? I rubbed the back of my neck. Or possibly someone's wife? I'd noticed that she was wearing a wedding ring, but I felt sure she wasn't married. Even at her age, just the wrong side of fifty, I found her girlishly pretty, the kind of woman who needed little makeup or time to look beautiful. She dressed with the taste and confidence that came from sophistication and money. But I couldn't figure her out. Maybe it was simply that she'd reacted to me as a doctor who'd seen her at her worst, and that made her appear vulnerable, timid, and lacking in confidence.

Other joggers ran between us. She waved from the water side of the walking track, and I smiled in reply. Life with a classy woman like her would be a dream. She was smart and polished. Except when she was lying or biting her nails. She seemed to hide behind her oversized sunglasses so it was hard to tell what she was thinking, but I knew there was chemistry. The nurse I'd lived with after Carla moved out had been good for me; I needed to live with someone I liked, who could cook fabulous meals, eat with me every night, and be up and console me when I came home drunk with empty pockets. But I'd blown that relationship too.

Like all the others, Carla was a fire sign, boisterous, vivacious, and enthusiastic about everything. She'd had more energy than anyone I'd ever met, and she made me feel alive like no one before or since. It didn't matter whether she could sing or dance well; she did those things because she loved to. For Carla it was the same with every activity. With Joan, I knew instinctively she wouldn't participate in an activity unless she'd already mastered it.

Joan and I headed for the elevators at the stern. When she bent to double knot her runners, I crossed back to her side. Her butt was tiny. There was no panty line under the beige shorts. I pictured her lean legs, the hamstrings pulled taut as they wrapped around my waist. She grabbed at my arm for balance as she stood up.

We walked counter-clockwise, and I pointed out the sign that read, Three laps, three kilometres. "So that's our total today," I told her. As we neared a set of wooden double doors, I suggested stepping inside to see the gym since she'd mentioned yoga earlier.

"So what's up there?" she asked, her hand shielding her eyes as she gazed into the windows.

"There's a staircase. On the lower level is the gym," I said. "You're looking at the top level where there's space for spa treatments, a nail and hair salon, a whirlpool and saunas." I took her hand and led her through the door, down the spiral staircase, and into the gym.

"Give me a second." Joan picked up a copy of the schedule for the week's exercise classes. We peeked in one of the studios. The Asian couple we'd shared the elevator with yesterday had places at the back of the yoga class. Today the woman's hair was pulled back in a severe, high ponytail. She stood at the top of her mat. In one fluid movement she bent down from tadasana (mountain pose) to forward fold and then to flat back. Her hair flew as she moved from high to low and up again. She held her downward dog for a long time. Her husband, equally flexible and trim, shut his eyes while he reached around and comfortably hugged the back of his calves.

"I haven't exercised in so long. I have to get back into it." Joan stretched one arm up and over her head while she bent her torso to the other side.

I joked that I could help by giving her a real workout, in any part of the ship she liked. The banter stopped abruptly, and her smile faded. She should have laughed it off but didn't. I should have apologized, but I paused too long. We walked on, the silence becoming awkward.

We stood in front of her door. I heard a clock ticking loudly. She wouldn't look at me and I gave up waiting. Joan pulled her key card out of a pocket and flipped it over and back a couple of times, staring down at it. What had happened to the sophisticated woman who dressed to the nines, lied with a straight face, and played jokes on defenceless tourists? She looked like a schoolgirl; her little feet close together while she picked at her cuticles and bit her lower lip. A flush crept across her cheeks.

"I'll see you later," I said, hoping it wouldn't be anytime soon. By time her door closed, I was stabbing the elevator button. I kicked the ashtray-cum-trash can that sat between two banks of elevators. The can, on top of which the Royal Caribbean logo was pressed into the sand, toppled over, spilling over the gold-and-blue carpet. I righted the metal container and stepped over the pile of sand when the elevator arrived.

# CHAPTER 9

## *JOAN*

Was he a jerk or a pig? It was hard to tell. His humour was crass, especially given we'd only just met and that had been primarily because of a medical issue. Maybe I'd have a nap before lunch. I took a big breath in and exhaled through my mouth, making that whoosh sound that was supposed to signify a state of relaxation. I wasn't there yet. I changed out of my clothes and donned a fluffy white robe. Although this sea of people was as much what I'd been seeking as the sea-and-sand holiday itself, I felt desperate for the solitude of my cabin. I placed my camera on the table to make sure I'd see it and remember to grab it when I went out next.

I rubbed a hand over my closed eyes. Earlier, I'd felt happier than I had for a long while, but widows were expected to be sad. To look sad. To feel sad. I knew I shouldn't feel guilty for feeling beter than sad. What a crazy world. Joe wouldn't want me to feel anything other than what I felt. Society's expectations of appropriate behaviour for a young widow be damned. I had no one to answer to. I took my paperback outside.

Sun  covered more than half the balcony. I moved one of the chairs, sat down and crossed my feet on the other chair. My eyes began closing right after I found my place in the book. My mind drifted to the hours Joe and I spent reading and discussing Internet articles about his disease.

"When the time comes, just tell the kids that my death came the day the cancer was diagnosed," he'd said.

"Brain cancer isn't like other types of cancer." Joe showed me a case online in which a man's personality changes had made him so paranoid he began walking around his house with a knife, with his wife and kids there.

"And I won't lose the fortune I spent my life acquiring," he'd said.

"I don't care about the money!" I yelled.

"That's why I have to safeguard the kids' inheritance!" Joe screamed back. I let him convince me that one day someone might feel they had reason to take control of Joe's business. Who would that be? Me? His shady brother, Phil? Could I see myself ever going to court to prevent him from making some unwise decision? Of course not.

"The only regret I have about my short life is that I didn't meet you earlier." Joe's words brought fresh tears, happy tears. I wiped them away and pulled at my dripping nose. For a moment, I forgot how down I felt.

Unable to concentrate I left the balcony. With the curtains closed, the bedroom was dark, and I crawled under the covers of the freshly made bed. Sad voices filled my head, the beginning of another dreamless rest. After much tossing and turning, I rolled over in frustration to look at my watch. I wondered just how long I'd lain there, not sleeping.

What? Four o'clock? I'd missed another dining room meal and wasted another afternoon.

I got myself up and out the door. The elevator opened onto the shopping street, more commonly known as the promenade. The blue domed ceiling gave it an airy outdoor feeling. I stopped in front of an artist's easel; the picture showed a man holding a tennis racket in the foreground and high ocean waves in the background.

The artist stopped and looked up at me. "You haven't seen this yet, have you?"

"Truly? There's a tennis court's on the top deck?" I said.

"Yes, on deck twelve. It's encircled with high green netting," said the artist. "You can't miss it."

But that morning, I had missed it, I realized. I scanned the glass counter in the Seattle Coffee Café. The tuna salad sandwich on rye smelled scrumptious. I licked my fingers after dabbing at the caraway seeds remaining on the plate. Suddenly Sam appeared at my side, a crooked smile tugging on his mouth. A good-looking tall blonde stood behind him. I was glad I had on my dark glasses and that there were several other people in the café eating alone. I straightened my posture.

Sam leaned close, so close I could've kissed his baby smooth-looking cheek. I smelled the rum from the pina coladas he'd been drinking. "Looks to me like you're still hungry. Join us."

"Looks to me like you've got yourself a burn," I said. His neck above the thin white linen shirt was bright red.

"I'll stay out of the sun if you stay and have coffee with me," Sam said. His wink destroyed the exquisite flirtatious moment. I reminded myself that I wasn't a flirt, that I was not only a grown woman but a sophisticated newly widowed young woman.

"Thanks"—I picked up my large camera—"but I was just leaving."

As I neared the elevator, I heard "Hello, again." We exchanged flashes of recognition. "I'm Amy." The Asian woman from the yoga class held the elevator door for me. "Whatever happened with the red-headed man who followed you down the hall yesterday? Tall, handsome, and American, I'd guess."

"Yes, we've definitely met." I laughed as I got inside. "That'd be Sam." I told her about the tour he gave me earlier and mentioned we'd seen her and her husband in the yoga studio.

"Hmm," she said. "I thought it was you. My husband Li is a more dedicated yogi than I am, although I practise at least once daily. Both of us are very health conscious. And your name is?"

"Pardon me, I'm Joan." I stuck out my hand. I told her I was somewhat health conscious—at least I didn't eat red meat—and that I loved yoga too.

"Li and I take our health regimen seriously. Maybe too much so," she said. "It's not just the yoga. You have to commit to good health: regular diet, exercise, and sleep. Only seriously disciplined people make this a lifestyle choice." Amy looked down, blushing.

I noticed a cluster of broken blood vessels on the side of her nose that she'd tried to cover with a light dusting of powder. "I dislike preaching. The people who talk the most often have the least to say, and yet here I am doing it myself."

"That's okay."

"For Li, it's like a religion. He believes one's success in life is a reward for one's commitment or degree of discipline. Although he's rigid, he's a very wonderful husband and life partner," she said.

"Me thinks the lady doth protest too much," I said quoting Shakespeare.

A scowl crossed her face and I realized I didn't know her well enough to be teasing her.

I jumped as a bell rang, a piercing bell. Just my luck. This cruise was not turning out to be as calm and restful as I'd expected. "So how long do you think we're going to be stuck here?" I asked.

"They will be telephoning the elevator in a minute—I've had this experience before. We might as well relax." Amy slid to the floor, her short legs extended as she bent low over them in a comfortable stretch.

She sat cross-legged in a half lotus. "I'm committed to being lean and maintaining good posture. That goes a long way toward looking tall, I've learned."

It was true. In a seated position, she seemed tall. "Can I take your picture?" I asked. She smiled that toothy smile. "I used to do photography professionally. I'm not some kook."

She placed her palms in prayer position and looked down at her tiny hands, thumbs and index fingers pressed together. Amy sat in a meditative, relaxed posture and didn't react to the sound of the camera shutter. She moved into a full lotus and placed her hands, palms up, on her knees. She had to be at least seventy: serious, disciplined, reserved, yet warm. I saw three hardcover books in her bag: the two in English were by Bill Bryson and Oscar Wilde.

"Turn your head to the side," I said. Click, click, click. "Can you balance on your left leg, grab your right ankle and pull it in to your butt?" Click, click. "Dancer's pose." Without being asked, she stood up in mountain pose with her hands together and back arched. Click, click, click.

I was in my groove and resented the interruption of the ringing phone. Amy balanced on her tiptoes to open the small box in the wall above the brass plate containing the fourteen floor buttons. A circular microphone extended from there on a spiral cord. She twirled with the cord wrapped around her small form. Click, click, click.

I could hear the voice on the other end saying the elevator would be put in motion and to expect a small jerking sensation. The voice then apologized for the inconvenience and asked if additional service was required.

We laughed together at the silliness of the message. What did they think—that we wanted room service in the elevator? I handed Amy her book bag and put away my camera.

"Thanks, that was fun," she said. "I've just been to the ship's library. It has huge windows. I'm sure you'll get better pictures there because of the light."

"Maybe but I'm more drawn to interesting people than scenery," I said.

"Will you join me for daily yoga practice for the rest of this week? You don't smile when you take your pictures and this would be good for you," Amy said.

"Do you think you could ask your husband to model for me?" I asked in return.

Amy touched my arm. "You should try daily yoga practice." She pointedly ignored my comment about her husband, putting an end to my series idea.

Skeptical about the yoga but not wanting to disregard her question, I answered, "Trust me, nothing will make me feel better, not anytime soon. Maybe my photography." I gazed up. We were almost on deck twelve, the pool and track deck.

"Try daily yoga and judge for yourself at the end of the cruise," Amy said.

She extended her delicate hand. The briefest hint of a smile crossed her porcelain face. I accepted the challenge, extending my hand for a firm shake. I knew my five remaining days on board wouldn't make a difference to my mental or physical health, but I wanted to photograph both Li and Amy. A small bob of her head took the place of the expected nod. I wondered if I could catch those subtle movements and changes in expression with my lens.

As we exited the elevator, I asked Amy if she knew where the tennis courts were. I wanted to see these for myself. "I think I'm going to be getting lost all week," I said.

"Not to worry. You'll fit right in." Amy paused before leaving my side. "I want you to meet my husband Li. He plays tennis. Meet us for drinks in the Champagne Bar before dinner, say 7:00 p.m.?"

I began to shake my head and then reconsidered. Why not?

# CHAPTER 10

## *RACHEL*

After I rounded this corner, I'd let myself slow down into an easy jog. It was hard to look attractive and fit while panting and slobbering like a Great Dane. I pulled my tongue back into my mouth. Shoulders back, tail tucked, posture erect. I pulled in my abs and pushed my way through the crowd and up to the bar.

My gaze rose above the walking track to scan the windows on the deck above. In the curvature of the roof bar on thirteen I pictured a variety of men.

Since cruises were notoriously weight-gain-alert zones, I'd come aboard a little under my usual weight. My bestie, Frieda, was terrified of cruises for that very reason. I had other friends who I'd asked to join me, but they too feared ballooning several sizes and swore they'd never get on a cruise ship. Didn't they have any self-control? All you really needed was a healthy amount of discipline.

At the Prow Bar, I swooped in onto a vacant stool. There was a bottle of Bain de Soleil suntan oil sitting there. "Soda with lime, please," I said. "So where ya from?"

"Philippines," the bartender said. "Someone left that here. Go ahead and take it if you want." The bartender flashed me a brilliant smile.

"No thanks, but I'll use a little. They'll never notice." We smiled conspiratorially. I watched the parade of sweating speed walkers, joggers, and ambling, fully dressed older couples. How they paced themselves on the track paralleled how they organized their time in general. The beauty of cruising, from my perspective, was that I unpacked once, yet I moved around lots. I was never alone unless I wanted to be, yet there were large or small group activities to be a part of any time I wanted.

A stranger approached and ordered a screwdriver for himself. If his hair had been its natural colour instead of dyed black he would've been a very handsome man. Well, that could be fixed, I thought. I arched back, resting one elbow on the bar. Then I heard him say, ". . . and for my wife, a soda and lime."

I turned away and stared at the disappearing ice cubes in my glass.

I felt a tap on my shoulder. It was the nice-looking stranger. I smiled at him. But I couldn't help staring at a dark stain near his ear.

"You're using suntan oil. Don't you know how much it increases your risk of skin cancer?" he said.

I smirked. "Well, I do know, and I'm not worried about what may happen when I'm eighty. If anything happens before, it'll be because of skin damage from my teens." I paused, rubbing some oil over my other arm and letting him admire my muscle tone. "The sun damage done years ago can't be undone," I informed him, shrugging. My eyes moved to the top of his head. "Then again, some things can be undone." He stomped away.

It was late afternoon. The sun, although low in the sky, was still in my face as I walked west. The woman strolling toward me looked so much like Frieda. Could she have gotten onboard without me knowing it? I broke into a run and threw my arms around her bird bones. She stiffened like something was very wrong.

# CHAPTER 11

## *JOAN*

"Hey," I said, my voice quiet, controlled. I eased myself out of the bear hug. I grabbed for my camera. The wide strap slipped down my arm, and I pulled it back to the top of my shoulder. Her dark, frizzy mop was smothering me. In a throaty, deep voice, she apologized. I wished she'd keep her voice down. There were a million eyes on us. I tried to step around her.

She caught hold of my arm and laughed. "I've been accused of being forward, but that was a little much . . . even for me. I'm so sorry," she repeated. She looked skyward and laughed at herself again, shoulders raised, arms outstretched, palms up, indicating the humour of it all. It was a hearty laugh emanating from the gut. I liked that about her. Her laugh turned into hiccups and ended with a very unladylike snort.

"I'm Rachel," she said. "Let me buy you a drink." I started to shake my head, but she was already pulling on my arm, insisting. "I'm a health nut—don't drink or smoke or do drugs. Yet I manage a full portfolio of vices: I'm a sun worshipper, a chocoholic, a sex addict, and an online shopper par excellence."

I agreed to the drink, because I found her entertaining. The bartender who saw us approaching had Rachel's lime and soda ready before we reached the bar stools. Hmm.

"And my friend will have a Pimm's lemonade. You'll like it—it's mostly lemonade with a little liquor and garnished with strawberries, mint, and cucumber. It's popular on the continent."

What a pretentious turn of phrase. Did I look British? She certainly wasn't.

I watched as the bartender mixed my drink. The coiled, wide canvas strap of my camera formed a cushion to protect it from any wet spots on the sleek wooden counter.

Rachel raised her glass. We toasted to friendship. She clinked her glass against mine with such force that she spilled the cold contents all over me. "Ah, I should have warned you . . . I'm a klutz."

"It's okay. I was a mite hot anyway," I said, flicking the excess wetness from my sleeve.

"Sorry about that. So give," Rachel said, motioning with the curled fingers of both hands, as if asking me to move closer toward her.

"What?" I said, draining my glass. The Pimm's was delicious.

"Well, I know nothing about you, but you know my name, that I'm American, and that I have vices." She smiled and her eyes twinkled. "People always say my New York accent is strong. I've offered up all my secrets, and you didn't even have to ask. Now give me the goods on you." She pushed her curly black hair back behind her ears. The breeze pushed it forward. The late afternoon sun no longer seemed very warm.

"Joan. Canadian," I said, and for good measure added, "young widow."

"I'll drink to that," Rachel said. "Only I'd add 'happy'—happy Joan or happy Canadian named Joan."

We clinked glasses again. "Hey, you left out 'young.' I don't look young to you?" I demanded with a serious expression. I was no match for Rachel, but I had a sense of humour too. "I'm definitely too young to be widowed. How can my life be over already?"

"Are you nuts?" We gravitated to two lounge chairs, our backs to the pool, facing the ocean near the railing. "With today's lifespan stats, you're hardly middle-aged—you've got a whole life ahead of you. It may sound crass, but aren't you looking forward to that?" Rachel asked.

I had no idea. I felt bad even thinking about it. "Not in a big rush, but one day I'll probably remarry. I think it's normal and expected that I be sad and alone for a good long time." I held my hands together on my lap, rolling one over the other. My skin felt dry.

"That's just plain dumb." Rachel said. "How long has it been since your husband's death?"

"Joe, his name was Joe." I swallowed. "Just a year."

The truth was I was more focused on death and dying than on life and living. In private I put off thinking about Esther's Alzheimer's, but I knew it was there, a worry I would need to deal with and that I attributed a recent seizure to.

I blinked, realizing Rachel was talking to me. "Did Joe love you as much as you loved him?" she asked.

My mouth hung open, a confused look on my face as I tried to figure out where she was going with this line of questioning.

"Well then, he'd want you to be happy, that's all. It's not the same for me." She held back her unruly hair with one hand and searched her pocket for a hair tie. "Augh!" she let it fly in the wind, whipping around the front of her face. "I've never been in love, at least not that I know of. I get lucky, but that's not the same." Rachel's laugh rang false. "My problem is I'm easily bored with the men I date. Some kids get ADD in school and can't sit still in one place doing one thing. I've got a related disease dealing with one person in one place all the time."

"You've probably been told this before, Rachel, but it's possible the right guy hasn't come along yet." I looked around the pool and studied the men. "Okay," I said, noticing her downturned mouth, "there may not be much at the pool this late in the afternoon but I'm sure—"

"Oh, I know it'll happen one day," she said. "I'm like your Canadian Mounties. I always get my man." She laughed so hard, she had to make a run for the bathroom.

When she returned, Rachel raised and lowered her thick eyebrows as if she were Groucho Marx. She was a hoot, as Rebecca would say. The sun had almost gone, and so had the heat. "I'll get us towels to use like shawls so we can stay up here long enough to catch the sunset," I said. The towel hut was situated around the pool past the crowd by the bar.

A grey-haired man with a big bouncing belly stumbled off his bar stool, nearly bumping into me.

"Hey, hey!" he called, raising big paws to my shoulders.

This can't be happening, I thought. Not twice in one day.

"Here I am, Mike. You looking for me, honey?" A woman my size sashayed toward us. Her attractive one-piece black swimsuit had a plunging neckline. The material clung to her ample chest like two triangular jib sheets stretching from the back of her neck to her waistline. The drunk man released me to face what I guessed was the familiar voice of his wife.

"God," I said loudly.

The woman rushing toward him slipped on the wooden deck, one straight leg out. Cartoon - like she passed underneath his outstretched right arm. Her other leg was held at a right angle like an athlete running hurdles. She slid to a stop in the pool.

There was a brief moment of silence while the crowd waited. But she came up laughing and sputtering as if it were all one big joke. The man had sobered up somewhat. He bent down, his stomach resting on his fleshy kneecaps, and stretched one hand out to her. The laughing woman yanked on his proffered hand until he tumbled into the pool on top of her.

Thankfully, they were quieted by the mouthfuls of water they unceremoniously spat out. I continued on my way to the towel hut.

"Well, aren't they the perfect match for one another? I bet they're married," Rachel said when I got back.

"You think?" I said. I turned my head to see them snuggling in the water like newlyweds. The woman's legs circled the man's thick waist; his head was burrowing into that concave soft place between the neck and shoulder.

"I've seen worse-matched couples," I said. "I saw them at lunch. They must have a volatile relationship, a bona fide Martha and George."

"Yes, I saw them too; they're exactly like Elizabeth Taylor and Richard Burton from *Who's Afraid of Virginia Woolf?*" Rachel nodded and tilted her head to the side.

"Come on, Rachel, surely you're not envious of them," I said.

"Right now, any relationship would be better than no relationship. Any wealthy, good-looking guy with a keen wit would suit me. Hell, now that I'm older, I'd even omit 'good-looking' from my requirements."

"But wealthy and witty still stand. Now aren't you a discriminating woman?" I smirked.

"Let's be real. I have needs—sexual needs, material needs, physical needs. Most of all, I get horny, and I enjoy the lust that comes with a new relationship." She stared at me, assessing my reaction. "Men are sexual beings, and so are women." I almost laughed when she said, "I'm one of those people who don't need therapy to get in touch with their inner self. I give myself license to explore freely."

"You're too funny," I said. "I have far less experience than you. My marriage was very brief." I told her I was forty when I got married and willing to try for kids, but Joe already had two grown children, was sixty, and felt he was too old for it to be fair to either him or a child.

"Sure," Rachel said. "He might have ended up a grandfather and a father at the same time, with the twenty odd years between the generations."

"Ah, you've been communing with my late husband," I said, smiling.

"Dark humour; a very good sign of adjustment." Rachel said. "I'd guess most of your friends are no longer working because they probably have the same financial status and social position you do. It's time to downsize, get involved in new hobbies, take up an old interest, travel, have adventures, and live without obligations. Change your outlook—a new chapter is just beginning."

I didn't want to admit she sounded like my therapist. "That's exactly what I'd want right now . . . if Joe were alive to do it with me. But I don't want it right now." I shook the ice around in my glass, tipped it back, and sucked on the lime wondering if taking the cruise wasn't a sign I did feel ready.

"How satisfied you must have been with your father figure-cum-lover," Rachel said.

"Hey, that's a cheap shot. My father wasn't even in the picture long enough for me to know him. You know nothing about me." I'd adored Joe and hadn't seen him as older. Who I'd fallen in love with was the most handsome, sexy, and admirable man I'd ever been lucky enough to meet. I turned away from her.

"I'm sorry, that was a little insensitive. Your husband must have been pretty special for you to feel as you do. Can I ask what it was that took your husband so early, or is that too difficult a topic for you?"

I pulled my hand away. "You just subjected me to a microscope and now you're asking if it's too soon to ask a personal question about my husband's death." My mouth moved but at first no sound came out. "Cancer." I rubbed two fingers over my chapped upper lip. "You know, you're the first person I've confided I'm a widow to. I mean on this ship—not at home obviously." I tasted blood and realized I'd been pulling on the skin at the side of a nail again. I forced myself to place both hands by my sides on top of the towel. "Just this morning I told another passenger I was a divorcee."

"Oh, why'd you do that?" Rachel asked.

"Well, I don't want men to think I'm here to hunt for a new partner, like some women are known to do on cruises."

She laughed. It sounded harsh. "Oh, like me, you mean?"

I apologized immediately. She punched my arm, the bruised one, and I grimaced.

Rachel didn't notice. "Just kidding. I'm going to make some guy a very lucky man so I have no hang-ups. In all likelihood, he'll be getting the better deal."

I knew if anything, it'd be companionship I'd want. "I don't recognize other needs like you do."

"Bullshit," Rachel raised her eyebrows.

"I don't how to think of myself. 'Single' sounds too young and 'widowed' sounds too old," I said.

The wind picked up. "Stay. Have one more for the road?" Rachel said. With a nod from me, she made a beeline for the bar.

When she returned, we continued our discussion comparing lonely to independent, and monogamous to promiscuous. Rachel and I were more alike than she wanted to think, or so I thought.

She lathered more sun lotion on her body although the sun wasn't hot any more at all. "I'll never play the mild mannered classy hostess who's an intelligent sophisticate. "You might, because for all I know, that may be you for real but I'm more of an in-your-face, fun seeker of the needy-greedy lover variety — the kind that likes fucking and being on top." Rachel's loud laugh told me she meant it and she knew how outrageous she sounded.

I tried not to appear shocked by her language. I didn't know people who talked like her. "It's different for me," I began. "For one thing, I have less of a Type A personality than you, and second, I'm a widow and you're not." I knew she'd be thinking the similarity was in our both being single, but I'd experienced great love and she never had. My nose itched and I had no tissue. I used the napkin my drink had been sitting on. "I'm not sure how long you're supposed to mourn, but I know I'd feel guilty about getting over Joe too soon. It'd suggest I didn't love my husband enough. And I really did . . . love him, that is."

"Fuck . . . Joan, you've got nothing to feel guilty about. Why care so much about other people's opinions?" For Rachel, appearances mattered only to busybodies with nothing important to worry about. And such people were pathetic. "I think it was a reporter, who said, 'Life is too short for pity parties: get busy living or get busy dying.'"

Heat flushed my cheeks. I curled my hand in to allow my thumb to reach a loose hangnail on my pinky finger. Somehow I pulled on it and felt the sting of torn skin at the cuticle. The towel blew off my legs, and I ran after it.

Rachel had finished her drink and was working on mine when I resumed my seat. I was annoyed that she did that. It bothered me that she spoke as if she was talking to a child. "All that counts is being true to yourself."

Now who's quoting Hamlet? Well, paraphrasing, I thought. Touché, Rachel.

"If you're ready to continue living, three cheers for you." She closed her eyes. "If you need to wait before getting intimate with men, so be it. There are no absolute rules. Live your life your way." She flipped her hair up away from her neck, and it moved wildly around her head.

I knew that and envied her freedom of spirit. Right then I wanted to see my first sunset at sea. I reached under my cot and pulled my camera out. Rachel watched me fiddle with the focus and pause, my fingers poised. I expected to see that pink ball turn orange, then yellow and finally white. I didn't yet know what colours I'd find blending on the ocean surface.

"Ah, the sunset," Rachel said, having opened her eyes and noticed the direction of my gaze. "It happens real quickly, so keep your eye on it. It's amazing, the spectrum of colours you see near the horizon."

A touch of pink and mauve threaded through the line where the ocean met the sky. I snapped twice.

Rachel tapped my arm. "Let's go. I'm cold. There'll be another sunset tomorrow."

I was feeling cool too, and besides, I remembered I had plans to meet Amy.

At the elevator, Rachel asked another of her direct, personal questions meant to shock me. "Do you want to have a great big orgasm this week? I may be able to help." She ran her tongue along her lower lip and then her upper lip.

The old man who joined us in front of the elevator gasped. He coughed till he turned red, and I hit him on the back a couple of times. He flapped his free hand in the air and moved away as quickly as he was able.

"Rachel!" I said, both appalled and amused. "You did that on purpose." She hit the elevator button again and rubbed the goose bumps on her crossed arms, a big grin on her face.

I stared at her, trying to decide if I was upset with her or upset I'd missed most of the sunset.

When the elevator opened on ten, I learned that Rachel occupied a stateroom one floor below me. Before she got out, she asked my table number so she could find me after dinner.

"Wait there, and I'll come over so we can go together to the theatre tonight," she said.

I agreed as the elevator doors closed.

# CHAPTER 12

## *JOAN*

Christ, why had I sat outside with Rachel for so long? I needed to unpack. Washing my hair and covering up my bruises was going to take time, never mind finding something to wear. I was due to meet up with Li and Amy in less than forty-five minutes.

"Hey, Joan, wait up," Sam called, exiting the other elevator on our floor.

"Sorry. I really have to rush," I said.

"Okay, but"—he held my arm, holding me in place outside his door—"do you have plans for tonight?"

He looked good. He'd had time to shower, shave, and change since I'd seen him earlier. "I hope you're planning to go to the Palladium Theatre tonight." When I didn't reply right away, he insisted I let him accompany me to the show. "I want you to have a better night than last night," he added. "You'll see, the time is going to fly, so you have to make each moment count." He tapped his white plastic key card against his wrist, looking straight at me. "I want you to forget we met over a medical issue."

I had forgotten we'd begun with a doctor-patient relationship because it now seemed inconsequential. It wasn't as if this was the beginning of anything important. Why I felt the need to prove I wasn't just blowing him off I didn't know. "Look, I met a woman named Rachel who I've made plans with. You're welcome to join us if you choose."

"Great, I'll escort the two of you, then," he said. I noticed for the first time a single dimple in one of his freckled cheeks. He was so damn cute for a grown man and so different from Joe.

I jumped when his hands moved quickly to either side of my face and he brushed his lips across mine. It didn't feel like a kiss, not a real kiss, but I suppose it was. I just stood there trying to figure out what had just happened when his door closed behind him and I found myself alone in the hallway.

# CHAPTER 13

## *RACHEL*

The older Asian man sitting next to me at the craps table captivated my attention. His long leg had brushed mine inadvertently when he sidled in to replace another player. He was interfering with my concentration. Beneath his fine shirt, I saw certain neck, shoulder and arm muscles contract and expand. His state of fitness was incredible given that he had some twenty years on me. I was losing more than I was winning. We both held fast to our places around the table as a crowd closed in on us. I made a late pass line bet and swore under my breath, more embarrassed than anything.

"Don't worry," he said, leaning my way. "That mistake only hurts you, so no other player will be annoyed." He patted my hand. I should have left this table three throws ago, but he kept passing me the dice to throw. I held them below his mouth, and he breathed his kisses into my closed palm. He wore a platinum wedding band, and I figured his wife was some statuesque beauty circulating nearby. When I was forced to move on, I tipped the croupier generously and hoped my Asian friend had noticed.

He scooped his chips into two paper cups, slid my stool out for me. I threw my hair over my shoulder. He passed me by the slots. "Allow me," he said, holding the door leading out of the casino and into the bar. I noticed his slim black pants, which hugged narrow hips. Like a connoisseur of fine tailoring, I noted the starched pale blue shirt, the French cuffs and the Gucci belt. He must have noted my drink earlier because he told the bartender to get me another Bloody Mary. We each picked up our glasses, and I expected him to make a toast, but instead he put a slim arm around my waist and guided me to a private banquette near the windows. His salt and pepper hair contrasted with his black eyes. He'd rolled up his sleeves, revealing hairless arms. The glass he held dripped condensation, a small trickle slipping from his wrist to his elbow. In slow motion he deliberately drew a cloth along his forearm. His cuffs, I noticed, bore embroidered navy initials, although deciphering them was impossible because the characters were Chinese.

"Do you have a name?" he asked. When I answered, he asked me to tell him something interesting about Rachel Gordon.

I thought I'd gone to heaven. His long thin arms were muscled. I wanted them around me. I felt the heat from his thighs. I followed the lines along his forearms. The contours of those muscles, like ropes twisting beneath the skin.

His conversation was to the point. His English, while impeccable, was stiff, like someone whose first language wasn't English. "To be clear, tonight is not for us," he said.

Disappointed, I took my hands off the table and dropped them on my lap. His hand found mine and held it on the bench seat. His thumb stroked the top of my hand. With every single movement and touch, my senses were excited. He knew the effect he was having on me. He asked the waitress to bring him a pen and paper.

"My name is Li. I am very happy that you allowed me to buy you a drink and tell you how lovely you are."

He was both vague and to the point. Was he trying to be mysterious, or was he unsure of his commitment to the woman who presumably wore a matching platinum band on her ring finger? No, Li wasn't the type to contrive to be mysterious.

"Rachel Gordon, you are quite different. You have that French *joie de vivre* attitude. Indulge me; write something about yourself that I can't tell just by looking at you."

If I had a conscience, its voice was drowned out by his presence. I told myself, as I had many times before, there's no such a thing as a "home wrecker." I squeezed his hand. When a man wandered outside his marriage, it was a sign of an unhealthy relationship.

I truly believed it was never "the other woman's" fault. Without hesitation, I wrote down my cabin number.

"Ah, there's my wife now. I'll have to excuse myself. And Rachel," he touched his index and middle fingers to his lips and pressed them to my mouth, "I promise to find you again before the cruise is over." I stayed in the dark booth at the rear of the piano bar and held the note over the flame of the candle. Why hadn't he taken it with him. Vanilla wax stuck to my finger, and I inhaled its sweet scent. Then I rubbed my fingers hard against one another, leaving a pile of wax shavings on the ebony table. I walked to a bar stool, opposite to where Li and his wife sat. She greeted him with the side of a pale cheek. I felt glad to see how meagre the competition was.

Looking in the mirror behind the bar, I studied her. She reminded me of a porcelain doll, lovely but unimpressive. I noticed she wore tiny ballet slippers, so I assumed she was a practical woman. Li didn't belong with a practical, demure woman. I could tell she didn't have what it took to hold onto him. She wore her long hair tied into an austere chignon at the back of her head. Although she was short, her posture was regal. She might have been a dancer when she was younger, but no, she was too short.

I ordered another Bloody Mary and turned to watch. I wasn't sure if it was Li I was trying to torture or myself. She handed Li a grey linen jacket. Shocked, I watched Joan approach their table. I turned back to watch them through the mirror behind the bar.

"Li, Amy, how good to see you. That dress is—" The two women kissed on both cheeks. When Li's wife smiled, I noticed too many teeth between her thin lips. As Joan and Li locked eyes I took the opportunity to slip away unnoticed.

Back in my room, I showered and spent extra time on my hair. I tried for a lighter than usual touch with my makeup and put on my favourite LBD, the iconic little black dress. Mauve threads woven into the spaghetti straps added just a hint of colour. I liked the final look and answered the door, ready with a sensual smile. A gloved gentleman stood there, holding a box from the H. Stern jewellery shop on the promenade. I took it inside to open it in private.

# CHAPTER 14

## *JOAN*

I walked through the noisy casino and found Amy and Li in the Champagne Bar, sitting close together on the same side of the banquette. Her soft skin glowed in the warm candlelight from the table votive. The peaceful, happy expression on both their faces led me to guess they were very much in love. I called their names to warn them of my approach because I felt as if I were interrupting an intimate conversation. Amy grinned, and then her expression changed. The waitress approached with a tray bearing one water glass and a bottle of Perrier, along with two flutes and a bucket holding a bottle of champagne.

They both rose when they saw me. I commented on Amy's chic sheath dress and took the seat opposite them. Li came around the table to pull out my chair.

"Take your jacket," Amy said to him. She threw the linen jacket roughly across the table, and it hit a wet spot in the centre of the table. He grimaced and jerked his head as though he'd been slapped. He shook his jacket and hung it around the back of the other chair on my side of the table.

"Please ask for another glass for that Cristal," she said, her voice too soft, too sweet. There was a disconnect between their voices and gestures. I looked back and forth between them but there were no clues as to what had happened before I'd arrived. Li nodded and signalled the waitress.

The tension made me uncomfortable. I picked the polish from a few of my nails, happy that at least I was wearing only clear polish and it wouldn't show.

Amy's picked up one of the champagne flutes. "And why are there only two glasses on the tray Li?"

"Easy," Li said, a hand on top of hers. She flicked it away.

My eyes searched my purse as I rummaged around for a mirror and my lipstick.

Li leaned towards Amy and warned, "I won't have you getting drunk in here again." He emphasized that last word, 'drunk', looking directly at me. Mortified, Amy stared at the tabletop. My heart went out to her. I reached for Amy's hand. Amy didn't notice; she was looking down. In the mirror behind her, when I had first sat down, I thought I'd seen Rachel. I looked for her now, but she was gone.

"To my husband and our first true vacation together in ten years of marriage," Amy said, her voice strong. She raised an empty flute.

I grabbed the Perrier and poured sparkling water for the three of us. "To vacationing," I said, we clinked glasses.

Thankfully, the waitress returned with an additional champagne flute. Then the conversation resumed; "Don't misunderstand Joan, Li travels frequently on business; we do not travel as a couple." The waitress opened the bottle, let Li test it, and poured the three fresh flutes.

"To health, happiness, and prosperity," Li said. His thin lipped smile was stretched taunt.

Li and I sipped our champagne while he asked where I was from and if this was my first cruise, two questions commonly heard among fellow passengers. Amy drank hers quickly and then a second glass as if she needed a thirst quencher. "To change," Li said, raising his glass especially high, as if that was toast-worthy.

"Well, I'll drink to that," I said.

"I'm going to get us some limes," Li said, excusing himself.

"Is something wrong?" I asked. "Do you want me to leave, Amy?" My fingers began rubbing over the tip of each nail in turn. All five fingers on one hand were devoid of polish already.

Amy shook her head. In Li's absence, she confided that they had their difficulties. "I helped him become the big man he is today.

He knows it but acts like it never happened, and I have too much pride to remind him." She didn't seem to enjoy the champagne. She poured herself a third glass but spent more time twirling the glass, watching the stream of bubbles rise to the top of the flute than sipping it. I got the feeling she was drinking just to annoy him but I couldn't be sure.

"Where did you two meet?" I asked.

"He'd been a country boy on a scholarship when he came to the Delhi School of Economics where I was doing my masters. I was his tutorial teacher."

"My God, Amy. So you were the older woman who seduced Li." We laughed.

"Don't laugh—it was a serious problem for his parents," she said. "But now, Li Chew is a distinguished CEO of a major Asian computer company that trades on the NASDAQ, the TSE, and others."

I looked at my watch before searching the room for Li.

"Oh, Li does that. He goes to the bathroom without telling me or goes wandering to avoid a scene in a public place. He could have legitimately received an urgent business call." She looked around before resuming the thread. "Sometimes, I hear his voice coming from a washroom or stairwell, wherever there is quiet, and he's having an intense conversation in a foreign language." She tucked some loose strands of hair inside her chignon and pulled a mother-of-pearl hairpin out of her purse and placed it strategically. "Thank goodness I've learned to entertain myself for long periods in a bar alone." She laughed, but the sound was more of a cackle, not light-hearted at all.

"That would upset me to no end," I said in earnest.

Amy's blank expression seemed frozen in place. "Li wants me to be jealous, and I am," she confessed.

"I'm afraid to ask, but is it other women or actual business demands that impose on his time so much?"

"We have paparazzi following us in Hong Kong," Amy said. "He's too recognizable to be having an affair and get away with it in our country." She shook her head and smiled her closed mouth smile, the one that gave nothing away. She'd clearly thought of this before. Amy raised her thin pencil- drawn eye brows.

My thoughts wandered to our conversation about how much he left her alone while he travelled but it wasn't my place to remind her of that. If I knew Amy better ... maybe, I'd say something. Regardless, I felt sorry for her blindness and her unhappiness which she couldn't acknowledge, not even to herself.

"You mean if I subscribed to *Fortune* magazine, I would know his face?" I said, changing the focus of the conversation. I sipped my drink. "This is the very best, isn't it?" She nodded with a closed mouth and I wondered if she did that because of her teeth.

"Exactly."

Joe was occasionally recognized, but it had never been a problem. I thought about it.

"It's simple," she said, "in our country, there's no assumption that behind every powerful man there's a dedicated, intelligent woman. In the western world, magazine coverage includes family photos and interview coverage of all family members, especially when a spouse has been influential in the business operation." Her eyes welled up with tears. "Since my family bankrolled his research and I shared intellectually in the development of the software it is particularly upsetting that Li does nothing to acknowledge my contribution." I passed her a tissue from my purse as her tears continued to flow.

"Help me to understand, Amy. Is it Li, or it your culture that denies you the recognition you deserve?"

"Both, I think," she said. She shook her head, undoing tendrils from her tight chignon. "It's both, but Li likes it this way, I can tell." She rolled one long loose strand around a finger.

She swirled the last mouthful of Cristal around her glass before draining it. "I love the feel of those bubbles inside my mouth," she said. "Bring me a Cab Sauv," she yelled to a waitress passing by. She upturned the Cristal inside the champagne bucket. I didn't know how we could have finished the whole bottle by now. If Li didn't get back soon, she'd be well into the red and too tipsy to even walk into dinner tonight.

Amy drummed her fingers on the table. I looked around and checked my watch.

"Don't worry; he'll be back any moment. But do me a favour— don't ask him where he was. I never do," Amy said.

I moved beside her on the banquette and squeezed her hand. Again I noticed how small and smooth it was.

"Have I told you about the four pillars of a healthy home according to the great Li, CEO of the Chinese version of America's Google search engine?"Without waiting for a reply, Amy continued, "An immaculate, uncluttered castle, loyal worker bees, weekly psychoanalysis, twice-daily yoga, and a diet rich in fish, fruit, and vegetables." I nodded stupidly, not sure what else was expected. Her lips were stained red, making her teeth appear a little yellow.

When Li returned carrying a water glass, his face had become softer and his tone friendlier. "It makes me glad to see Amy enjoying another woman's company. Ordinarily, I prefer small yachts or private planes, but the cruise ship, her preference, allows her the chance to mingle with all kinds of people." I looked at him, scrunching up my face at his condescension. Amy noticed it too and turned her back to him.

"Don't pay any attention to him. He's what Americans call 'snobbish.' But there are lots of other reasons to love him. You just have to keep reminding yourself what they are." She laughed, a little too loudly.

He looked at me and bowed slightly. "I apologize for abandoning you for so long." He scowled at the upturned empty champagne bottle and picked up the wine to check how far into it we were. "I socialize with business people who are used to my behaviour."

"I socialize with my therapist," Amy said. She's interested in me and fortunately, doesn't have any inclination to share her problems." She laughed and began to cough.

"Shush, Amy. Not so loud," Li said. He left to get her a glass of water.

"Thank you." She tipped it back too quickly and swallowed. Water dripped off her chin. Amy used her napkin to dab it and apologized for her sloppiness, not at all resembling the woman I'd photographed in the elevator earlier. "And guess how my wonderful husband reacted to the suggestion of marital counselling?"

Li stiffened in his chair. He poured himself a glass of water and silently offered to do the same for me.

Amy's light tone couldn't hide the animosity; "Li said his schedule was too full for that."

He cleared his throat. "Do you know I'm sitting right here?"

My therapist and I often meet outside her office at a restaurant of my choosing and she won't ever let me pay for the meal. Isn't that unusual?"

"Not when you pay her exorbitant bills, it isn't," Li said.

Without thinking I said, "*I Never Promised You a Rose Garden.* Remember that movie?" They both looked confused. "It had a depressing theme. The point it made was that to be master of your own destruction is preferable to any method of destruction imposed by another. Or at least that's how I remember it." Li and Amy still looked confused.

He said, "Smile, darling. I'm giving you what you most wanted: my time. And I'm sitting here with you in spite of the fact that you're insulting me in front of our new friend."

I gazed at Amy. She was sipping her second glass of red wine and had consumed maybe three or four flutes of champagne. LI took the glass out of her hand. She batted her heavily mascaraed lashes.

Her tears had dried up, leaving marks akin to train tracks down each cheek. There were dark circles under her eyes that I hadn't seen when she'd arrived earlier.

"Are you married, Joan?" Li asked.

I looked down at my wedding ring and twisted it around and around before answering. "My husband passed away last February." It was a statement of fact, now entered into public record.

"Well then, here's a woman Amy can relate to," Li said, his eyes twinkling with amusement. "Amy informs me she often feels like a widow." His hairless, perfectly oval face didn't change as he scanned our expressions. Although he was an attractive man, at the moment, I didn't find him likeable.

Amy slid along the leather seat of our banquette and stood up. Li and I sat in silence, not saying a word untill she'd returned from the bar with a bowl of nuts. "I think this wine has gone to my head. I'm feeling a little queasy," she said. "Shouldn't ever drink on an empty stomach, Li tells me, but he also reminds me, shouldn't eat unless you're hungry. I'm always thirsty but never hungry. So what's a woman to do?" She popped a handful of mixed nuts into her mouth.

Amy leaned in. I expected a private word, a whisper, but instead her voice rose, the slurring attracting the attention of many strangers. "At home the only private time with my husband I can count on is during our morning yoga practice." She rested her head on the back of the upholstered bench seat. Soon she stopped talking. Amy had fallen asleep.

"Can I get you anything else?" Li asked.

I couldn't believe him. I looked around the room for a familiar face, but of course there'd be no one to help Amy or me. Where was Rachel when I needed her? I used my teeth to even out a nail that had cracked up the centre. I hated when that happened. With all their talk about a healthy lifestyle, they had a strange relationship.

Li stood and unrolled his cuffs, doing up the buttons. He slipped on his jacket, moved to Amy's side, and placed one arm around her waist. Li then pulled Amy upright by shoving his hip against her chair and tilting her towards him. She immediately became alert, rising on her own.

"Leave me alone," she said while she struggled to move his hand from behind her back.

"The way I see it, I'm a widow of a different kind," she said, standing upright as if nothing out of the ordinary had happened. "Li isn't sick with any fatal disease other than ambition."

"Come on Amy, it's time to go." With his hands on her shoulders, he said, "I love you and am going to try to give you the best three week holiday."

Amy and I walked side by side with Li a step ahead. "Did I tell you we're going to a yoga retreat for two solid weeks in Florida after this cruise on *The Liberty?*" She rose on her tiptoes and tried to place a kiss on Li's cheek but only succeeded in getting a lipstick mark on his shirt collar. His mouth twisted, unkindly.

I had to try to keep my face expressionless. Their acrimonious relationship made me wonder why she wanted Li's company. Amy threaded her arm through mine and quickened her pace. I struggled to keep her upright and avoid us both weaving down the hall. "You're wearing flats—I'm not. Can we please slow down?" I said.

Amy told Li that I played decent tennis, but walking was not my forte. She laughed.

Li stopped and turned. He seemed to be assessing my strength.

"I haven't watched you play in years, Li. Probably because you play in the office gym. Why not decide upon a time tomorrow with Joan, and I'll be the cheering squad?" Amy said.

"But which of us would you cheer for?" he asked, stepping in and hugging her.

I slowed down and walked behind them. I could see Li's fingers softly moving across Amy's forearm, near the elbow.

"Wait," I said. "I'm up for a game but we can't schedule tennis tomorrow. It's our day in port . . . Belize. So when should we book the court?"

I figured I'd need a practice day, so I suggested Thursday, before we blew kisses to each other and moved into the Rembrandt Dining Room.

# CHAPTER 15

## *JOAN*

The maître d' asked my table number, then instructed a young waiter to escort me there. The Rembrandt was a mammoth three-storey restaurant. I'd seen part of it at breakfast, but it looked different with the dimmed chandeliers and candlelight. I faltered when I saw my table with seven strangers. The group seemed pretty well paired off. If this didn't work out, I'd blame Ian and Rebecca. The kids had insisted on this choice, worried that if I sat alone I'd come home more depressed than when I left. I looked at the bunch of matronly women and old men and doubted they were capable of stimulating conversation. Besides, the kids were wrong; I wasn't depressed.

The first man to extend his hand was an elderly, presumably retired naval officer. "Submarine, Korea, 1950–53," he said in response to the scrutiny I was giving his lapel pin. It was a long brass bar covered with three rows of coloured ribbons. He introduced his wife as Laura and explained they were from the Isle of Man. The two other couples at the table had flown to Miami from California. Susan, the loud, big busted woman I recognized from the pool this afternoon sat beside her sleeping husband whose face I didn't get a look at. Their traveling companions, Sharon and Mitch, were very close, old friends.

"Not old people—old friends," Susan said and then chuckled at her own joke. "Sharon here went to grade school with me." She raised her glass to Sharon who toasted their friendship back. "Come sit, Joan. Have some of the wine we ordered."

I shook my head. "Already had some in the lounge, but thank you," I said.

The other person to complete our table of eight was a single male traveller who declined to offer his name.

The waiter came to inquire about my beverage of choice. When he'd gone, I introduced myself.

"I'm Joan, from Canada. This is my first cruise," I said, inviting small talk from my tablemates. The adjectives "happy" and "single," and the noun "widow" came to mind. Laura was the friendliest, which was surprising since it's usually Americans who are so warm and welcoming.

When everyone had ordered, Susan asked the already familiar question: "And how are you enjoying the cruise?"

"I'm finding the variety of activities almost overwhelming, like going into a Toys "R" Us store these days and trying to find the perfect gift among the zillion options they have."

Sharon reminded everyone that you can't do everything and have a relaxing vacation.

"We don't sit in the sun like many other people but mostly we find shady spots to read or listen to lectures and go to the gym frequently when it's a sea day. We only do those three things." She looked to Mitch for confirmation.

"Precisely my point," the officer from the Isle of Man chimed in. "Some people want a restful vacation, and others crave stimulation, games, and activities. Here you have the best of both worlds. Choices and more choices."

Laura raised her hand in the air, her fingers positioned as if she held a pencil in her right hand. "I make a list, each and every day over coffee." Her husband told us they didn't always stick to it but it was good to know when those activities of particular interest started and where they were held.

"Mike and I are like that," Susan said. "One day we do next to nothing except fool around in the pool," she looked at him and winked in spite of the fact that he sat with his eyes closed, "and the next we're on the go; from the casino at ten, to lunch at one, to a dance class at two, to the art auction at four, and then to side-by-side manicures at five thirty." Susan turned to Mike for agreement. We could all hear him snoring.

"I'll take him upstairs and put him to bed," Susan told the table. "Clearly, Mike had too much sun and alcohol today. It was a do-nothing-but-drink kind of day." She looked at him lovingly, not at all embarrassed.

The big man on the other side of Susan got up to help her hoist him out of his chair.

"Will you be able to manage? Do you want me to come with you?" he asked.

"No, I'm fine, Neil," Susan said.

I watched them leave. Mike stumbled and fell into a diner seated at the table next to us. The irate young girl called out, "Jerk! Watch where you're going," but Susan ignored her.

"Neil," Susan called back to us, "meet Joan. You haven't even said hello to her yet. She lives in your old hometown. Make friends while I'm gone."

I felt my dining companions look to me for a reaction and I felt my face turning red. Neil raised his hands in the air as if he'd given up and moved into the seat vacated by Mike, which put him next to me. The waiter rushed over to provide a fresh napkin, cutlery, and a water glass.

Neil extended his hand, took mine, and lightly brushed his lips across my knuckles. "Nice to meet you, Joan. You've got to excuse Susan. I certainly have." He laughed to himself. "For example, at the pool today, she walked around asking every lady who wasn't wearing a wedding ring if they might be interested in meeting a nice black man—me! Now what kind of a sell is that? Nice, my ass. Does this nose look 'nice'? I've been in more barroom brawls and pro rings than I can count." He laughed again.

I knew it wasn't false bravado because, joking aside, he was in fantastic shape; his thick neck was corded by bulging tendons, and those muscled arms were the real McCoy. His face was so dark I couldn't read his expression. A memory came to mind: Joe had had a signed picture of Mohammed Ali in his office, although I couldn't remember how he'd acquired it. Maybe the memory was significant. I picked up my Diet Coke and took a big sip but it went down the wrong way and I spat it up. The dark liquid fanned out across my plate and the surrounding white tablecloth. Neil laughed before apologizing and asking if I was all right. The couple from the Isle of Man looked disgusted. Laura picked up her napkin and dabbed at her face as if my projectile spewing had come close to soiling her space, which it hadn't. Her purple nail polish caught my attention.

"Can't take me anywhere," I said, trying to bring a little levity to the situation.

"Way to loosen up a crowd, Joan." Neil applauded. "So where were you last night? Entertaining some other lucky group in one of the specialty restaurants? You do any other tricks?" he asked.

I nodded and continued smiling. I pushed my chair back to let the wait staff deal with the mess. Changing the topic, I said, "So Susan says we're both from Toronto. I take it you moved away a long time ago."

"Yeah," Neil said. "I moved when my career took off, but my father lives there, so I visit often. And where exactly do you live?"

Once appetizers came, everyone's attention was diverted to oohing and aahing over the attractively presented food.

Susan returned and dominated the conversation immediately. "You know, I think the sun must affect the absorption rate of alcohol. Mike isn't always this bad, is he?" Meaningful glances volleyed around the table like a hot potato. "People tend to overdo their drinking in the sun. Don't you agree?"

"Susan, we've talked about this before," Mitch said. "Drinking till you pass out? He shouldn't be doing that regularly." He played with his napkin under the table.

"Oh, don't be party poopers," Sharon said. "We agreed not to discuss anyone's drinking problems during this trip." She used the first two fingers of each hand to indicate quotation marks around "drinking problems."

"This is a farewell party for my buddy Mike and alcohol," Mitch said. "Remember, you two, we agreed not to get on his case at all during the cruise."

Neil elbowed me softly. "Would you mind if I took off my jacket?" he asked.

The question startled me a little.

"A problem developed soon after I took up boxing—I haven't been able to buy jackets or coats off the rack since I was around ten. In a pinch I do, and then I regret it. Like now, I can barely move my arms." He shook his arms away from his body.

"So do you generally eat in places where jackets aren't required?" I said.

"Uh-huh, except on cruises. That's the one rule the ship enforces, and I like to use the dining room at dinnertime. I have a few tailor-made suits, but who wears suits anymore? So when someone marches over to tell me to put my jacket back on, don't be embarrassed for me."

"Ah, not to worry. I don't get embarrassed that easily," I said.

Neil told me this was his second voyage with the *Liberty*. "I find it especially good for a single man," he said.

"Any reason other than the obvious?" I asked. "Meeting single women?"

"No, no . . . no." He tilted his head, and a small smile turned one side of his mouth up. "Joan, you're a surprise. Are you always this direct?"

"Heavens, no. I'm just having fun with you. I guess I feel comfortable being silly with you."

"Some things I prefer to do with other people but I don't need to be in a relationship to have company when cruising," Neil said. "Like now . . . dinner table conversation, or later, discussions with people who've been at the same theatre." He called the waiter over and ordered a drink.

Those were the same reasons I came on board.

I picked up my napkin and dabbed my lips. My steak had been cooked perfectly. Even the vegetables were crisp, surprising considering the kitchen was dealing with some fifteen hundred passengers; mind you, there were two seatings.

"So are you one of those who love dress-up nights? I suppose most women do," Neil said.

I smiled, thinking I did actually look forward to an occasion to wear something fabulous. I hadn't had the opportunity to dress up in a long time.

"That's what I figured," he said. "Not me—I'm afraid I don't own a monkey suit."

Before I could interrupt, Neil went on. "Yeah, I know I can rent one on board, but they don't suit my body type. There are enough options for both dining and dancing that I don't mind missing the formal occasions." While I'd been talking with him, I'd overheard the others talking about the excursions they had booked for our first port, Belize. By this time, our plates had been cleared and the waiter was circling with a coffee thermos.

"I'm beat. You'll have to excuse me," Neil said, glancing around the table. "Have a great day in port tomorrow. See y'all at dinner." He pushed in his chair. I watched him, curious to know more about him. Later, I'd google both Li and Neil.

# CHAPTER 16

# *JOAN*

Neil seemed to have made quite an impression on the women at our table. "I mean, if you were a fisherman and wanting to haul in something really special on this voyage . . ." Sharon's voice drifted off as she stared at his retreating form.

I frowned and shook my head; I knew what she was suggesting. "No, not me. I didn't come here looking for a man."

Susan added, "Yes sir. That man is all man—keeps himself in good shape."

"Well if looks aren't incentive enough"—she looked at me meaningfully—"he has deep pockets. He was quite successful in his prime." She cleared her throat and took a swig of her wine. "I myself wish I'd met him some twenty years ago. Even then, I was loose as a goose and into men of all colours." Susan laughed and told the group that this was no exaggeration.

I sighed with relief when the conversation reverted to a discussion of tomorrow's excursions. Susan asked me which one I'd booked for our first port of call.

I had nothing organized and knew from their conversation I'd regret it if I didn't arrange something quick. I asked everyone at our table to keep a lookout for my friends, explaining that Rachel or Sam might show up before I returned.

I stepped out of the line every few minutes, wondering why it wasn't advancing at all. Only one option was left by the time I made it to the counter. A crowd of people exiting through the main doors of the dining room forced me to take a circuitous route around the room back to my table. An unfamiliar twinge of jealousy pulled at the corners of my mouth as I spotted Rachel and Sam, rubbing shoulders at my table. She was, quite consciously I was sure, presenting him with a good look at her full chest. She shook out his pocket handkerchief and pushed it back in place by running two long fingernails into his breast pocket.

"There. That's better," she said, apparently aware of my proximity without having turned her head. "If you must make such an outdated fashion statement, the very least you can do is form a proper puff."

"Thanks," Sam said. His twisted smile angled away from Rachel as his sparkling eyes met mine. He smiled a greeting and asked if I wanted to help polish off the bottle of red he'd ordered in my absence. I shook my head. "You look great, Joan." His simple, sincere compliment wiped the smile off Rachel's face. I felt glad before chastising myself for being so petty. Rachel raised her brows as if to ask what I thought of her flirting. I wasn't sure how to answer.

"Oh my God. You're blushing, Joan," said Rachel. The chill I felt toward her increased with each adolescent remark and gesture.

I looked around the almost empty dining room. "Are you two ready? I think we should head to the theatre or we'll end up with seats at the back behind some pillar."

Sam stood immediately, but Rachel remained sitting, swirling the wine in her oversized goblet.

"Let's just finish this, huh, Sam?" she said, as if I weren't even present. He moved behind her chair and began sliding it out for her.

"Okay, okay. I get it," she said, rising.

"So aren't I the lucky one?" Sam said, not skipping a beat. "I'm going to parade two beautiful women, one on each arm, down the main thoroughfare of this ship. You know what I always say: the only thing better than escorting one beautiful woman is escorting two."

He offered each of us an arm. I cringed and rolled my eyes at his corniness. It seemed so out of character and underlined my impression that he was pretending to be someone he wasn't.

Rachel grabbed my arm and pulled me into the washroom. "You're going to blow it. Sam is somewhat interested in you, but trust me, he'd be more interested if he thought you didn't like him."

"Rachel, you're ridiculous. Because I'm not interested," I insisted. "He helped me when I banged my head yesterday. That's it. "

"Well, it's changed." She refreshed her lipstick and smacked her lips together. "And you're interested — you just don't know it yet."

"Come on, let's go," I said, placing my palm against the washroom door.

"Just remember: the first relationship after a marriage is only a dry run in the bull ring. It's just a stepping stone to get your feet wet in the pond you've been out of for so long. You don't actually swim till you get to the sea," Rachel said.

"Your metaphors are tedious," I said. "If what you're trying to say is that, if anything, this thing with Sam will be a meaningless relationship, just say so."

Rachel blocked the bathroom door and faced me. "That's exactly what I've been trying to say." I moved her out of the way to let another women enter. "You just need to get laid." She leaned against it and with arms crossed stubbornly in front of her said, "You know, I've never slept with an Asian. I've tried a black, an Egyptian, a Jew, and a Russian. But I've had my eye out for an attractive Asian for a long time and the opportunity seems to  have just presented itself. Funny, huh?"

Strange aspirations, not exactly funny,I thought.

Rachel extended her arm and brought it up close to her face. She was staring at her jewelled bracelet. It looked extremely delicate on her big boned wrist. "Hey Joan, you want to know how I got this?"

"Not if it involves a sordid tale of infidelity or racial ignorance."

"You're the one who's racially ignorant," Rachel said. She punched me in the arm and I winced. "I'm the one with experience."

"Enough!" I said, covering my ears." I want a decent seat, and I'm leaving."

The diamond and emerald bracelet sparkled on Rachel's wrist as she pushed the washroom door open. I was sure I'd eventually hear the story behind it.

"I'll go ahead and get us seats," I said, leaving Sam or Rachel to walk the rest of the distance to the theatre. I wasn't sure I wanted the company of either of them. It was going to be an early night for me.

An hour later Rachel and I exited the theatre singing, "Life is a cabaret, old chum, come to the cabaret . . ." Sam shushed us half-heartedly.

One of Rachel's hands was up in the air. Her hips shifted as she performed a salsa move forward and back. "So, amigos, you two up for a little salsa in the Bolero Bar?"

"Not me," I said. "I can't dance salsa very well at all."

"Well I can teach you," Rachel said, tugging on my hand. "Come on, I can tell you've got your second wind." Rachel's smile begged me not to disappoint. She made puppy eyes to reinforce the message.

I hesitated. I had slept through my first night and had promised myself I wasn't going on this trip to sit in my room and read, which was exactly what I'd do if I returned to my cabin now. "Why not?" I said, "but you can't laugh at me."

"Terrific," Sam said. "The bar's open until two every night." He tapped the crystal face of his watch and pointed out that it was only ten thirty. "Too early to hit the sack."

I yawned and told them I'd stay for an hour.

Soon after the three of us found seats at a ringside table, Rachel came around my chair and held out her hand to take mine and lead me onto the dance floor. "Watch" she said, dramatically using two fingers of one hand to point to both of her eyes. She turned around and with her back to me stepped forward, swivelling her hips to the right when she placed her right foot forward, then shifting her weight and swivelling her hips to the left when she stepped forward with her left foot and so on, before she added arm motions.

After a two-second demonstration, I said I'd got it. I started to laugh when I found myself mimicking her swivelling hips, sweeping arm motions and facial contortions. They all melted together in a dramatic sing-along to "Mambo No. 5." I joined in when they got to the chorus, the words to which I didn't realize I knew: "A little bit of Monica in my life, a little bit of Erica by my side, a little bit of Rita is all I need, a little bit of Tina is what I see." I sashayed back, exhausted and sweaty, to the table where Sam sat continuously applauding.  Rachel danced on, moving forward and back and in small circles with one hand in the air.

"Drink?" Sam asked.

"Diet Coke," I said, "Thanks."

After I'd finished my drink, I told Sam I wanted to head out. He insisted on walking me back upstairs.

I placed my hands around my mouth to be heard above the music. "Rach, I'm going upstairs," I yelled.

"Why so early? You turn into a pumpkin at midnight?" She shook her head as if she were disappointed and told us she wasn't going to argue because she was meeting someone else later anyway.

"I'll be here for another hour if you want to come back, Sam," she called.

Sam didn't respond but I knew he'd heard her just as I had. My hand was held firmly in his and he gently rubbed the top of my hand with his thumb. Before I knew it, he was leading me to the elevators. The ride to the tenth floor was silent, and for once the elevator was empty. At my door he shuffled from foot to foot. I smiled self-consciously, my knees locked so tightly they hurt. I fiddled in my little clutch to find my key card, giving myself time to decide whether to offer him my cheek or my lips. Should I shut my eyes?

Sam took the plastic key car out of my hand, kissed me on the cheek, and pushed the door in for me. He had turned around and left before I realized that he'd said good night and I'd said not a word.

Lying in bed, I identified my mixed-up feelings. Guilt because it had only been a year since Joe died and my family would probably see my interest in another man as inappropriate. If truth be told I felt a touch jealous, because I wanted to know if Sam had gone back to see Rachel or if he'd gone elsewhere. I also felt guilty about not saying anything to Rachel about Amy and Li. If she were somehow involved with Li— that would be awful. But had I done anything to feel guilty about? Would I feel guilty if I slept with Sam? . Did I miss being held firmly and feeling a lover's hot breath on my neck? All of a sudden, the answer was very clear. Yet knowing the answer to that, wouldn't let sleep come any sooner.

I did miss Joe, more than I could say. But he wasn't coming back. No one could predict my shelf life, but I wasn't due to expire any time soon. So of course I should miss sex; reputedly, I was in my peak years, but in reality I only missed the idea of being passionate. I was scared to expose my middle-aged body to someone new. Tears flooded my eyes again, just when I thought I'd seen the last of them.

At the sink I held cool water up to my swollen red eyes. I don't know when I'd come to the decision that Sam was a safe person to get intimate with and get this over with. I'd never have to see him again.

# CHAPTER 17

## *JOAN*

## *Monday, February 3, 2003*

## *Day 3, Belize*

As soon as I entered the room, I saw Amy and Li warming up on their matching yoga mats. Li's forehead met his shins. Amy was also bending down, palms on the ground. With one hand she pointed to the mat beside her where she'd saved me a place.

Louisa, our instructor, introduced herself, cutting off any further conversation. I followed her instructions, trying to clear my mind of all else. "Allow your legs to spread wider than hip width," she said in her Spanish accent. "We begin and end our yoga practice in savasana, or corpse pose." The music was soft, in sync with Louisa's tone. "Roll to your right side and gently push yourself upright to mountain position. Inhale; circle your arms backwards, up to the sky, and bring your palms together as you dip back. Exhale; fold forward, softly bending your knees, your hands to the ground. Inhale; flatten your back, lift up halfway. Exhale; release; forward fold, head to your knees. Inhale; your right leg back and then the other; downward dog . . ."

I thought of all the times I'd done this, every morning, next to the bed while Joe opened the curtains, padded down to the kitchen to put the coffee on, and returned with half a toasted bagel and coffee mugs on a tray. Joe had munched his bagel, watching with an interested smile and waiting patiently.

"Oh, I love when you get in the cobra position. Lying on your flat stomach, your chest raised, head back, your little chin jutting out as much as possible. Your neck becomes long and slender, and it begs for my kisses." Joe often used to interrupt me before I finished the forty-minute routine. That would never happen again.

Now, Louisa looked around the room, meeting the eyes of as many participants as possible without breaking the flow. I saw her eyes settle appreciatively on Li and then dart to Amy. I didn't have time to think about that as she began the next salutation. "Again." During the third sun salutation B, Louisa said, "Now hold that down dog."

I smirked and began coughing as excess saliva slid forward in my mouth. I tried to swallow, which was hard since I was bent upside down. I smiled, picturing Joe that time when he'd laid down on his back underneath my downward dog. He was agile and fun. Saliva dripped on the mat, and I collapsed laughing, looking anything but serene.

A few seconds later, I was calm and moving into pigeon pose. A painful spasm attacked my back thigh muscle. I clumsily unfolded both legs so I could knead the cramp. It wasn't going away. I heard a loud moan and realized it was me. I knew my behaviour in class was odd, and I felt self-conscious.

"Here, let me help," Amy said, speaking quietly. "Take deep breaths." She expertly rolled the hard muscle between experienced fingers. "I bet you're dehydrated. I'm surprised I'm not, given my drinking last night. I made you uncomfortable and owe you an apology. I shouldn't have—"

"Ah. Finally, it's gone. Thank you," I said, cutting off any reference to her embarrassing behaviour of the night before.

During the final savasana, I tried to let my body relax, pushing all thoughts away, but it was no use. I pictured myself undressing in a dark room. I squeezed my eyes shut, straining to identify the male silhouette standing within arm's reach. Did it belong to Sam, Joe, or someone else? Louisa clicked her finger cymbals together. I rolled over and opened my eyes. I saw the pair of twoonie- sized brass discs that were attached by wide elastic bands to Louisa's right hand index finger and thumb. "Namaste," she said, bowing her head.

"Namaste," came the response of the class.

I hopped up and began rolling up my mat. I hugged Amy and promised to catch up with her later.

"Don't you have time to have one drink before you rush off." Amy asked.

Li rolled up her mat. I explained that because of my Belize tour, I barely had time for a shower. "Definitely later," I said as I left.

The various excursion groups met in the Pavilion Theatre. The sanctuary tour was one of the top picks for Belize. Almost half the people in the room wore circular stickers of neon green or pink but there were many other colours used to identify the other tour groups.

I looked around at the people in the room. Susan and her husband, wearing red stickers, were all smiles, waving as if we were close friends. Neil, unmarked by any sticker, sat near them. His eyes met mine, and he smiled brightly. Even with his broken nose and ill-fitting clothing, Neil was extremely attractive. He was the opposite of Sam, who was pale and had a slight build. I had no doubt Sam, had he been there, would have been dressed like a Ralph Lauren model, whereas Neil wore comfortable clothing, baggy jeans and an overly loose black T-shirt. He held a bunched-up light grey sweatshirt in his fist. I wondered if Rachel would like to meet Neil.

When my group leader stood up and raised his neon pink lollipop stick, I fell in line. I felt like a child on a school excursion. The rest of the travellers would be doing the very same thing, but that somehow failed to make me feel less juvenile about following the lollipop stick. The gangplank off the *Liberty* was a metal bridge attached to a small tender.

"Why do we have to drop anchor and take the tender in to Belize City?" I asked Louisa, who happened to sit down next to me on the small motor boat.

"Simple," she said. "The water depth is very shallow along the pier . . . it's inadequate for a ship like the *Liberty*, whose hull hangs deep in the water."

"Hmm." I rested on my elbows and faced the sun. My hand trailed in the cool turquoise water as we motored to shore.

"Test, test." A heavyset local fellow tapped the mike. "I'm going to use our fifteen minutes on the tender to tell you a thing or two about Belize," he said. As he spoke I began taking pictures of the pastel-coloured houses with their long lines of washing along the shore. Our guide best represented the local colour in my opinion. I focused on him, his dreadlocks with hemp woven into his hair, his colourful shirt and jewellery made of leather. He exuded an easy going personality with his sing-song voice and warm smile.

"Hello and welcome," the young man began. "My name is Willy and I was born here, just outside the city limits of Belize City. Belize was first inhabited by the Mayans in 900 AD, so if you have time, take in the museum or climb a Mayan ruin before heading back on the tender." His travelogue held my attention for a few seconds only. He ended by informing us about the tender travel options back to the ship. We were free to stay on shore up to 11:00 p.m. if we wanted. "Remember," Willy said, "tenders run back and forth all evening but don't get left behind. That could prove very problematic for you."

"There are wonderful local seafood and Caribbean restaurants here," said Louisa, "and the mall contains duty-free stores, but in reality the deals aren't so great, so beware."

I thanked her for the warning. It was much the same in all the islands. "Yoga was great this morning. Enjoy the rest of your day," I said as I preceded her off the tender.

As I walked down the pier, I noticed Rachel and Neil sitting on the edge of a fountain, hips touching. Well, that didn't take long, I mused. I felt envious and put on my big glasses.

The coach bus was air-conditioned, and I was fortunate to find the last window seat. The main Belize government buildings, hospitals, libraries, poor and wealthy districts, were identified by our tour guide while the bus meandered through the narrow streets. I was glad to see less disparity between the rich and the poor than Joe and I had noticed on other Caribbean islands. As we neared our destination we heard about the charitable organization that ran the sanctuary and cared for their collection of animals injured in the wild.

In the animal sanctuary parking lot, our guide distributed cold water bottles. The howler monkeys unnerved everyone. Once we could identify them, it wasn't as bad, but their piercing cries sounded as if they were fighting one another right next to us. Several older travellers rushed ahead, hands clapped over their ears. A teenage girl leaned against the cage, mocking her parents, who cowered together far away from the noise coming from the monkeys. Just then a small reddish-brown monkey jumped from the canopy of branches overhead. He clung to the wire cage by one arm, twisting the girl's long curls in his wrinkled black paw. He shrieked louder and more shrilly, competing to be heard over the girl's screams.

"Fuck!" The scream was muffled, but the terror was obvious. "Help me . . . help!" This time her voice had more power behind it. Her parents stood frozen. The tour guide rushed over and took a knife from her pocket. "No!" the girl yelled.

Her mother finally sprang into action. "What, what, what are doing? Just shoot it, for Christ's sake." The mother was as panicked as her daughter.

The raised knife slashed through the air, freeing the girl from the monkey's grasp. The girl with half a head of hair chopped off fell into her mother's arms. We stood transfixed as the sounds of the hysterical girl and her mother's faded away. The bus driver and the father trailed behind, heading back toward the bus. The girl held her hand over the side of her head where it must have felt almost bald. The rest of us broke away and continued meandering through the footpaths again. We were all extra cautious to keep a safe distance from the cages.

A colourful pair of toucans caught my attention. They perched on a stand made of an old tree, out in the open. I rushed to unpack my camera and snap a few good shots through the greenery, from the side of a tree, and up close through a veil of palm fronds. I ran to catch up to the rest of the tourists, who had passed me along the path.

An umbrella of foliage shielded the dirt path from the sun. The piercing shrieks of the howlers made everyone jumpy. I was shivering, and not just because we were walking in the shade. The thing was, you heard them before you saw them.

"These animals arrived from Panama," our guide explained. He told interesting stories that likened each animal to a refugee in need of sanctuary and health care, and I believed him. At the end of a circuitous path was a long cage within a tall wire mesh enclosure. This was where, for twenty-five dollars, visitors were invited to have their photo taken inside the cage with a wild animal. This time, I looked at the guide and saw him for what he was: a storyteller. I kicked the dirt. I shook my head at the other naive tourists my age. The animals must have been heavily sedated. I felt the ethical wrong doing of drugging these animals so strongly I wanted to storm out of there but I had to wait. My head turned to look for someone to talk to but I had a change of heart. And what kind of person would get into the cage with a black panther or a gorilla? I drained my water bottle, thinking about the irony of promoting this place as a sanctuary for animals that had been hurt in their natural setting.

I closed my eyes as soon as I was seated aboard the bus. The subdued conversation of other passengers included fragments that rang true for me: ". . . the ethics of drugging the animals they were supposed to be helping . . . desperate to generate funds . . . it isn't all black and white . . . can't sue . . . charity."

"I'd sue if it would help but—"

I jumped. The voice of the teenage girl's mother came from right beside me.

"Poor baby. She's going to be emotionally scarred for life," she said. "I just might sue them."

This was supposed to be a quiet day for me. I resented all the hysteria. With challenging wide eyes, I said, "She's calm and feeling better now, correct?"

"Not much. That was horrific." I looked at the girl's mother, guessing something American would be physically obvious about her. She began to sniffle and wiped her nose on her sleeve.

"It was an unfortunate accident — could have happened to any one of us," I said. I was in no mood for further discussion and put in my head set cutting off further discussion. I felt a hard elbow in my ribs. "What the—." I pulled my ear buds out.

"You don't have to say anything else." She hopped up, and seconds later her husband claimed the seat next to me.

I rushed to get off the bus when it stopped in front of the duty-free stores in Belize City. As predicted, they were a disappointment. I checked the sidewalk in front of the duty-free mall for the girl and her parents. The coast was clear. I made a run for a bar on the beach.

It was an ideal spot to watch a sunset. "Ha," I said, laughing at my stupidity. I'd have to turn around and face the interior mountain to see the setting sun going down in the west since the patio bar and restaurant faced the Caribbean Sea . . . due east. No matter. If I waited long enough, I'd see something scenic, as the moon was already brightening slivers of the inky water.

"What can I get you, miss?" the bartender asked.

"Would you have a Beaujolais?" I asked. His confused look was answer enough. "Or I know, I'll have a small pitcher of sangria." And here I was, sitting at a bar alone, for the first time in a long time. Before this trip I'd thought about seeing my friends again, and even made a list of all the single, divorced, or widowed women I knew. Many of these women were acquaintances from book club or card night or yoga, but organizing something the way Joe used to plan vacations for us and another couple was too much work . . . for me  . . . for now. I felt lucky to get on this all inclusive no-worry cruise. My glass was empty. How did that happen so quickly? I leaned my elbow on the bar and held my head in my hand. The last big trip Joe and I had taken was when our group of four couples took the three-week winery tour in France. The more I thought about it, the more I fell in love with cruising.

"Thank you." I sipped my drink and recalled Joe's last night alive. I remember his comment on the wine we stored downstairs.

"We have a few good bottles of wine in the cellar. Let's use one of them before . . . you know?" Joe said.

I shook my head. "Why bother opening anything? You said you can't taste it. Remember?"

We ate at home, or at least I ate. We finished the whole bottle smiling and being silly. I restrained myself from telling Joe how exceptional the wine was. It was so ironic that I knew nothing about wine before I met Joe and now that we'd gone on that winery tour I was somewhat of a connoisseur. Yet I couldn't share my appreciation of fine wines with him. I enjoyed my chicken too, in spite of the fact that I saw Joe just moved his around on his plate rather than eat any of it. Later we watched an episode of *Law and Order* on television in the bedroom. I leaned towards the centre of the bed to kiss him lightly and then he turned away from me and I turned on my light to read.

Part way through the night I shuffled, half asleep, to the bathroom. The bottle of anti-nausea medication that was supposed to be taken an hour before Those Other Pills (as I had come to think of them) lay empty on top of the counter. I stopped myself from looking for them and groped my way back to bed. My eyes wouldn't stay closed, but I forced myself to lie still, not look at Joe, not allow myself to know if it was done or in progress. He'd decided he didn't want any teary goodbyes, and I'd respect that, not let myself dwell on that decision, not then. Tomorrow would be the worst day of my life. I remembered making a long list in my head. The hours ticked by, like the second hand on a watch clicking into position ever so slowly, methodically. Lack of sleep and the stress of averting my gaze until 5:00 a.m. had done me in. Eventually, I'd leaned over Joe and gone numb. I wished I could go back to sleep, just get a few hours before making all the calls, but it was impossible: there was no one else to do it.

"Señora, can I pour you more? You have a whole pitcher here," the barman said.

"No, *gracias*," I mumbled, blinking back the tears. I pulled my head away from the past, refocused my gaze, and caught sight of the hostess. I needed a table and some food to counteract my very real feeling of nausea.

# CHAPTER 18

## *SAM*

That afternoon in Belize, I noticed the blue shutters that surrounded the tall, thin windows of the local bar and hotel. I cupped my hands and peeked inside. Unoccupied booths filled most of the interior space. I hopped up on a stool.

"Just off the boat, huh?" the man one stool down joked.

I laughed good-naturedly. "What was your first clue?"

"Clean shoes," the man answered, as if the question hadn't been rhetorical.

A cute woman, maybe twenty, wearing short shorts and a butter-yellow blouse, climbed up on the stool on my other side.

"Dora," the man said. He pointed to me, making the introductions. "Meet Mr. Smith." I lifted my hand to the brim of my imaginary hat. He stood up and dug his pocket for some change.

I faced the man who stood, about to leave. "Clean?" My glance at Dora made it clear I was asking about her.

"Uh-huh. Checked monthly by the local doc. No worry, no cry." It was the skinny black bartender who answered. He broke into song with the first few lines of Bob Marley's "No Woman, No Cry" before enjoying a good laugh. A second later he reverted to the blank look he'd worn when I walked into the place. He stared at the glass in his hand, rotating it as he polished it.

Dora closed the curtains, but the light pouring in the window seemed just as bright as before. Her thin arms wrapped around my neck. I hesitated. Naked and hairless, she looked too childlike. I flipped her over. Dora raised her bum in the air. Her fingers clutched the sheets. My arousal was obvious, and I plunged deep into her, enjoying my time there before I exploded into her darkness. I rolled over, breathing loudly, wanting to hear the voice that accompanied that small body. Before we'd made any eye contact, she moved away from the bed. "Where are you going so fast?" I asked. I was unsure whether she understood English.

*"No problema,"* she said. "Fifty pesos, *por favor."*

After a minute, I nodded and paid up.

Dora placed her money on the water-marked bureau. Naked, she resumed her postion on the bed, fanned her hair out over the pillow and lay on her back with her legs held up in the air, wide apart.

She motioned me toward her and let me know another go-round would cost fifty more pesos. It was a surprise to realize how little pleasure she'd had. I grabbed my khakis off the chair back, found a few extra pesos for a tip, and walked out on her. I was stepping on top of the white leather at the heels of my sneakers as I came down the staircase. They were probably wrecked for good.

Minutes later, I saw Ellen come out of a bookstore a few doors down. She was holding a large shopping bag. "Well, well, well. Hmm, what have you been up to? Sampling the local delicacies?"

"You got a pickle up your ass or something? I don't get it," I said.

"First on board and now ashore. Why am I not surprised?"

"Ellen, what business is it of yours if I want to get laid?" I reminded her of an evening years ago when we'd visited Nassau on a previous cruise and partied with a crowd of locals we'd met at a Carlos' N Charlie's restaurant. I wanted to try a threesome, and Ellen arranged it and participated at the home of a woman we'd just met. Now if that wasn't mixing with locals, what was?

"I'm just protecting the ship where I live and work and making sure you don't infest our staterooms with any creepy-crawlies."

Dora walked by us and smiled. Ellen must have noticed because she added, "You know, I don't want to see you bringing some kind of disease to our female passengers."

"Jesus, Ellen." I pushed my aviators farther up my nose, then took them off and squeezed the bridge of my nose. "What's gotten into you? It's Joan, isn't it? Don't deny it. I saw you with her. Remember, I've seen that look before." I stopped tapping my glasses against my leg and used a cloth to wipe the lenses before putting them on again. "Joan's either widowed or divorced but either way she's not your type." When I looked up, Ellen was no longer standing there.

# CHAPTER 19

## *JOAN*

The bartender put my sangria pitcher and my glass on a tray and accompanied me to the entrance, where the hostess stood. "Where would you like to sit?" she said.

Familiar faces from the ship were scattered around the rattan furniture. I pointed to an empty table facing out to sea. The perimeter railing held small lanterns every few feet. The setting was glorious, and for once, I didn't mind the idea of eating alone.

Barracuda, a favourite of mine, was the catch of the day. I couldn't eat half of the huge serving they brought me. Whenever I started to feel happy, a heavy weight descended on my shoulders, wiping the smile off my face. It wasn't right that Joe was dead and here I was, a year later, enjoying paradise. I was sure I'd feel less guilty if I were back in the darkness of my lonely room. The waiter was too busy to notice me waving. Instead, I caught Ellen's attention. Even with her broad shoulders, angular features, and oversized men's shirt, she looked feminine. Her platinum hair was cropped short and spiked at the hairline like that of so many current pop stars and fashion models. She certainly didn't look like a nurse tonight. It took me a moment to realize she'd stood up and was striding with her wineglass toward me.

"Well if the mountain won't come to Mohammed, Mohammed must come to the mountain." She sat down and sipped her wine. "You don't mind, do you?"

"No, of course not," I said.

She dusted the bread crumbs off the table and asked if I'd ordered dessert yet.

"No dessert for me, thanks. But you go ahead. Order me coffee when you get his attention," I said. "I'm going to the washroom."

I walked around her chair. When I returned Ellen reached over and stroked my bare arm. I looked up, confused. "I saw you taking photographs on the ship," she said.

"Just practising," I said.

"You a photographer?"

"Used to be. I stopped when I married my husband Joe."

"Maybe you can take some shots of me. I did some modelling as a teenager, but my parents found out and put a stop to it."

Her eyes roamed over my breasts. It made me uncomfortable. "When Joe died," I continued, pulling on my sweater, "I gave it up. It's like I'm rediscovering an old favourite toy again." I inhaled and tried to be my most honest. "I want a strictly R and R trip with no commitments on this trip. Sorry."

"Well, we can talk about Sam if that's a more pleasant topic for you." Without waiting for a reply, she said, "I can see why he's attracted to you, but I don't understand what you see in him." She scrunched up her smooth face. "Maybe it has to do with you being a widow. You did just say you're a widow, right?" I nodded. "Let me tell you, with Sam, you're scraping the bottom of the barrel." The waiter brought our coffees and a crème caramel for Ellen. "I'd hate to see you hurt, is all."

I gazed at the moonlight casting a runway-like path across the surface of the dark water to where we sat. "I'm not in the market for another mate, Ellen. I just want a holiday, and that includes meeting new people." I unpacked my camera, adjusted the lens and blocked her voice out by snapping a sequence of shots. With the large black lens up to my eye, I could lose myself for short periods and feel a sense of freedom.

"Excuse me," I said. Ellen nodded, unsurprised. I took my camera to get a different view of our crowded floating restaurant. From the sand, I put the diners in a haze and focused sharply on the background, just the opposite of what most photographers would have done. I was very pleased with my composition. And although

I hadn't intended to, I took several shots of Ellen in sharp focus, the background a blur and a counterpoint to her beauty. She could have such an amazing career in modelling if she were willing to leave the ship and live in a cosmopolitan city, I thought. As soon as I regained my seat at our table, I bubbled over with enthusiasm over this brilliant idea, my credentials, contacts, and so on.

"Interesting," Ellen said a few minutes later. "I'd have considered it ten years ago, but it's too late now. Thanks for the vote of confidence, though." She ran her index finger around the inner rim of the ramekin dessert dish to ensure she hadn't left any. She stared at me while licking her finger dry. "Who would have thought you'd be more of a risk taker than me?" She waved the waiter over and asked him to bring us hot coffee. "You seem so self-assured, more alive and confident when that camera is blocking your face."

"Hmm" I said, aware there was truth in her observation. Was I one of those people who had no strong identity without a specified role like wife or photographer? Did I require a role to confirm my worth? Too many serious questions. My head spun and I knew I shouldn't have finished the pitcher of sangria alone. "Tell me about you. How did you come to work on a cruise liner?" I said, switching topics. I rested my head on my hand, not caring that my elbow held a place of importance near the middle of the table.

The waiter circled back and refilled our coffees. I swung my hair off my damp neck.

"There's not much to tell. I graduated from a midwestern college when there were no jobs for nurses in my town. I didn't have the money to get first and last month's rent together, so moving to another city was out of the question. I applied to all the cruise liners." She finished her coffee and dipped her spoon in her dessert. She licked it slowly, making me think of Rachel. When she finally looked up at me, I could tell she saw the lack of interest I was trying to hide.

"Room and board are deducted from your gross salary on a ship, so you skirt the rent issue. You get a great job with all kinds of benefits." She wanted to order another crème caramel.

I rolled my eyes and waited until another small serving of dessert was placed in front of her.

"I saw that, your expression," she said, pretending to be mad. "I love this stuff, can't get enough of it." Ellen dipped her spoon in her small bowl and took one lick at a time, savouring the taste this time. "Sam's the type of guy who'll act like he cares for you. He reciprocates your affection one day and acts cool to you the next. Believe me—I've seen him in action on other cruises."

If I hadn't been tired I might have been more tactful. "Are you in a relationship, Ellen? I'm starting to wonder if we're talking about someone else and not Sam at all." She looked over my head, then down at her water glass. Her chin dropped a little, which hid her expression. She scraped the edges of the bowl to finish her dessert.

"Yesterday, not today." She laughed, watching my expression. Ellen shook her head from side to side. "Louisa and I have been in a relationship for months, but today I called it off. She still doesn't want others on the ship to know that she's not straight but of course everyone does."

She waited for me to say something. "That's awful," I said touching her hand.

"I hate this kind of bullshit," Ellen said.

I nodded. I understood perfectly.

She pulled at her beautifully coiffed hair. In so doing, she crushed the pretty wave that created the volume. "Louisa is an adult, living a lie and therefore acting like a child." She reached inside her cross-body bag and brought out an e-cigarette. The steamy fog formed a spiral as she exhaled. "Louisa needs to come out about who she really is. At least I used to think that was our biggest problem."

The humidity was causing my hair to stick to my neck. I held it up with one hand and fanned my hairline with the other. "You'd find more gay women in a big city, but that's obvious. Maybe it's time to get off this ship. I knew lots of people of all sexual orientations when I worked as a professional photographer for a big magazine."

"That's like saying some of my best friends are Jews."

I blushed, knowing she was right. When the bill arrived, I was glad to see the waiter had already separated my order from Ellen's.

"Back to your earlier point, Joan; you've got to remember, the pond I fish from is smaller than yours, so the odds are high I end up single. "You're right though Joan, living on a ship does restrict the numbers of suitable partners I meet. I might think about a change." She picked up her mug and held it without sipping.

"Well, the odds are higher I don't end up with Sam. This is just one week out of my 'ever after'." I said.

The hostess offered us tequila shots on the house on our way out. We threw them back and tipped her.

On the sand, Ellen leaned on my shoulder and took off both of her sandals. I did likewise, commenting about my good balance, thanks to yoga. Then I lost my balance and nearly pulled her down on top of me. When we got it together we held hands and walked on.

"Hmm, maybe you're right," she said. "I should put down roots if I want to have anything like a normal life—live in a cool city and maybe own a loft somewhere." I detected a hint of excitement and looked at her in time to see a big grin. The humidity had flattened her hair and softened her features.

"So the idea is growing on you already," I said.

We let go of each other's hands and ran toward the tender, where people were boarding. Ellen sat close beside me in the bow. The wind whipped my shoulder-length hair around. She held my hair in her hand and inched closer, hiding from the wind while burying her chin in my neck. "Your hair smells nice. You don't mind me snuggling, do you?" I shook my head, happy to show her I was no homophobe. I heard her throaty laugh and understood the questioning looks on the faces of some fellow travellers. I didn't care what they thought. Rachel would have been proud of me.

"It's been nearly a year since your husband died. Right?" Ellen said.

"Hey, your mouth is near my ear. Don't shout."

"I was just wondering if you miss the sex." Like Rachel, Ellen expected me to be totally open.

I shook my head. It wasn't the place for such a private, personal topic, even if I were so inclined. The similarity between Ellen and Rachel hit me. They both liked shocking strangers. I turned around and cupped my hands close to Ellen's ear to tell her about Rachel. Ellen had met her on that first night, the one I'd slept through. Not surprising.

"Do you know Rachel is bi? As in bisexual?" Ellen said.

I didn't know if she was trying to shock me again or what. "I don't know who you think I am," I said, "but I don't share personal details about myself or my friends." I pushed my hair behind my ears and tugged my fingers through the knots, pulling at them angrily. A few strands of hair caught in my ring, and the tears welled up.

"Well, there's nothing to get upset about. Christ, I only know about Rachel because that's who Louisa cheated with." She breathed heavily into my ear.

The motor on the tender cut out. We sidled up to the metal plank. Crew members stood at the ready to help each passenger to the *Liberty*. I wanted to flee. Life with Joe was uncomplicated. I knew who I was. I knew who my friends were. I knew what role was mine to play, and it seemed I knew how to be happy. Although I was on holiday, I found myself at this moment a knotted ball of frustration and anxiety. Why?

Ellen caught my arm as I fled. "Stop hyperventilating. It's unhealthy."

I don't know why I agreed to go to the rooftop lounge.

"Relax Joan. You seem to want to shoulder other people's problems. Can't you see you've got enough of your own issues to deal with?" She looked at her watch. It clearly wasn't how she wanted to be spending her late night hours — counselling. The Spanish coffee took the chill off the night. My tongue flicked against the sugar rim. I wanted to savour it and make it last. I was expecting Ellen to apologize for getting so personal in her questioning; for some of those things she said about Sam. She didn't. Instead she persisted, "You never answered my question—do you miss the sex?"

I frowned. My voice rose, a sure sign I was feeling defensive. I wrapped my arms across my chest and tucked my hands under my armpits. "I can't say I've thought about it. But I have considered the double standard that exists. If a recently widowed man finds someone to bed, his friends congratulate him. A woman in the same circumstances is crucified for that same behaviour. It's not right."

"Crucified? You're being a little dramatic, aren't you?" Ellen's voice mocked me.

Although it was perfectly cool in the rooftop bar, I felt flushed. I pulled my hair up off my neck. I was having another hot flash. My mouth was dry. The room swam. Ellen hopped up to get me some water. I took a few deep breaths to calm myself and swallowed slowly. Eventually, I pressed the point that there's a common perception that men need women and can't take care of themselves. Ellen was beaming as though I was flattering her personally, her independence and strength.

"So accept it," she said. "Men are needy, we're not, so we, meaning women, belong together." I smiled but wasn't sure if she was serious or not. My coffee had cooled. There was no more cream floating on top. I pushed it aside. It wouldn't taste like Spanish coffee anymore.

"You're definitely hetero," Ellen said, an insincere note of flippancy evident in her voice. "I'll leave you to your thoughts of guilt, love, and envy." She kissed me on the cheek. "Good night, Joan. I've got to get up early tomorrow."

When she'd gone, I waved the waiter over and asked him to replace my coffee with another one, a heavily laced Spanish coffee. What the hell—it would help me sleep.

# CHAPTER 20

## *JOAN*

Hushed voices and a 180-degree view of the moonlit sea were the perfect setting for my mood. Down below on the track were a few couples walking hand in hand in the night air. A shiver moved down my spine as the familiarity of a particular couple's silhouette caught my attention. The tall, slim man could have been anyone but the shoulder-length curly hair of the woman — I gasped. I remembered it well because I'd almost suffocated in it yesterday. I had to look away.

The band returned. There was no interlude between the soft recorded music and the loud country-rock. I stepped outside the bar where the music seemed softer. I was thinking about Esther's Alzheimer's, when I'd get it, not if, and whether I felt I'd lived enough, a heavy topic I took all too lightly. Leaning with lousy posture over the wooden railing, I sucked on my torn cuticle and contemplated my options.

I thought about Joe and that climactic discussion we'd had during our third week of appointments with the palliative care doctor. We were discussing his first love: golf, of course. Dr. Gold advised Joe that his balance had deteriorated. His new recommendations included a cane: an end to days spent on the golf course, and an end to days spent on the driving range too. Joe wiped tears from his eyes with his knuckles. His voice cracked as he railed against the unfairness of that. I wanted to comfort him, but there were no words. And when the doctor described what the next change would look like—the change in personality—well, that was the moment of decision. Joe swore he wouldn't be around when that day dawned.

My voice cracked several times while describing the prettiest blue sky we'd had all winter and the green shoots breaking through the wet earth. "Those are snowdrops, and crocuses. Stay with me and see them next winter." I pleaded.

And he said he knew what snowdrops and crocuses were. He brushed the tears off my cheek, but his tears were long gone. "Let's do something special tonight because tomorrow I start focusing on dying."

I'd screamed, "No!" right there in the parking lot. "You think I want to celebrate tonight?"

"That's okay," he said, as if he had to comfort me. "You can save that extra special wine for my funeral and shiva." He walked to the passenger side of the car and got in. I made up my mind not to waste time arguing after that. I was more than a little hurt that he didn't want more time with me  but I came to accept it. More than that; I came to realize I'd have done the same in his situation.

I'd always thought life was about making choices: what to study at school, who to date, when to go out and when to stay home, where to travel and where to avoid, whether to accumulate material stuff or whether to acquire experiences. My weekly manicures were no longer needed, as there was nothing left to polish. My weight dropped although I gave up the gym. I lacked the motivation to do anything. What Joe wanted was clear, and if the truth be told, I came to want it too.

"One day, I hope I'll be able to forgive myself for that," I said aloud.

"Who are you talking to, pretty lady?" a man asked. He reeked of liquor.

I ignored him. I moved along the railing away from the fumes coming off his clothing.

He was weaving on the spot. "Ah, poor baby." He leaned close to me. "You look so sad." Yellowed fingers took hold of my chin. His whole hand smelled. "Have you been crying?" he asked, bending close to my face.

I pulled away. "Don't touch me!" I yelled, stepping back.

"Don't you remember me? I remember you—so much that I missed you at dinner tonight," he said. I could have sworn I'd never heard that voice before, never seen that leering look. He grabbed my upper arms and pulled my face up to his.

"Ah, you're Susan's husband," I said. I recognized him as the same comatose idiot who'd sat at my dinner table last night. "You're drunk. I'll get someone to come help you."

"Nonsense. I'm fine. Just been enjoying myself." He squeezed my breast and then moved his hand to my shoulder.

My right hand swung forward, but he moved his head and avoided the slap meant for his cheek.

"See, my reflexes are working just fine." Mike raised his eyebrows, waiting for me to argue.

"That hurt," I said, giving him a push with both hands. "Where's Susan?"

"Wanna see just how fine I am? If I was drunk I couldn't do this, now could I?" He stood up on a wooden deck chair. If his weight wasn't evenly distributed, it would tip. My eyes moved to the wooden railing, which came up to his hips. Mike wobbled, smiling like a mischievous child, unaware of the danger. I looked around for help. "I'm going to jump if you don't go in there and dance with me," he said.

"M-M-Mike, get down."

A small and silent crowd gathered.

"You're going to fall. Take my hand," I said.

One side of the chair tipped forward. He used his legs to tip it in the opposite direction. The chair teetered. In slow motion he swayed back toward the rail, his arms circling like a bird about to propel itself into flight. I screamed. He overcorrected, swinging his body forward and down. Mike crashed headfirst into the umbrella table stand next to the chair he stood on. Its concrete foundation turned red. Automatically, I bent down into the pool of blood spilling from his nose and ear. I touched his neck and felt nothing except the incredibly hot temperature of his blood. I ran to where a red wall phone hung.

"I've called," Ellen said, removing my hand from the telephone and replacing the receiver on the hook. I looked up and saw Louisa standing nearby.

"See you downstairs later," Louisa said.

A flurry of activity like bees around a hive swirled near Mike. My hand moved as if to swish them away. I felt dizzy.

Someone else bent down.

"Don't touch him. His neck could be broken," Ellen told the stranger.

I just stood, watching and weaving from light-headedness.

Ellen crouched near his body and picked up his limp wrist. When she stood, she told everyone she'd felt a pulse and we should go on with our evening. As those carrying the stretcher headed for the elevator, I noticed she still wore the outfit I'd seen her in earlier. It remained spotless.

# CHAPTER 21

## *SAM*

I lay in bed, thinking it hadn't turned out to be a good day at all. Belize was better the last time I visited. It was my own fault because I'd been too lazy to plan on doing something with someone. The Mexican whore was a disappointment. I needed to know that I'd left a woman feeling good and satisfied. You'd think I'd be more secure by now. Carla had known which buttons to push. She used to tell me I was a lousy lay or that I was nothing special in the sack. But then she'd apologize and say she made it up to get me back for gambling away the trip-to-Paris money.

I rolled over and closed my eyes. Ellen popped into my head—the sexiest dyke ever. Why did speaking with that bitch make me feel so defensive? But I knew why. It all went back to when I found out Louisa was bisexual; I just figured Ellen was too. So hitting on Ellen was an honest mistake. I hated her knowing that I'd wanted her so much. I'd confided in her about Carla and my screwed-up marriage, hoping for a sympathy fuck, but I couldn't even get that. Fuck me, I thought, and got out of bed.

I pulled on a sweatshirt and grabbed a blanket, which I threw over my shoulders. The breeze on the balcony was balmy, the humidity now gone. I lit the lantern and placed it on the little table next to the chair. I was lousy at identifying the star patterns. I'd tried learning the constellations, but I was never absolutely sure of the names I gave to particular patterns. Carla had told me I was wrong often enough that I gave up and stopped trying to impress anyone with my so-called knowledge.

My Cruise Control lay on the balcony table under an empty glass. Tomorrow's yoga class was at one. If I couldn't be romantic by pointing out the stars, or throw oodles of money around, I could at least be in respectable shape. I was pretty good at yoga actually.

No sooner had I leaned back and stretched my arms than I jumped straight out of my skin. I heard screaming coming from a higher deck. I threw on my jeans and ran down the hall. When the elevator doors opened, I saw Joan, white as a sheet and covered in blood. "My God, what's happened? Are you all right?"

"It's not my blood—it's Mike's." I shivered. There was no emotion in her voice. I had no idea whose blood it was, but it didn't matter; at least it wasn't Joan's blood.

She stood gazing down at her dress, a stunned look on her face. The elevator door began to close. I grabbed her hand and pulled her out. She stumbled into my arms. I held her and patted her back untill her breathing became steadier. She dropped her key card, so I picked it up and led her inside her cabin.

"Sam, Sam, it was awful. Blood was gushing out of his head."

"Shush, let's get you cleaned up and you can tell me about it after." Once inside her room, I said, "Stand here for a sec." I slipped the long sleeveless dress over her head before guiding her a few steps back to sit on the vanity chair while I ran the tub.

We didn't say another word till I'd gotten her out of the tub and into a clean oversized T-shirt. I'd had to shampoo her hair and remove the butterfly bandage over the cut from the seizure the other day. I took her hand and sat her down on the side of the bed while I brushed out her wet hair. She moved as if in a daze, not offering a word or a direct glance. I towel dried her arms and legs sofltly.

"Sam?" she said, finally looking up at me.

"Hmm?" I answered. Her eyes looked enormous. Her skin had regained some colour. "It's okay, Joan. You don't have to say anything. No one is accusing you." I thought for a second and then asked who this Mike fellow she mentioned was.

"He's someone who sits at my dinner table, but I've only been there at the same time as him once." Tears streaked her face. "I guess there was another time when I saw him and his wife horsing around in the pool." She looked up at me standing over her and wiped away the tears. "I didn't do anything."

"No, of course not." She pulled at her nose, reached for some tissue, and blew softly. She held her head in both hands.

"I'm calling room service to get us a tray of tea." After giving her room number, I followed her to the side of her bed.

Joan sighed, her chest deflating and her shoulders slumping all at once. I pulled the covers back and helped her get into the bed. Her head rested on the big pillows, and she stared at the ceiling. I heard the ujjayi breath. Thank God for three-part breathing and knowing how to control anxiety. Stress and epilepsy made a bad combination.

"Blood and drama seem to follow me wherever I go," she whispered. Her head jutted forward and her chin dropped close to her chest. All posture collapsed unto itself as she caved in a moment of raw weakness. I could hardly bear to look at her, to let her see me looking at her. As if speaking to herself, she said, "I thought I'd left that part of life at home. . . and now Mike." She rubbed her closed eyes and opened them, blinking in rapid succession.

"What are you talking about?" I sat next to her and put an arm around her, rocking her like child.

"First Joe and now Mike. Two men dead and I'm involved," she said, as if that explained all.

Mike was a fellow passenger, but who was Joe?

"You don't know for sure that this Mike is dead, do you?" I asked. When she shook her head, I told her I was sure in both cases these were accidents, that no one was to blame." I put a hand under her chin and moved her face up so I could look her in the eye. "You bear no responsibility." I squeezed her close to me. She was so small. Poor Joan was shaking. "Joan, relax. Breathe slowly. You know how to do it."

Her neck rolled forward and around in a circular motion before she reversed direction. With her eyes closed, she seemed to be talking to herself: ". . . teetered off a chair . . . split his head open or . . . punctured—" She began to cry and sniffle. I went into the bathroom and brought the garbage can and a box of Kleenex back. I saw her Purell on the counter and used some before returning to her.

"I'll call the infirmary for you. We'll find out how he is." I picked up the phone, but no one answered at the other end. "Here, turn yourself around a bit and I'll massage your neck and shoulders." She didn't need convincing. Her little oohs and aahs made me smile. That's all I've ever wanted from a woman in exchange for my efforts. She was facing away from me, so I didn't see her expression when I asked if I should know who Joe was. She didn't answer, and it was then I guessed.

"Look," I said turning her face toward me, "people have accidents. People die. It's all part of the natural course of events that we just have to cope with." I picked up the garbage can from the floor so she could throw away her used tissues.

"Nice speech," Joan said. Her angry tone and straight posture made me move away from the bed. I didn't know why exactly, but she was upset I'd referred to the loss of Joe and the accident with Mike as having nothing to do with her. I'd tried so hard to be helpful, and this was where it got me. I carried the trash can back to the washroom.

"Sam, you have no idea how much blood there was pouring out of his head."

"Yes, head wounds do bleed a lot and often look more serious than they are. You should know that better than anyone." I saw she remembered her seizure. It seemed like a lifetime ago. We were strangers then.

The knock at her door made us both jump. I answered and accepted the tray from room service. Before the door closed, a crew member in whites, looking very officious, glided in. I stood by while the uniformed officer questioned Joan.

Shortly after he left, I put the empty tray in the hallway outside the door. Her answers had satisfied him and had left her exhausted. I checked my watch and automatically yawned. It had gotten quite late.

"I don't think I'll be able to sleep," she said. I wondered if she was asking me for drugs or simply commenting on her distress. I found the music channel on the television. It showed two categories: Classical and Fireplace Folk. I chose the second. Joan's smile of appreciation told me I had guessed correctly.

First my left shoe, then my right, fell from my feet as I shook each leg over the edge of the bed. Joan and I set our backs against the headboard. She rested her head on my shoulder. I could get used to this, I thought. The Fireplace Folk track had many songs we knew the words to. Here and there I sang the odd line from the Bob Dylan tune playing, and when I stopped she added another line or two. The same thing happened when Joni Mitchell's "Big Yellow Taxi" played.

"Those aren't the right words!" Joan teased. She smacked my leg playfully. The bloodshot eyes remained, but she'd loosened up like a woman stepping out of a tight corset. Together we found ourselves singing to Leonard Cohen. She looked up at me, her lips curled ever so slightly, the natural colour back in her face. Simon and Garfunkel began "Bridge over Troubled Water." She propped herself forward so I could stretch an arm around her shoulders. She snuggled in close. I leaned back and closed my eyes. Soon I heard the sound of her slow, even breathing. She'd fallen asleep.

I opened my eyes but hesitated before moving. I didn't want to blow the chance I had to make a go of things with Joan especially now that I knew for sure Joe had died and she was a widow and I could conclude that she was not a poor widow. I took pains to pull my arm back and lower her head onto the pillows. I let myself out of her room and hoped that in the morning she'd think me the perfect gentleman. She was a wonderful person and I wanted her to think the same of me. I smiled feeling proud of the kind of man I was.

# CHAPTER 22

## JOAN

## Tuesday, February 4, 2003

## Day 4, aboard the Liberty

It was unusual for me to wake up in a room filled with brilliant sunshine. I looked down at my wristwatch and verified what I already knew; it was late. One of these days, I'd make it into the dining room for breakfast.

Today was the day I was allowed to get rid of the bandage at my hairline. Facing my image in the bathroom mirror, I suddenly remembered last night: the accident; Sam; how he'd stuck me in the bathtub, washed Mike's blood off my body and out of my hair.

I wet my hair and took my time blowing it dry. Looking like me again lifted my spirits. I picked up my camera. My 5D Mark II hung from a heavy strap around my neck. I pulled the camera strap higher on my shoulder. It hurt, reminding me of my bruises and where I'd fallen during Saturday's seizure. In frustration I plopped back on the bed. My feet dangled while I banged my head back on the unmade bed and fresh tears flooded my eyes. I didn't have Joe to carry my beach bag with the sunscreen and the water bottle and my yoga mat. I had to do it all myself. At least photography didn't require a daily commitment or schedule this time around. I closed my door, wearing a white baseball cap and carrying my beach bag over my shoulder.

The Café Promenade was packed with late risers. I jostled my breakfast tray among the crowded tables, not having seen a single place to sit. Luckily, I spotted Neil sitting with another couple from our table. He waved me over.

They were discussing Mike's accident. "You remember Mitch and his wife Sharon, from our table?" he said.

I nodded. "Actually," I said, interrupting them, "I was there, so I may be able to help fill in a detail or two." I took a sip of my coffee, which burned my tongue. "Ow! Whoa, that's hot." I smacked my lips together, apologized, and then described the order of events, ending with Mike banging his head.

"So you're suggesting Mike was showing off for you last night?" Mitch said.

I flashed a look at Neil. I didn't like Mitch's accusatory tone. His face became redder and redder and he said, "You can't be suggesting he's responsible. There's no way you get off scott-free."

Neil told Mitch to calm down.

"So why didn't you get him down, call for help before he knocked himself out?" The blond Californian leaned forward, his saliva spraying across the table surface. "You think you're too good for the likes of him, don't you? You probably pretended you didn't know him," Mitch said. "Why didn't you go try to find Susan?"

I paused and bit my lip until I tasted fresh blood.

"Take it easy, Mitch." Neil smiled at me. Turning back to look at Mitch and Sharon, he said, "Joan's telling us what she saw. Everything we've heard suggests Mike had an accident when he was clowning around, and Joan just corroborated that story."

"I know your type. You just didn't want to get involved, did you? What you did was leave the scene of an accident, which is a crime." Mitch nodded to Sharon, as if she should be proud of him.

She lowered her head and held her double chin.

"The nurse and a stretcher arrived before I left the roof, for your information." I knew he was desperate for a punching bag, someone to blame, but I'd be damned if I was going to let him use me. I finished my coffee and stood up.

Neil ran a hand behind his neck and over his chin. "We know you bear no blame, Joan. We're just worried, is all." He looked at Mitch, who'd gone mute. "Mitch is sorry he dumped his anger and frustration on you, aren't you, Mitch?" Neil said, standing up beside me.

Mitch snickered. With his sleeve he wiped the spittle from the corner of his mouth. Then he waved his hand as if he were dismissing me. "Jeez, Neil, you sound like a teacher settling a playground argument," he said.

I should have walked away but I had to have the final word. "There's no argument here, Mitch. After all, Mike was pretty inebriated when he got up on that chair. He wobbled it on purpose to impress first me and then a whole group of people who happened to be outside the rooftop bar. Any one of them could be another witness if you want one." I put my hands on my hips, and looked up to meet his eyes. "It seems Mike regularly allows himself to drink to excess." My chin jutted forward, daring him to contradict me.

"Whoa! Miss Holier-than-Thou, is it? Who made you judge and jury?" Sharon's eyes became huge, and her cheeks turned red. Her strong voice took me by surprise. She was her husband's best defender, right or wrong.

"I'm just saying, sooner or later, someone will be asking where his friends and his wife were last night at one in the morning."

Mitch and I stood nose to nose. I could see his nostrils expanding with each breath.

"Joan, let's get out of here." Neil pulled me away. As we walked, he began to lecture me. "You know, I recently spent an afternoon poolside with Mike so, like everyone else, I know he can be a sloppy drunk. "But," he said, "if he was as intoxicated as all that, it's more likely he would've passed out in a chair, like he did at dinner that night. That's more Mike's style than pulling stupid antics and tempting fate."

I wondered if Neil was poolside that day Rachel and I observed Mike and his wife Susan falling over one another into the pool. "Well, is it possible he was faking the drunk routine?" I asked. I had to relearn a simple fact: people were who they wanted you to think they were. "Maybe Mike was just flirting in a way that felt safe. I could have run into his arms to make sure he walked away and didn't fall. Maybe he was counting on that." I looked at Neil, and he ruffled my hair.

"You were good, standing up to Mitch like that. I didn't know you had it in you to be so assertive." I smiled inwardly, thinking the old me was coming back. We walked down two flights of stairs, turned a corner and saw the sign Infirmary. I squeezed Neil's arm. He knew I wasn't the person Mitch and Sharon thought I was.

Ellen was writing on the clipboard chart when we entered. "Hi," she said. "What brings you here?" The infirmary was busy with wheezing and coughing people. It was standing room only.

"Hi," I began. "I can see you're busy. We just want to check on Mike Cole. He's going to make it? He's fine?"

Ellen told us he was sleeping.

"Oh my God. Tell me he's woken up since last night," I said. Neil steadied me, and I bent around her, trying to see into the rooms with open doors down the hall.

"Susan is with him now." Ellen looked at her clipboard. "Mr. Brown, go into examination room two, please," she called to the people on chairs.

A man in jeans holding a bloody cloth up to his nose excused himself as he passed between us.

"If you want, I'll tell Susan you're here and get her to come talk to you." She called after the man with the bloody nose, "Mr. Brown, I said room two, not three." She rolled her eyes.

"We don't want to wake him or disturb her for that matter, but that sounds like a bad sign," Neil said.

"I'm going to be sick," I said. "Tell me he's going to be okay."

Ellen stopped what she was doing and held my gaze. Her confusion was clear. "If it was anything really serious, I couldn't say . . . but Mike will be fine. He's had a concussion, but he's been woken every hour all night. No wonder he's tired."

She called another name and said, "You know what? I'm tired too."

"So will he get released today?" Neil asked.

"He'll need a CT scan at the nearest hospital. Then we'll know if there's a bleed or anything else." She wrote something on her paper. "That's when we'll know how serious the situation is." She finger-combed her hair as she scanned her list again. "Mr. Humphrey, room eight," she called as another man stood up.

"Thanks for the update about Mike," Neil said. "Tell him Joan and Neil were here, would you?"

Before she could answer, we heard an alarm coming from the hall. I heard thrashing and the sounds of bed springs bouncing. Then Susan's voice screaming for help. I knew what was happening. Friends who'd witnessed my own seizures had described the sounds and the frightening contortions of a convulsing body. Poor Mike. Poor Susan.

# CHAPTER 23

## *Joan*

At two thirty that afternoon, I ate lunch at the poolside barbeque. Perspiration soaked the back of my sleeveless T- shirt. I saw Rachel get up to go to the bar and she seemed to be checking around the pool deck for me. The day was perfect —a smattering of fluffy white clouds, a gorgeous shade of blue overhead and a hot eighty-eight degrees.

"There you are. Sweet Jesus, where have you been?" Rachel said she'd had a hard time saving me a chaise next to hers and didn't think she could have done it much longer. "I'm dying to go to the bar and get something. What do you want?"

"I slept in and then went to yoga," I told her. I didn't think she heard me but she returned with my water and her cranberry and soda in no time.

"You're kidding. On a beautiful day like today, you choose to exercise indoors in a gym? Why not do laps in the pool?" Rachel's sweat made her body glisten. There were beads of perspiration lining her upper lip, and I offered her a tissue, motioning to make it clear what I expected her to do with it.

"Rachel, relax, I'm here now," I said as she wiped her lip. "Yeah, that's better." I felt no need to tell her about Mike's accident, the infirmary, or my commitment to join Amy for regular yoga.

"I prefer facing the ocean," I said.

"I know. You're anti-social." Rachel huffed.

I had no intention of disputing that. I opened my sunscreen and began smearing it all over. "You're really red around the edges of that bikini." I pointed to her chest. "It's because it's a different cut than the one you wore yesterday. Take some of this," I said and held the SPF 30 out toward her.

"No, Mom, but thanks."

"Seriously, Rachel, sun damage to skin is way more unattractive than an extra pound or two." I told her I thought a little fat on an older woman went a long way toward filling in wrinkles.

She snorted. "Me? So I'm an older wrinkled woman, now, huh?" For some reason she was acting as if she were seriously offended. "I might be obsessive about my exercise regimen, but I'm much healthier than you. You practically starve yourself, have no natural immunity because of all that hand sanitizer you use, and are likely anemic to boot." It was Sam, not me, who was obsessive about his use of hand sanitizer, but I couldn't be bothered to prolong the argument and clarify  every little thing. None of this really mattered. Why?

"Okay, calm down, Rachel, Let's not fight about it," I said. I looked around, hoping we hadn't attracted any attention. I realized my shoulders had crept up around my ears and I lowered them.

Rachel's face was beet red. She wouldn't give up. "I saw the plate you left in the dining room the other night. You play with your food rather than eat it. Little cubes of meat were spread around strategically." Her finger was tapping her temple.

I put my hands up in surrender. Joe had always said the best way to put an end to an argument was to apologize and admit guilt. The truth often didn't matter. I looked at the sky and then searched for my sunglasses.

"I just do that when I'm being polite about not eating something I don't like."

But she didn't accept my logic and wouldn't let it go. Her retort was instantaneous. "Really? If you were at a friend's home, I might buy that. But here, on the ship, you're afraid to insult the chef or the waiter?"

Why hadn't I taken Joe's advice and admitted to an eating disorder or something, if that was what she wanted to hear? I couldn't do it. "I'm being honest," I said. "I just hate it when the waiter comes over and asks, 'Is there something wrong with your meal?'"

Rachel's face softened. "Never mind; let's stop arguing. But for the record," she said, "I count this as a win for me."

I stood, straightened my towel, and lay down on my stomach, facing the magazine I'd laid on the deck in front of me.

"Where's your suit? Who comes to the pool in a gym clothes?" Rachel asked.

"I wore this for yoga today. The shorts work for tanning too. And soon I'm meeting Sam for the destination lecture," I said. I gave my attention back to the magazine. Only seconds passed before Rachel pulled out one of my ear buds.

"Do you ever feel suicidal?" Rachel said.

I turned over and looked at her. "Are you serious?"

"Absolutely."

"Well, in a matter of speaking, I think about my death, so yes, but I'm not depressed, and I'm not thinking about it now." I felt something sharp and knew I had a broken nail that would drive me nuts or lead me to bite it and even it out until there was nothing left. I dug in my bag for an emery board. "Why'd you ask?" I said.

Rachel pulled her hair back into an elastic. She used the edge of her towel to dry the line of perspiration on her top lip and at the top of her chest. "It was a guess," she said. "You take life way too seriously, as if everything has to have meaning. Try staying in the moment and you'll be a happier camper."

"Thanks, Freud."

She slugged me in the arm, and my iPod fell to the tiled deck. "What the—?"

"Sorry about that." She looked at her watch and told me I had five minutes until the Cozumel lecture. Rachel passed me one sneaker, and I found the other on the right side of the cot.

"Do you see now why I didn't change after yoga?"

"You and your schedules," Rachel said in a disapproving tone. "You're actually more of a social butterfly than I am—or so Ellen tells me—and now I believe her." I eyed the blue sky above, not wanting Rachel to see what I thought of her having discussed me with Ellen or having intruded on Ellen's relationship with Louisa."I'd like to hear that lecture too. Can I join or is this a preamble to a more— ?"

"Don't be dumb. Rachel, we've got to rush. Sam will be waiting." I grabbed my white zippy and did it up.

She sat on the side of her chaise, hesitating. "I'm attracted to Sam, just so you know, —I just don't find poor doctors appealing," she said.

"Okay, Rach, get your sandals on." I tapped my foot and checked my watch again. I was on a holiday and checking my watch a little too often.

"No, I've changed my mind." Rachel was smiling and looking past me. Intrigued, I followed her gaze. A silver-haired man sitting at the swim-up bar was wetting his cigar with his tongue and looking straight at her. Rachel leaned over to the side, one breast almost popping out of her bikini top, and opened the sunscreen bottle I'd left there. After rubbing her long fingers across her chest and neck, she swung her hair over to the side. She was the queen bee performing her ritual dance. "I know what you're thinking, Joan," she whispered, her lips hidden by her curtain of dark frizz, "but I can't resist a challenge. Stay here and watch."

"No thanks, I've got my own date," I said, shaking my head as I left the pool area.

# CHAPTER 24

# *JOAN*

"No, I'm not cutting the line, sir, just meeting someone farther ahead," I said, my eyes searching for Sam in the long line leading to the pavilion's double doors. He hugged me hello and told me he'd started to worry I'd forgotten the destination lecture. He commented on my yoga shorts and said he'd planned to do yoga too but had been busy doing nothing. We laughed. His single dimple showed in one cheek. He took my hand and pulled me along.

During the talk, they showed slides highlighting the Spanish presence in the history of Cozumel. Terracotta tiles, white plaster, arches, and adobe-style buildings abounded. Cozumel, like many Spanish towns, was home to numerous plazas with statues of Cortés, Columbus, and other explorers. About six of the excursions involved snorkelling and boating. Four tours were of an educational nature. Several slides showed adventure tours, which appealed to a certain group who cheered. Our speaker recommended that people book tours to get the most out of the short amount of time they had ashore. He alluded to the beauty of the land discovered off the beaten track but stressed the risks of renting a private vehicle.

"What is he referring to?" I whispered to Sam.

"When a low-life sees a rental licence plate, he knows there's a tourist aboard with more money than a regular local. In other words," he said, breathing in my ear, "the tourist has a target on his back." I shivered before pushing Sam's face away from my neck. He moved back a bit and continued whispering. "In a lot of these poorer countries, the rental car agencies advise if you've been hit from behind in a fender-bender, don't get out of the car—keep driving and return to the agency."

I filed that away, not wanting to allow fear to guide my choices.

Later, we sat in the Café Promenade and discussed our preferences. I pointed to the open brochure. "Can we rule out the old Mayan temple and the diving excursion?" I asked.

"We think so much alike. I wanted to cross those off the list too." Sam asked what I thought about the tour of El Cedral.

I had to admit it didn't even sound familiar.

"Remember the slide showing the ruins of the oldest pyramid in Cozumel? There was a small adobe building there where a tour of how tequila was made and free tastings were offered," Sam said.

I made a face. "Nothing is free, Sam, Were you born yesterday? You can be sure they try to sell you all the varieties of tequila they include in their tastings." I was feeling less sure that we did think alike. "I think that diving excursion would have been fabulous but how could they do everything they promised in a half a day when the excursion offered a dive lesson, a long boat ride out to sea, a dive and time for the return trip back?"

"Well, a lot of people were signing up for it," Sam said.

"Only a fish would spend the kind of money that trip cost for a half day excursion and probably a short dive." I made a face and raised my eyebrows, embarrassed to have to spell it out: "I've paid less for a full day dive in the Bahamas, if that helps put it in perspective," I said.

Sam rubbed his chin.

I opened my mouth and closed it. Nobody likes a know-it-all. I shook my hair of my neck and tied it up with an elastic. Maybe our best option would be to just get off the ship where it docks in San Miguel and find a grocery store. Then we'd fill a picnic basket and go find a pretty beach on the other side of the island. I explained my idea to Sam. "But taking a cab is impossible because you can't rely on the driver coming back on time. Will you agree to renting a car?" I smoothed my hair which the humidity was making wavy. I was self conscious of the back and blue bruise on my forehead and caught Sam staring at me, lost in thought. I didn't really think he was looking at these imperfections.

It seemed a delayed reaction but Sam jumped out of his seat. "Terrific." He planted a big kiss on my cheek. "Perhaps they just gave those ominous warnings so passengers would spend more exorbitant amounts on day trips booked with the cruise's excursion desk." Sam hugged me tightly.

"This is the best idea," I said squeezing him back with arms that ended up encircling his waist.

He reached across the table and grabbed his pop can but paused before taking a sip. "I suppose you want to get me alone in a deserted spot."

I hit his arm with the island map they'd passed out at the lecture. "Am I that transparent?" I asked, batting my eyes like a schoolgirl. He laughed and said he'd be back as soon as he'd made plans to get us a car.

The private outing was something Joe would have suggested to me, only he would have hired a car and driver. It was a money issue, but I was also determined not to become like Evelyn, my widowed friend back home, who spoke of her late spouse as if he'd constantly had a better idea than any of us still living. It was "Charlie used to do this" or "Charlie would suggest that."

I once said to her, "But Charlie's not here, sadly, and a new friend may feel—"

"What the hell, Joan," she'd said, "as if I'd ever want to pick up anybody's dirty socks again."

Minutes later, Rachel appeared and asked, "Is that the island map they handed out at the end of the lecture?" She drew close to the café table.

I nodded and saw her look around for Sam.

"Well, well, well," a familiar voice said. I glanced over to see Neil.

"I didn't know you two knew each other," Rachel said. Neil shrugged, spilling the two drinks on the tray he held.

"Yes, just luck; we were seated at the same table day one," I said, smiling at Neil. I took the tray from him. I barely knew Neil, but I liked him. He wore burgundy sweatpants and a grey loose fitting T-shirt bearing the *Liberty* logo.

Before I had the chance to ask, Neil explained how he and Rachel had met. He had acted as her windshield on the tender that carried them both to shore in Belize yesterday. I could just picture her, cozying up against his wide back as the tender plowed through the waves to shore. Could it have been Neil I'd seen her with last night? No, the man was tall and slight.

But I remembered seeing Rachel and Neil together on the edge of the fountain in the town square in Belize.

"It's amazing how many different people I come into contact with in just one day." Rachel wanted us to be curious about her popularity, but there was nothing mysterious about it. I stood up to refill my Diet Coke, but she stopped me. "I'd met Neil already, but today he swooped right in and saved me from a lecherous guy by the pool who seemed to think I was some kind of bimbo. Can't you just picture it?" She looked at him and batted her eyes.

"You're such a cliché," I wanted to say. "Why is it you constantly have to deal with that problem?" I raised my eyebrows and headed off to the counter, laughing to myself.

When I returned, Sam was back.

"So Joan, have you heard anything more about Mike?" Neil asked.

I shook my head, and we told Sam what we'd gleaned from our visit to the infirmary.

"I've been asked to accompany the helicopter carrying Mike, as have most doctors on board. The *Liberty* can't continue understaffed. I found out the captain contracted another passenger to take responsibility for Mike during transit from Cozumel to Miami. The cruise lines always do in these circumstances." Sam took his glasses off the top of his head. He ran his fingers through his thick red hair which made me want to touch it.

"Why would anyone give up the remaining vacation days on a paid cruise?" Rachel asked.

"Simple. The doctor who volunteers and his or her traveling companion if there is one, are offered an additional full week free cruise as well as substantial compensation for the work involved. If desired the traveling companion gets to complete this week too. Not a bad deal, I'd say." Sam's eyes widened.

"Wow," I said. Had he given that up to be with me? I knew he wanted me to think so. His green eyes sparkled like the light reflecting off the Caribbean Sea.

Rachel cleared her throat. She looked from one of us to the other. "Who's Mike?" she said.

I chose that moment to go to the washroom.

"So you knew this Mike guy well?" Rachel said when I returned.

"No. He was the drunk we saw acting like an ass in the pool yesterday." Her smirk told me she remembered him and Susan well. "Although we were seated at the same table, I'd never been introduced to the drunkard," I said and turned to look at Neil, who didn't seem to believe me.

"Joan," Neil said, "stop calling him a drunk." He rubbed his face, which was covered in five o'clock shadow.

I was tempted to apologize, but I hadn't done anything. "It's definitely unfortunate that he had a serious accident. I'm sorry if I sound like I'm lacking in compassion."

Sam rubbed his Purell cleansing gel over his hands and said he had a lot of news to share. "I rented us an air-conditioned car, which was hard to get." I hugged him, and for a second I hoped he wouldn't invite them to join us. I heard Neil say he'd be happy to share the cost of the car.

Rachel hugged me, and I angrily pushed her frizzy hair away from my nose. She didn't notice. "We need to make a list so we don't forget any essentials: books, magazines, drinks, your SPF, my cosmetics . . . maybe fresh clothes for later," she said. "It might get cool if we stay there and eat at a local place."

Touching my hair, I remembered my appointment. Tonight was a formal night.

"Much as I'd love to stay and chat," I said, "I want to try to get in a half hour with the ball machine. Gotta go."

"Tennis ball machine? Now? Why?" Sam said, looking confused.

"I have a game planned for the day after Cozumel and need a little practice. Really gotta run if I'm going to have enough time." I blew a kiss and began walking.

"Wait up," Neil said. "I'm going there too."

We weren't that far when we heard Sam shout: "You two make plans for the four of us tonight, all right?"

I waved a hand above my head.

"What do you think about meeting in the piano bar for trivia at ten?" Neil said picking up a small gym bag. "I'll be eating in the cafeteria tonight. I couldn't stand another night in a penguin suit," he said.

"Men in tuxedos do not look like penguins." I punched his arm. "Goodness, I get it. With arms that developed, you really can't buy an off-the-rack suit."

We walked around other couples, who took tiny steps down the hallway. "I'm not sure why it bothers me, but I don't want you thinking poorly of me," I said.

Neil knew I was talking about Mike again. He gave me a friendly squeeze. "Such an old-fashioned phrase. All's forgiven," he said. "We've moved on."

That had been Joe's attitude—he'd never wanted to talk anything to death. When we reached the gym, Neil headed off to the free weights, and I asked a staff member to set up the ball machine for me. I didn't want to look foolish in front of Li and Amy. When it was time, I headed up the staircase to the hair salon. I settled into the chair of the stylist assigned to me and had a much-needed power nap.

# CHAPTER 25

## SAM

### *Wednesday, February 5, 2003*
### *Day 5, Cozumel*

It didn't look like my room. Judging by the sun's brightness, it was early but not that early. I yawned loudly, squeezed out a little gas, and stretched both arms, fingers splayed above my head. Surprised by an awareness of heat, I opened my eyes wide and looked at the sleeping form next to me. How drunk was I last night? Fuck—the blackouts were getting serious. I had to cut down on my drinking. Joan gave no indication she was aware of me or the fact that I'd just farted in her bed.

I set my long eyelashes to work, covering her neck and shoulders with butterfly kisses.

"Ooh, that tickles," she said, turning over and greeting me with a welcoming smile. She pulled the sheet up near her neck, just as she had the first day we talked in this very room, her room.

"How much do *you* remember of last night?" I asked, emphasizing the word "you."

She told me we'd returned here around three thirty in the morning. She avoided saying what I wanted to know, enjoyed seeing me try to weasel it out of her.

"Okay, so tell me," I joked, "did I behave well last night?" I turned my boyish charm on full blast.

"Yes, you were really good," she teased. "You fell asleep in that chair. A few hours ago, you got up to use the bathroom, draped all your clothes on that chair, and climbed into bed. And you stuck to your side of the bed like all my favourite sleepover guests."

I relaxed, proud of my behaviour for a change. We lay on our sides, facing one another. Joan's natural beauty took my breath away.

She threw a leg over my hip. I leaned toward her, slipped the strap of her tank top down, and kissed her neck. Cupping my palm, I held one small breast in it. The nipple was elongated and sensitive to my touch. She broke from our kiss to moan softly. She pulled away, manoeuvred herself onto her knees, and sat astride my hips. Joan crossed her arms in front of her and held the bottom edge of her tee. I expected her to pull it down to cover her thighs. Instead she pulled it up and over her head and tossed it away. She leaned over and opened the bedside table drawer on her right. My jaw dropped to observe her flexibility and her obvious preparation; she withdrew her hand; a condom in her grasp.

Instinct led our hands on a journey of discovery. We rolled to exchange positions. I held her wrists pinned above her head and used one hand to travel up her side and around her firm deltoid. "Very impressive, Ms. Sax," I whispered. She exhaled, and her hips rose. I bit her ear, conveying the depths of my arousal. Both of us began to breathe faster, louder. I stopped hearing anything but the crazy beating of my heart.

Her laugh surprised me, and my eyes flew open. She toppled over me onto the bed. Joan sighed and wriggled her body in a big stretch. "Ah, I feel alive. I'm exhausted," she said."You okay?"

"More than okay," I said. I stretched my arm out and Joan lifted her head so that it rested on me somewhere. I grinned so widely it hurt. Joan had paid me a great compliment: she felt good.

She didn't stay there long though. She hopped up to wash her face and dress. "Come on, lazybones, let's grab a coffee. We've got a full day today, starting with yoga."

"No, today is Cozumel. Let's have a long shower together."

"I don't know about you, but I'll be showering after yoga. If you don't want to come—" Joan looked up at me as she tied her laces. I bumped into her, my hands going to her hips. For the second time this week I thought she was too good to be true. So far I hadn't seen Joan's flaws, which led me to think I should be on guard for a big letdown.

In the exercise room, Joan placed her mat next to a familiar-looking Asian woman. I interrupted their conversation to introduce myself. The woman bobbed her head but said nothing in reply. Then I went in search of my own mat, annoyed that Joan hadn't thought to get one for me when she'd retrieved her own. I'd become secondary to the Asian couple.

To make space for me, the couple separated. I ended up lying down between them.

"Thank you. I'm Sam," I said, a second time to the woman.

"So you said. That's my husband Li, and I'm Amy," she said. Her close-mouthed smile appeared genuine though reserved. They made an unlikely couple; even in casual attire he appeared more confident, affluent, and sophisticated than she did. About five feet in height, she swung her head, and her long greyish ponytail swung to her side. She looked at Joan and then back to me. Then it clicked. We'd first seen her in the elevator shortly after arriving. And she and I had sat next to one another at the casino bar the other night. Partners in heavy drinking following heavy losses. When I'd left, she was asleep, her loose long hair spread over the polished wood.

I looked to the side to catch Joan's attention, but she was prone on her back in savasana. I tried to clear my mind, relax, and enjoy Louisa's steady coaching and soothing voice. I knew Louisa well and had to focus not to think too much about our last conversation. I cringed recalling when I'd told Ellen how irresistibly attractive she was; only to be informed she was more interested in Louisa than me. Although it was over a year ago, I felt sure Ellen had told Louisa about it.

I glanced at Joan's form. She maintained perfect alignment between her shoulders, glutes, thighs, and ankles. The straight line her body formed suggested steady practice. I willed her to notice my form, my muscled calves and tight small butt, but she was concentrating and not on me.

I remembered her naked, walking to the balcony to spread the curtains this morning. If it hadn't been a port day, one where there was an urgency to make the most of every minute, I was sure

I could've convinced her to come back to bed. Louisa called the name of a difficult position, which I performed impressively. How could I impress Joan if she never looked? The sound of the round brass finger cymbals Louisa wore on two of her fingers ended our session, and I sighed with relief.

"Louisa gives a good workout, doesn't she?" Joan said. She wiped her brow with a towel and said she suspected I went to a yoga studio regularly.

I put my hands in the air. "Guilty as charged," I said. So I guess she'd sneaked a peek when I wasn't looking.

"Remember, be on deck eleven at ten o'clock," I said to Joan. Amy and Li approached, and I held the door a minute more. "Maybe if we're not all too exhausted after our excursions today, we'll find you in one of the bars tonight," I said to them.

"Of course, Sam. We'd be delighted. If possible, find us in the bar adjacent to the casino, the Champagne Bar. We'll keep an eye out for the two of you. But if you're too tired when you get back, then tomorrow," Li suggested.

"Sounds great," Joan said.

"In the meantime, enjoy Cozumel," Amy said.

# CHAPTER 26

## *SAM*

From the top deck of the *Liberty*, we had a good view of San Miguel, the port city of Cozumel. I cleaned my aviators on the shirt I wore over my bathing suit. Three docks extended off along the right side of the wide pier. On the opposite side, several small fishing craft bobbed in the bay, creating a picturesque scene. The first slip, nearest the shore, stood empty. In the second slip were three ships tied up, one behind the other. The cruise liner the *Princess* sat closest to the main dock. Next was the smallest of the three ships, a Norwegian vessel. Her guests waved madly, clearly excited to commune with other cruisers. The third one was too far behind to identify it.

The *Liberty* sat in the third slip. Rachel and Joan approached us lugging four pairs of fins, masks, snorkels. My hands were on my hips and I groaned. "Joan, you're crazy if you think we're taking all that stuff with us."

"Come on, Sam. Don't be such a sourpuss." Rachel shoved me, and I took a step back, still l scowling. "Don't you think it'll be fun, Neil?" She told him she wanted to build shared memories with him. I trusted Neil to see through that malarkey.

"For God's sake, it's not like we're hiking with all of this. We're renting a car. Cozumel is known around the world as a fabulous spot with incredibly clear waters and the most colourful fish," Joan said.

I've snorkelled here before and it was a gorgeous spot, but I didn't want to carry all that cumbersome equipment. I looked at Neil, hoping he'd be the one to veto the idea.

Neil took a snorkel from Rachel. "This is pretty good stuff, Sam. See here—it even has a purge valve for when water gets into the mouthpiece."

"Thanks a lot, Neil. You just want to get laid," I said, turning toward him.

"And you're just lazy," he said.

"Quit it, you two. You can return your stuff to the sports deck at the bow, but Rachel and I are taking our stuff and planning on using it." Joan sat in one of the chairs and tried to reorganize the bag she was carrying.

"Obviously, the fins aren't going to fit," I said. I shook my head, annoyed with myself for giving in so easily. "I'll carry them." Four towels were sticking up out of Joan's bag already.

Neil and I sat at a table, repacking the beach bags with the snorkelling masks at the bottom and the linen napkins and cutlery we'd borrowed from the dining room on top. We thought the girls would like this. We had to sign the items out, and if we didn't return them by a certain time, our accounts would be charged. In our second bag, we'd packed shorts, sunscreen, and magazines.

"I don't know why you bothered with all that. We could have just bought paper plates and plastic cutlery and not carried it," Joan said.

I rubbed the back of my neck. My plastic water cup was empty. I overturned it on the deck and stomped on it. Neil looked over. I shrugged and stared back.

"Sorry, Joan. I figured the less we had to buy, the fewer the stops we'd need to make in town and the quicker we'd get to the beach. Just trying to please." I exaggerated my gestures to make her regret her criticism.

She leaned over, held my chin up, and kissed me on the mouth. "It'll be more fun your way. I'm the one who's sorry. I am really anxious to get to that secluded romantic beach." How ironic those words would seem later.

"Is anyone bringing a cell?" I asked. I had expected someone would.

Joan dug into her windbreaker. "I think it's neat to go 'unplugged' as they say, but I do have this."

She showed me a little wristlet attached to a strap in the zippered pocket of her terry cloth jacket. "I like to travel with several credit cards." She laughed. "But there's no one I need to call and I don't intend to get lost, so I'm not bringing my phone."

No big surprise there. I already knew how she felt about technology. While not a neophyte exactly, she refused to be connected all the time. I figured I could do without my phone until dinnertime too and hoped my effort to do so would impress her. Actually, except for taking pictures I always left my cell in the room on board, so why take it with me now? Besides I knew she had her good camera.

"I'm sure we all brought adequate cash and a credit card too. My wallet's in the Royal Caribbean tote," Rachel said. "But if Joan wants to go on a spending spree and decide to spoil me, that's just fine by me," she teased.

Most of the crowd had cleared the gangway. It was time to get a move on. I cringed as I took hold of Joan's beach bag, the one that identified all cruisers because it was emblazed with the Royal Caribbean blue-and-white logo. Two cruises ago, I'd told a woman from New York to carry the thing herself because I wouldn't be caught dead holding that bag.

Neil held up his matching bag. "Look, we're twins," he said.

"You're an idiot. You paid for that?" I asked him.

"No," he said, clearly offended by the presumption that he had. "I got it as a prize in the Irish pub's trivia game last night. Remember? You got bored and left me and Rach there after the first round?"

Humph. I motioned for them to walk ahead of us, off the ship and through the cruise terminal. Rachel's huge black straw hat made me think of Audrey Hepburn, but she didn't have the body type. She was too big and bulky. It was Joan who had the long neck and small bone structure, even though she was much shorter than the Hollywood star. Hepburn had been a favourite of my grandmother and mother. I couldn't stop looking at Joan's outfit.

On a street perpendicular to the main street, just opposite the cruise terminal, we saw the sign of the rental car agency, just where we'd been told to expect it. There were no more convertibles when I'd made the arrangements, which was a shame. When Joan was seated in the front of our Kia, her cigarette-style ankle-length pants rose up her legs. Her sexy little ankles showed just above her tiny ballet flats. I couldn't wait to get us to the beach and watch her strip and show the bathing suit she was wearing underneath. If my gay brother could hear me now, I thought. I didn't realise I was so into her.

By eleven o'clock, the four of us had stepped out onto a covered parking lot attached to a Mega grocery store.

We had determined that Rachel and Neil would find fresh baguettes, cheese, an assortment of drinks, and ice. "If I don't find a sangria mix, I'll buy ingredients so I can make it," I heard Rachel say.

"Terrific," Joan and I answered. "Meet us back at the car asap," I called after them. Joan and I headed toward the deli counter to make our choices and completed our shopping in record time. It had become so hot I grabbed cold drinks to open as soon as I got outside the Mega.

I asked Joan to find the map we were given by Avis. "I might have put it in the glove compartment," I said. The site of El Cedral was at the southwestern side of the island. We drove in the opposite direction, crossing to the northeastern side at Middle Island Road. On this side, the waves were wilder, the reef closer to the shore, and signs lined the road, naming beaches separated by the odd tourist stand or restaurant. Very few people were in sight. " I flipped the pop can open and passed the others their drinks from the bag on the seat beside me.

A few motorbikes passed us, but there was next to no traffic, and apparently no hotels on this side of the island. The two-lane road led us around a jagged coastline of bays and unapproachable beaches. Rachel began hinting she felt carsick.

"So maybe you should come up for a little air. You two haven't stopped making out like teenagers since you got in the car," I said.

"Sam!" Joan jabbed me in the ribs. I wasn't sure if it was worse to sound jealous or just peeved that I had to concentrate so hard when Neil was clearly having the best of times. The bald tires, lack of seat belts, and sand blowing across the road worried me.

Under my breath, I told Joan that if Rachel threw up in this car, I'd kill her. There was only one lane in each direction. I rubbed the bridge of my nose. Joan described the scenery so I didn't miss it. Rachel complained about the ongoing travelogue she had to put up with, and I told her to stick her head out the window.

With the window open, we became uncomfortably hot. The car's air conditioning was shit, but it worked better with the windows up. I offered to pull over and was glad when Rachel said her nausea had passed.

"Good, then put the window up, for God's sake," Joan said.

I dared not take my eyes off the road. Joan kept describing things, the huge waves and the hibiscus flowers. "Ah we just passed Paradise Beach," she said. The windshield became spattered with the mist of the salt spray. Shit, the wipers weren't working. I wanted everyone to shut up. "There's Manatee Beach," Joan said as we approached the next sign. Let's try this one.

The car skidded. "Do you think you could tell me before we pass the exit to the beach?" I said, annoyed. According to the map, we were about to arrive at the lighthouse, beyond which were no more private beaches, just a few public beaches and those belonging to certain hotels on the western shore.

"I thought we were aiming for a secluded spot," Joan whispered, leaning in for a squeeze.

I put one arm around her shoulder, inhaled her fresh scent, and said, "Let you in on a little secret: all roads lead to Rome."

We came to a sign that read simply Beach and Seafood. I turned in to the parking lot and hoped for the best. Standing out on the dirt road in front of the restaurant was a line of shops showcasing handicrafts, Mexican embroidered blouses and dresses, straw hats, vanilla, tequila, and a variety of pretty shells. "I promise, we'll be back later in the day," Joan said to the men standing in front of their stalls. They probably had few customers a day and Joan had too soft a heart to ignore their pleas to look at their wares. Rachel, on the other hand, made it clear she couldn't wait to get organized and open the guacamole and salsa dips, corn chips, and beef fajitas. I agreed. We were all hot and hungry.

"What are you and Joan whispering about? We're dying of hunger." Neil said.

"I'm trying to convince Joan it's okay to ignore these locals." I gave Neil a look that suggested Joan was a little too much of a bleeding heart to be for real.

"But they're poor and not begging, just trying to earn an honest living. I want to help them." Her eyes were large and pleading, but I pulled her along.

"You can always buy something on the way back to the car later, all right?" Neil said. "Do you think we can walk through the restaurant? I see the ocean and a staircase on the far side over there."

No sooner had the words left his mouth than Rachel had walked over to the hostess. "Señora, could we walk through"—she pointed—"to get to the beach there?"

"What you think? This a sidewalk?"

Rachel promised her we'd be back for a meal later. The stout lady became gracious and waved us through, telling us to be careful on the steep stairs leading down to the beach. Finding the perfect spot took more time than expected. I intended to talk everyone into skinny-dipping, so we had to get away from the restaurant crowd.

"Oh, God. This is the most gorgeous beach. It's heavenly and not a soul in sight," Joan said.

I agreed. In the distance I could see an endless stretch of white sand devoid of footprints.

We picked our way first down the steps and then, just as carefully, across the thin coating of sand on the rocky extension of the reef that met this part of the beach. Some fifteen feet past the foot of the staircase, the sand felt soft and deep. Near the water's edge, its texture changed; my foot sank so deeply, I thought we'd found quicksand. There was no one to call for help. Immediately, I looked back to catch Neil's eye, but he was still on the hard, rocky beginning of the route I'd chosen to take. His eyes were glued to the surface of the ground. My adrenalin spiked, and I forced myself to breathe slowly through my mouth. I pulled my foot out and told Joan to head up away from the water a bit. Following, I sighed with relief when I was sure I'd found purchase on familiar hard sand.

"Look at that," yelled Rachel, who ran ahead toward a faded pink-and-mauve woven hammock hanging in the shade between two palms. In this little spot out of the glare were tall grasses.

"Yay!" I shouted, glad to see evidence that other visitors had enjoyed this spot.

"Someone's going to have a nice siesta there," Joan said.

"Yeah, me," Neil said.

Once the girls were safely ensconced on the beach, they began unpacking our picnic while I doubled back with Neil to get the Royal Caribbean bags and snorkel equipment.

Our picnic was fresh and everything was delicious, even if the corn chips they'd made in the store were a little too greasy. Miraculously, they were still warm.

"Did someone buy water bottles? It's too hot for more sangria but I've been so thirsty since we started eating," Joan said.

I offered Neil a drink because he was also complaining of being really dry. That's how the ice cube fight started. Neil missed the beer I tossed, and it slipped to his crotch. He thought it was intentional. Before we knew it, all four of us were engaged in a battle.

Neil jumped up at one point.

"Be careful! You'll get sand in our food!" shrieked Joan, covering the plates with one large towel. She and Rachel bent down to put the lids back on the open dip containers.

I called a time out, and a second later we were all dashing into the surf. The water felt cold, cold, cold. I faced the beach and realized we were truly isolated. There was the faintest hint that a dirt path had once existed through the brush on the hill behind the hammock. This was as secluded a spot as ever there was.

A half hour later, I was giving myself a rash. The sun had dried the salt water off and my skin felt uncomfortably dry and itchy. What I would have given for a freshwater shower. "Let's take the snorkel gear and go back into the water."

"Was that really you suggesting we snorkel?" Joan said, teasing me. She passed me a pair of flippers and took hers into the water. A wave swept over her, tossing her onto her behind. She flopped around on her back, trying to get each foot in a flipper. Rachel couldn't stop laughing at her. Neil got our attention by telling us we were missing the biggest manta ray he'd ever seen this close to shore.

Everything we saw blew me away. The sizes of the fish we saw were as impressive as their colours.

Neil said, "I'm going to take my book over to that shady area where the hammock is."

I looked at Rachel, the sun worshipper, and wondered whether she'd choose shade or sun—or rather Neil or sun. She looked sad but picked up her towel and moved toward him."Let's lie down together. I can handle the shade of those two old palms if you can." I watched them settle under the shadow of the cliff. On her side, face to face with Neil, Rachel struck a seductive pose, one of her long legs carelessly thrown over his hip.

Joan lay on her stomach, head to the side, facing away from me, a hat over the exposed part of her face. Flat on my back next to her, I burrowed into the sand, forcing a concave spot to conform to the shape of my ass. I twisted a little from side to side and tried to make myself comfortable. I sensed Joan was laughing silently at my wriggling. My eyes focused on Rachel. Her sculpted legs and toned arms suggested just the right amount of weight training. She wet her full lips, and I wondered if she was really as sensual as her moves suggested. My eyes caught her gaze, and I realized she'd been looking at me too. I had my answer; flirting was part of her personality. I held her look for a minute, calculating how long she could keep it up, but I lost the contest when Joan called my name.

"Sam, will you pass me a water bottle, please?"

Joan was so different from the type of women who'd always attracted me. It might be a sign that I was growing up. If not now, when, I thought. I remembered something my brother said, that I always went for women dumber than me and poorer than me. The only reason I let the woman on my arm get top billing in the looks department was because that boosted my ego. I shook my head, realizing how pathetic that made me sound, but I thought I should be congratulated for being so honest with myself. Joan sat up, sipped the water, and handed it back. "You finish it," she said, lying back down and this time facing my direction.

I lay on my side, resting on my elbows, and admired her perfect features, her youthful, calm expression, and her petite perfectly proportioned body. How different she was from Rachel.

"Why are you staring at me?" Joan said.

"Your eyes are closed. How—"

"It's your breathing. It's kind of warm and awfully close to my face." She smiled and pushed up onto one elbow, a hand under her cheek. Her small flawless breasts rose from the top ruffle of her bathing suit. Joan timidly reached toward my chest, her long thin fingers combed  my chest hair and I shivered like I'd never been touched before.  I turned away, distracted by a rustle in the grasses behind and above us.

# CHAPTER 27

## *Sam*

I looked at Neil at the exact moment he called my name. I sensed Joan sit up, attentive. Biting my lower lip, I felt in my pocket for my cell. "Shit."

Some rough-looking men were stumbling down the cliff from the road above. I had a lousy premonition that they didn't just want to share our picnic. I wiped sand off my hands, got onto my knees, and sat back on my heels, trying to look unconcerned.

A skinny old man led three younger guys in tattered cut-offs. A little kid raced around the others, sprinting toward the beach. He almost tripped over Rachel. "Uncle, here," the kid shouted.

Rachel lay on a towel under a palm, ear buds in, eyes closed, totally unaware of the danger at her feet.

Neil walked from behind the palm where he'd gone to take a pee and nudged her with his toe. She took out the ear buds. "It's okay, Rach. Get up and stay calm," he said.

The leader seemed frail and old, his vitality leached out of him, but he had his protégés, anxious to pick up the slack. He motioned for Rachel and Neil to move down the beach to where we stood. "Why don't we all sit together? You can tell us how you like our island." I noticed the disfigured right side of his face. Part of his nose and mouth had been completely cut away. His voice was deep and phlegmy.

I looked at the kid, who was helping himself to our picnic. A handful of tortilla chips spilled from his dirty fingers. The brazen little shit walked down to the water's edge with the whole bag and a litre of water.

There was nothing to be worried about. These were poor locals wanting to rip off some not-so-poor tourists. Two of the guys looked so similar; I guessed they were brothers, probably in their early thirties. Their eyes darted around the group, and they kept swallowing but avoided eye contact with us. Threatening tourists was a serious matter in Mexico. The little kid had the same smile as they did. The big guy with the darker colouring and dreadlocks was no relation. He was another story. A scary story. Joan took a step closer to me, and I put my arm around her shoulders protectively.

"Listen, old man," Neil began authoritatively, "let's send the women into the water to cool off." He tilted his head, nodding at the ocean. Joan stepped toward the water, but the old guy grabbed her arm and held her in place. Neil's vice grip tightened on the old man's forearm. "Let her go. Now."

The two of them locked eyes. I held my breath. Eventually, Joan's arm fell to her side and she rubbed it. It would be just Neil and me against the four locals, not counting the kid. I didn't like the odds. I'd had more black eyes in high school than there were marshmallows in a box of Lucky Stars. It came with the territory when you had a queer for a brother.

Neil crossed his arms in front of his broad chest. "Talk to us if you want, but let the women go into the water, away from here." Neil rubbed the back of his neck and under his chin where the perspiration had gathered in the creases of his skin.

"Sorry, amigo, we can't do that," the old Mexican said. The few teeth he still had in his mouth were badly stained. I heard the phlegm in his throat, and he horked in the sand. A series of coughs followed. The other men gave each other knowing laughs and slapped one another on their backs. I shifted from foot to foot, nearly losing my balance in the sand. The old guy looked up, and I recoiled at his disfigurement. I found him intimidating but forced myself not to step backwards.

"Why do you need them?" I asked, motioning to Rachel and Joan.

The old skinny man found this funny. He slapped his knee, laughing louder. After bending low, he toppled to the ground on top of our blue towel. He sat up, noticed Joan standing near him, and patted the space beside him, his meaning unquestionably clear. She didn't move. "Señorita," he said playfully. *"Por favor."*

"No, I don't think so," Joan said in a neutral voice.

"Do my looks make you afraid?" he asked.

Rachel plunked herself down. "I'm not afraid of you," she said. She held his gaze till he gave his attention to picking inside his one clear nostril.

"What do you want?" I asked, staring down at my seated adversary. "Listen, we've got Coronas in—"

"You hear that, amigos? The American thinks we stopped in for a drink."

I cringed. Blue veins protruded like tracks along his neck, down his arms and ropey legs. The sagging flesh jiggled as he reached for a crushed pack of Camels in his back pocket. "Want one?" he asked, shaking a cigarette from the package toward Joan.

Joan shook her head. She pulled the Royal Caribbean bag closer.

"Stop. You need something now?" the old guy wanted to know.

"Just this." She lifted her white zippy up before putting it on to keep from shivering.

Rachel shifted over to the cooler. She passed beers to the intruders. "Here, I'm sure we'd all be happy to give you our fancy watches. Just leave us alone," she said. She dropped her Cartier in his outstretched hand.

"Yeah, here," Joan said as she took off the gold chain around her neck and her watch too.

On wobbly legs, the thin man got himself upright. He moved the three items around in his palm. "That's a good start," he said, pleased. *"Gracias."*

One of the look-alikes snorted, covered one side of his nose, and did that thing where you blow to clear one nostril at a time. The green snot flew out with a honk. He looked at Joan to see her reaction since his mucus had landed just an inch from her foot. She raised her eyebrows for a second.

"I'm sorry we don't have more to offer," Joan said, her voice trailing off. She removed her diamond ring and the turquoise and silver one I'd bought her on the ship and placed those in his hand too. "Together these are worth a lot of money."

I kicked sand between my feet. Neil was watching Rachel and didn't seem as angry as me that the girls were offering up their stuff without even being threatened.

"How much money?" one of them said to Joan. The biggest of the three young adults squealed over the size of the diamond. They crowded around the stash in the old guy's open hand. "Miguel, come, look," the old man shouted to the kid.

I moved from foot to foot. It bothered me that the girls had given up their stuff before these buggers had demanded it. I took my sunglasses off and wiped between my eyes where the sweat had collected and put them back on. From underneath, I hit the old geezer's outstretched hand, causing all the jewellery to jump off his palm and drop into the sand. And then I kicked the sand around so they'd have to dig to find it.

"*Joder!* What'd you do that for?" the kid shouted. He dove into the sand and began digging. I followed his glance to his uncle, who was staring at me, the venom now pulsing through those ugly veins.

"*Comer mierda,*" one of the brothers said.

"Shit eater," I translated to myself.

"For fuck's sake, Sam. What're you doing?" Rachel yelled.

The old man used both hands to push me backwards, and I tripped.

Neil's reaction was to defend me by throwing his fist into the old geezer's chin. He fell to the ground and spit out a tooth. He shouted something in Spanish.

Someone grabbed Neil from behind while the big guy with rope for hair punched him over and over, right in the stomach. I froze. I was sitting on my ass, not a part of the scene playing out in front of me. The big guy who'd exhausted himself took a break, leaning on his knees and panting. Then he moved around Neil and aimed a high kick at his back, just above the waist. Neil's mouth twisted, the whites of his eyes looked both yellow and red intermittently and when he was  doubled over his pain became mine. The big Mexican pulled Neil upright, walked behind him and put him into a stranglehold.

Neil was no stranger to the move. He put both his hands on his attacker's fingers, trying to pry them loose.

I bent down, stood up fast and threw sand in the face of his attacker. Then I jumped on the big guy's back.

Joan gasped.

With one arm around his shoulders, I felt like I was riding a bucking bronco. I pulled with all my weight on his dreadlocks.

The kid, Miguel, and the old uncle and both of the brothers were on their knees, still searching for the jewellery in the sand.

The big guy with the dreadlocks released his grip on Neil. "Run!" I screamed. I grabbed Joan's hand. "Run, the way we came!"

"Our stuff!" Rachel shouted.

"Just go," I screamed again, pushing her ahead of me. The keys were in my pocket, and that was all we needed.

The two brothers trailed us for a bit but gave up. They were more interested in the jewellery.

Five minutes later Neil told me to pull over. He threw up over and over. I saw blood in the vomit. He lay down in the back seat with his head in Rachel's lap. None of us spoke. I dropped the others at a hotel I had seen before on the main street in San Miguel. After abandoning the car in the rental agency lot, I ignored the employee calling me and walked back to the hotel. Joan was the only one of us who had a credit card in her possession, so I assumed the room would be in her name.

I approached the registration desk with as much decorum as possible. I was, after all, standing in the lobby of a four-star hotel in nothing but a bathing suit, not even shoes. "Could you please tell me the room number of Señorita Joan Sax, *por favor?*"

"No, but I'd be happy to connect you on the house phone," the young woman said. "It's our policy not—"

"Yes, yes, fine," I said, moving to the adjacent wall. I tapped my swimsuit pocket, reassured to find I might not be totally at Joan's mercy.

# CHAPTER 28

## JOAN
### *Thursday, February 6, 2003*
### *Day 6, Cozumel*

Neil slept late, but when he opened his eyes, Rachel and I were sitting near him. Dirty sandals and a small pile of sand lay like a puddle at the end of the bed. His dark skin made it difficult to see the bruising, but his expression hinted at his pain.

"Argh" he moaned. Neil screwed up his face as he touched the white gauze wound around his torso.

"Sam, he's up. Come in," I called.

"Well . . . if it isn't our hero. So glad you've decided to rejoin the living," Sam flashed a little light in Neil's pupils, first left, then right. "Yeah, breathing's painful. The hotel doctor left you meds for that." He watched Neil touch the gauze. He nodded. "I know, in North America we don't tape broken ribs, but apparently they still do here. I wasn't going to argue with the local doc. If it bothers you, we can cut it off tonight, but with all that chest hair . . . it's going to really hurt coming off."

"Ouch," Rachel said. She picked up Neil's hand and kissed his cheek. "Let's get the three of us a drink. I wasn't sure you were going to survive the night, but now that you have, we can celebrate." She winked.

I moved to the end of his bed and wiggled his giant foot, sticking out from the light comforter. "Sam ordered champagne and orange juice with our breakfast order, but I didn't let them open the bubbly till you woke up." I accepted the glass Sam poured for me and raised my glass. "To Neil."

Neil asked for straight OJ and pain pills. "Never mind, I'll be right back, I gotta go . . ." He paused, a quizzical look on his face as the reality of his condition registered.

Sam was ready with an explanation. "Last night the doctor gave you a strong sedative and put in a catheter, since he wasn't sure you'd be able to get out of bed to go to the john if you needed to. You were in shock and might have suffered some internal damage." Neil pressed his lips together. "Without an X-ray the doctor said he was only guessing about the state of your ribs, and the catheter is only temporary."

"How temporary?" Neil said, checking under the covers.

"The doc is coming back sometime this morning to take it out," I said. I opened his drapes to let the sun in.

"Rachel honey, Joan, would you two excuse us, please?" Neil said. "I've got to pee."

We left Sam with Neil in the second bedroom and moved into the suite's main room. A breakfast trolley sat next to the window in the living room of the large two-bedroom suite we all shared. "Tea or coffee?" Rachel asked. She stretched out on the cream sofa and sipped her black coffee. She was so animated, talking with her hands about this beautiful hotel we'd landed in.

"Rachel, please lean over the coffee table while you're drinking. You're making me nervous," I said.

Was I the only one worried about how we'd rejoin the cruise? She sat forward after huffing like a child whose fun I'd spoiled. "Joan, since you're the only one who has credit cards, could you take money out of an ABM and give each of us a hundred bucks or something? It'd be less embarrassing for us. It'd be repaid of course, as soon as we get back to the ship." Rachel leaned forward, held her coffee cup in both hands, and held my gaze.

I told her we'd see after deciding how long we'd be here. "In the meantime, just charge to the room," I said. Neil called my name, but his voice cut out and we could tell it hurt him to yell. We joined him, and he switched to whispering and breathing through barely open lips.

The ice bucket filled with hot soapy water and a wet washcloth sat beside the bed. "I'm kicking myself for leaving my credit card and cash in the dumb Royal Caribbean bag on the beach. You know I'll pay you back for these medical costs, Joan," Neil said.

I waved it off. "I'm not worried about that, just about you. How do you feel? Will you want to go out today or lie here and regain your strength?" I asked.

Neil seemed to be thinking it over. He sat upright, breathing shallowly.

"We can stay here and then leave you to have a rest while we go get some sun," Rachel said. "We need to make a to-do list first." She found paper and pen in the desk drawer. She read aloud the first item she'd written down: clean bathing suits.

"Give me that," Sam said. "I've been composing it in my head for hours. Shoes. Did any of us carry shoes off that beach?"

We shook our heads.

"So see what you can find for us in the lobby shops or go down the street, but be as quick as you can. We need a few toiletries although the essentials are already here, care of the hotel."

Neil squeezed his eyes together and held the bridge of his nose.

"Do you have a headache?" I asked.

"We'll get pills for that, and suntan oil too," said Rachel.

"He doesn't need any more pills. Neil's already on serious pain medication that will do the trick," Sam said. He took my arm and led me into the living room. "Joan, I just thought of something. How're you going to manage without your medications?" Sam asked. He hugged me and drew his fingers through my tangled hair.

"It's all right, Sam. I always carry a two-day supply of anticonvulsants in a watertight little bag. I like to be spontaneous, so I'm always prepared. Hence the jackets with pockets, wherever I go." My hand tapped my side as I counted the days in my head. I figured I'd be in trouble if I weren't rejoined with my pharmaceutical supplies by Saturday night.

"Oh," was all Sam said. A long pause ensued. He released me, and I rose.

Rachel wore the bathing suit and cover that she had washed in the sink last night. She pulled a thread hanging from the neckline. I could see the wheels in her head turning. "We'll get to the beach today, won't we?" she asked.

Sam swallowed a bite of Danish. "Neil's sore and he needs rest and time to allow the torn muscles to repair themselves. However, he needs to get up and walk a bit regularly so nothing stiffens. Therefore, going down to the pool will be good for him, good for all of us.""

"I heard that. Why are you talking about me out there? Get in here." It was a struggle for Neil to speak up. He groaned. The three of us returned to his room. "I like that idea, so call the hotel doctor and tell him to get his ass up here," he said. He hugged his middle. His next words were spoken so softly, they were barely audible. "I don't want to waste the day lying in bed." Neil pointed at Sam. "Never mind that. You're a doctor—you take this thing out now. We'll discuss our options at the beach later."

By noon the four of us were sitting poolside around a circular blue-tiled table with an umbrella overhead. Rachel and I figured there were two options.

"Option one is to find a flight to Nassau tonight, Thursday, and be at the marina when the ship gets there in the morning. Option two, the alternative is to let Neil rest here, let all of us enjoy two relaxing days here and fly out on Saturday, the day the *Liberty* returns to Miami." I opened my eyes wide, begging the others to choose my choice.

"Judging by the long lines at registration last Saturday, the ship will be in the terminal all afternoon so we can collect our things anytime Saturday, up to around six. Isn't that when the *Liberty* left Miami?" Rachel picked up Neil's hand, kissed it and tried to get him to meet her gaze but he was thinking it through on his own. His pursed lips moved from right to left as he considered the pros and cons.

Sam twirled his watch and gave no indication of a preference.

"Joan and I like the second choice," Rachel said. "I've no desire to sit at the Cozumel airport. Let's face it; what's the likelihood of all four of us getting on a standby flight to Nassau?"

The pool deck was so pretty. The look was exotic but not overdone: a mix of colourful large planters sitting atop terracotta tiles. Along the pathway leading from the hotel to the pool and from there to the beach, there were an infinite number of shades of green. Silver green, kelly green, emerald green, lime green, forest green, yellow green, chartreuse, seaweed, olive. Sans sunglasses, I squinted into the endless distance, and wished I still had my good camera. Green became blue became navy became black. I caught sight of the turquoise water somewhere in the middle distance and felt the urge to test the temperature of the ocean.

Sam shook his head. "Joan, what are you thinking? We've paid for that cruise. We won't be getting any money back. And staying here is a fortune. Just look at this place." He ran a hand through his hair. In the sunlight, it looked strawberry blond. He shaded his eyes with the palm of his hand and looked at each of us in turn. "Then again," he said, "it'd be no good if just one of us got on a flight. I don't like that option either. And then it's possible we could all get stuck in Nassau and not get on a flight to Miami in time." He got up from his chair. "I'm hot. I'll get a waiter to bring us soft drinks. Okay?" Sam zigzagged toward the pool bar. He held his head to the side and rubbed his neck as he moved.

Neil had strong feelings against taking unnecessary flights. It hurt to breathe deeply, so through nearly closed lips he listed his concerns. He bent forward, arms hugging his chest. Being without sunglasses, he was constantly wiping sweat from the corners of his eyes.

"You okay?" Sam asked, returning with a waiter who carried a tray of colas.

Neil nodded. "Did you bring the meds down to the pool?" He watched Sam nod and held out his hand. "It's time, doctor," Neil said.

"Fuck," Sam said, slapping his forehead. "We can't travel without passports."

There was utter quiet except for the sound of a child running around the pool. "Cannonball!" the boy shouted.

"This isn't a joke, Sam. Can I have the pain meds now?" Neil asked again.

"Hey, Neil, did you ever lose your passport? I mean during your career?" Sam grabbed hold of Neil's shoulder. He released it immediately. "You okay? Sorry. I totally forgot." One look at Neil's face and he stopped to fish in his pocket for the pill bottle.

"Thanks," Neil said, his voice low and controlled. He swallowed the pills without water. He took shallow, quick breaths, and we waited.

I winced, just hearing the strain there. "I'm getting you water," I said, and he rewarded me with a weak smile. When I came back, I learned Neil had lost his passport on two occasions, but his experience didn't help us.

"Wish I had something good to say." He looked at Sam. "The first time it happened I had to wait overseas while my agent went back to the Canada, paid a penalty fee for fast-tracking the new passport, and then travelled back with it. The other time, I went to the Canadian embassy in Austria, but it took a three weeks in total to get a new passport and I couldn't go outside of Austria that entire time. It didn't make sense. Go figure."

"Shit," Rachel said, as if the problem was just becoming clear to her. "But this must happen all the time. The average Joe couldn't do what you did, Neil. They wouldn't be able to afford it." Then she looked at me. "And what if the person who'd lost their passport was travelling alone?"

It had taken a while, but it was sinking in; we couldn't buy tickets to fly out of Mexico without passports, period!

"We're fucked without passports," Rachel whined.

"Calm down, everyone!" I yelled, my hands pumping the air by my sides. "We'll figure something out."

Neil inhaled and groaned in pain. "I don't think these pills are doing anything."

Sam smiled. "Christ, Neil. Give it a little time. The dosage you're on would put a normal human to sleep." Sam switched arms to continue shading his eyes.

"I just got a brainwave. I'll be right back," I said, taking off for the lobby doors.

As I waited at the desk for the registration staff to locate the concierge, I thought about all the ups and downs of this eventful week. It had got off to a rough start with that seizure, but then I met Sam and we entertained ourselves teasing those whale watchers on the top deck. I had taken out my camera again, using Amy as my muse; she posed in the elevator when we got stuck. Although I'd lost all the pictures I'd taken, I'd rekindled an interest in both yoga and photography—not bad for someone who'd been a loner for the past year.

I didn't have a watch to look at and asked a stranger for the time.

A woman wearing a beige jacket and skirt approached me. "Excuse me, the concierge was in the restaurant dealing with a problem but will be with you shortly. He knows what you want to speak to him about."

"Thank you. I'm fine here."

There was a sign advertising a band in the hotel, and I thought about the night I let Rachel teach me to salsa. I had to admit it had been fun.

"Señora," a tall slim man said. His dark moustache covered his lips to the extent that I couldn't tell if he thought it was presumptuous of me to be asking him for such a favour.

Waiting for him to contact Western Union, I reflected a little more. Belize was a disappointment, but Cozumel, in spite of yesterday's events, was a jewel of an island. The little bit of snorkelling we did at the beach was well worth the argument I'd won with Neil and Sam over schlepping all the snorkelling equipment the ship had loaned us. And it looked as though we'd have two more days at this four-star hotel.

# CHAPTER 29

# JOAN

The sun blinded me when I stepped out of the hotel. Sam, Rachel, and Neil must have left the pool and gone to the beach. Neil was lying in the shade under a *palapa* on the sand, close to the steps leading up to the pool. He told me Sam and Rachel had gone for a walk and pointed where. I jogged on the sand till my energy was spent, and then I continued walking. Eventually I saw them at the far end of the beach, maybe three hotels away. I waved my arms back and forth over my head. They were standing facing me and clearly refusing to return my wave.

"Fine!" I yelled, and took off into the surf.

A short while later, Rachel's voice reached me from the shore. "Swim in." She held her hair back with one hand. "We were just teasing you."

Sam's voice was fainter. He said something like; "Don't bother." He walked a few steps farther. "You sure took long enough."

My hands feathered the water while I floated on my back. I stared at the cerulean blue overhead, a smattering of white threads high in the sky. A huge rolling wave lifted me up, and I giggled as if I were on a raft, about to be overturned. I could never get enough of this. Moments like these contradicted my depressive thoughts about my life's purpose being nothing more than my inadequate attempts to solve a series of problems: mine, my kids', and my friends. Not a very lofty reason to be put on earth. Could it be possible that there wasn't a purpose? That idea made the most sense. I pushed the serious thoughts away to focus on the cirrus clouds. I laughed, the English language was funny. I swallowed water and began coughing, choking and treading water furiously. My eyes struggled to find sky.

Sam rushed to the water's edge. "You okay?" he shouted. There were stark white marks where his fingers depressed his skin at his hips. I was above water.

"I'm fine." I exhaled. I began swimming in. My arms seemed weaker than usual. A wave slapped me in the face, forcing me back me out and holding my head under. I sputtered, broke through the surface gagging and made another attempt to reach the beach. The water smacked me in the chest, knocking my breath out, but I managed to crawl forward on scratched bleeding knees. I fought the receding water. Panicked, I opened my mouth to yell for help and swallowed more salt water. I couldn't drag myself through those last three feet.

A strong hand gripped my arm. Sam's eyes caught me in an iron grip. Together we both landed on our behinds on the beach.

"Didn't you see the flag?" he said, breathing heavily.

Rachel touched my shoulder and said, "There—it's red today. That generally indicates a strong undertow and danger." She sat on my other side, an arm around my waist.

"Well . . . it's all Neil's fault. I was envious of all the attention he was getting and wanted some too."

Neil walked toward us. He looked as winded as me.

"How are you doing?" I asked as we walked toward the hotel steps and the freshwater showers.

Neil admitted to being uncomfortable. "Joan, you don't look so good. Why don't you join me in the shade, have a cold drink and catch your breath for a while?" Neil poked Sam who walked ahead a little. "If you've any sense you will too, Sam." I watched Neil return to his place under the *palapa*. He'd saved a number of cots by spreading towels, magazines and a pair of new sandals over them. "Sam, you've got a bad burn, there. Don't you feel it?" he asked.

"That's exactly what I was thinking when I looked at you from the ocean, Sam." I faced him. "Honestly, you're badly sunburned."

"Sam shrugged his shoulders. "My skin shows it, but Neil's doesn't. It's not as bad as all that," he said.

Sam took my hand. I stood under the freshwater shower head at the bottom of the steps between the pool and the beach. He washed the sand from my back. He stood out of range of the shower's pinging drops but I didn't ask the obvious question. We moved to the chaises that Neil had saved for us.

I sat on the side of mine and enjoyed the sensation of my toes moving back and forth in the white sand.

"Joan," Sam said, "I've been thinking, who on board who might notice our, or better still, your absence? Maybe your tablemates or . . . I know, your friend Amy?"

"Oh, jeez, how could I forget?" I said. I stood facing Rachel's cot. "Remember that brainwave I'd had earlier?"

Rachel sat up on her cot and looked at Neil and Sam. "You mean when you took off in to the hotel? Where'd you go? What was the big deal, anyway?" Her frizz covered her face so I couldn't see her expression.

"Well," I said, "I had the concierge here cable the *Liberty*. I sent a note asking Amy and Li for help."

Sam rose. "So what's Li, a magician?" He raised a hand to attract the attention of a waiter walking in the next row. *"Cuarto cerveza, por favor,"* he yelled. He held up four fingers. *"Pronto."*

Sam paced until the waiter returned. He walked down to the water and back. "First off, you barely know Li," he said. "Second, I'd like to know what you think Li can do that Neil or I can't."

I looked at Rachel, wondering if she knew what I knew about ChewTech. She returned the look, a puzzled expression knitting her brow. If it hadn't been for the stock portfolio I'd inherited, I wouldn't have known about ChewTech either, and if I hadn't googled Li, I wouldn't have put his name and ChewTech together. I knew exactly how powerful and influential Li Chew was. I looked to see if Rachel was going to say anything, but she had disappeared.

I bit my top lip to keep from saying anything condescending, or worse, yelling at Sam. "Let's wait and see." I touched his arm.

"Want to go up to the pool level? We haven't tried the swim-up bar there yet." He pulled away. I grabbed my things and left him there to pout.

I dove into the pool. When I came up, I saw Sam marching across the pool deck and through the revolving doors into the hotel. Rachel had moved up to the pool level too. She was sunning on a cot at the deep end. It took me a few minutes to locate Neil. He was climbing down the ladder near the shallow end. He shouldn't have been in the pool. On his tiptoes he treaded cautiously toward me. He hugged his ribs, shielding himself from any water pressure.

"Ah." He breathed a loud sigh of relief when he got himself up on the stool next to me.

"It's pretty here, isn't it?" I said.

"Yeah." He ordered a soda and lime this time and asked if I wanted anything. "I'll sign for these," he told the barman. "Joan, I don't wanna keep saying this, but —"

"No, don't say anything, Neil. We'll work out the money later. That's the least of our worries."

"You saved us all yesterday. It's you we owe a big debt of gratitude to." He squeezed my hand. "I think secluded beaches have lost their appeal for me, forever." When I didn't respond, he stared into his drink and took a slow sip. "You know, Sam was especially brave. I'm a professional fighter, so it's instinctive for me to respond to a fighter, but for Sam it took real guts."

I tilted my head. Neil was squinting up at the beautiful fuchsia flowers hanging from each row of balconies on the hotel next door, the one with the neon sign, Casino.

"I bet that's where Sam went. He might need rescuing." Neil finished his drink, and I knew he wanted an excuse to get out of the sun. "I'll go see what I can do."

"Neil," I said, a restraining hand on his arm, "Sam doesn't have enough money on him to worry about. Maybe some change from our picnic shopping went into his bathing suit pocket, but that's it."

"Okay. I have another idea." His finger traced the edges of the square blue tiles on the bar's countertop. "I could use a nap, but before that I'd like to make a purchase. Will you spot me a hundred? I can't go much longer without a sweatshirt on my back."

"No doubt grey?" I said. "Take two C's if you want. There's cash in my room safe and I trust you more than anyone." I told him the safe number and Neil kissed the top of my head. "Tell Rach where I've gone." He tiptoed through the shallow end and exited by the ladder.

Rachel opened her eyes when I sat down on the empty cot next to her. "Where's Neil?"

After I explained, she said, "Good. I need a break from him. He can be so serious. He was telling me he's an atheist. I think that's weird. It's such a personal thing to share, don't you think?"

"Compared to what? Sharing your body?' I asked and laughed.

Her smile faded. "Tell me why you think Li or Amy will notice your absence."

I told her about the plans I'd made on board with the two of them, all of which I'd missed.

"My, aren't you the highly connected one?" Rachel swung her legs to the ground and perched forward, her face close to mine. "Did I tell you Li and I had met at a craps table one of the first nights aboard?" Her fingers encircled one bare wrist, and for a moment I thought she was telling me something meaningful. Rachel wet her lips.

I covered my mouth. "When you're outrageous you're funny, but what you're insinuating is disgusting. Amy is my friend."

"Well, if he's looking, he's going to find someone. Besides, it's too late for them." Rachel punctuated her statement with a defiant look. She took off down the steps toward the beach.

I lay down in the welcome silence. I must have gotten used to being alone — more than I realized. Over the course of this holiday I hadn't opened a book once, and missed the guilty pleasure of losing myself in someone else's troubles. I wished I had time for a massage to work out the stress. There was something wrong when you needed treatment for the pressure of having to please so many people. I closed my eyes, wondering where the closest Canadian or

American embassy was. I rubbed my closed eyelids. Should I go find a computer to do a search in case Li didn't come through for us? No, let someone else do that.

Rachel returned around five, which was when the concierge had told me to check in for a reply. "Come on, let's go," I said. "It's time."

"Time for what?

"Just come." I dragged Rachel by the hand as she tried to slip her feet in her sandals, nearly tripping on the terracotta tiles around the pool.

"Okay, so read it aloud," Rachel said when we finally reached the concierge desk and were handed the telegram.

It wasn't what we'd expected.

Upstairs, Sam answered the door. His chest was a mass of water blisters. He just stood there a dumb look on his face. "Don't say it. I know. I look like a boiled lobster." He turned around to display the extent of his burn. "This is what happens to me if I don't wear SPF and reapply it a zillion times. I was careless." He'd overdone both the sun and alcohol, it seemed, so he'd forgotten about the telegram.

I covered my mouth to hide my smile, but Rachel burst out laughing. She held the tops of her thighs, saying it would be Sam's fault if she wet her pants.

"You hear from Li?" Neil got up and came to us. Sam looked as though he had no idea what Neil was talking about.

"Stand back, Sam. Let us in, for God's sake," I said, giving him a gentle shove. "Li's made plans for us to get out of here. A yacht will pick us up at the Cozumel port authority at six tomorrow."

"A yacht?" Neil said, shocked. "We're taking a yacht to Nassau?" He sunk into the deep sofa.

"No," Rachel said. "Guess again."

Neil looked really confused, and Rachel laughed again. "What? You said a yacht," he repeated.

"Whoa, back up," Sam said. He looked dumbfounded. "Did I miss something?"

Rachel shook her head, and I grabbed a diet drink from the kitchen fridge. "Who wants one?" she asked.

Once seated on the L-shaped sofas, we told them the new plan. When it sank in, it was clear Sam was not happy. "So we don't get Thursday and Friday in Cozumel after all. Why'd you think it was okay to decide for the rest of us without asking?" He shook his head, lost his balance and fell into one of the wing chairs.

Rachel sat near him. "Don't be mad, Sam. Li's solution to have us sail from Cozumel straight to Miami and to bring us our passports there is our only option, short of staying put an extra week or more while we arrange new passports."

Sam picked up the Cozumel tourist guide off the coffee table. He turned page after page without reading.

"Sorry, old man. We asked for help, and Li delivered. What's there to be sore about?" Neil said. Rachel stretched out on the chaise portion of the sofa, letting her feet lie on top of the Neil's lap. "The way Joan explained it, we don't need passports to *sail* the Mexican waters. What we need is to have our ID before we step off the boat and on land in the States."

"Ta-dah! Problem solved, and solved in style, I might add." I moved over to the armrest of Sam's chair. I picked up his hand, but he pulled away.

He got up. "It's easy to give money away when you have tons of it." He moved to the other wing chair nearest Neil.

"Whoa. Sour grapes or what?" Neil said, kicking Sam's foot.

Sam sprang up. Neil rose too. Sam's right fist shot out passing over his left shoulder. Neil's fancy footwork and blocking were his only defence.

Neil hopped in a bouncing rhythm, both of his hands curled into balls. They circled between his mouth and his neck. He stopped. "Hey, man, you got a problem! You never . . . you hear me? . . . *never* pick a fight with a fighter." Neil tilted his head a little to one side. "Get out of here."

Sam opened his mouth to reply but changed his mind. Head down, he walked into our bedroom and quietly closed the door behind him.

We looked from one to the other. I shook my head and followed Sam. He stood by the round table in front of the window. I noticed a Visa card and moved over to see whose name was on it.

"It's mine," Sam said." He plopped on the bed, raising his arms overhead so his head lay in his interlocked fingers as he spoke to the ceiling. "I couldn't risk having it rejected in front of everyone. Besides, you'd already checked us in when I arrived." He chanced a look at me, but I kept my face expressionless. "Next door at the casino this afternoon, I was able to buy a hundred dollars' worth of chips." He shifted to the end of the bed, pointed toward the bureau, and grinned. "And I turned it into a hundred and fifty."

My gaze shifted from his strange euphoric expression to the mess in the room. A mini-bar-sized tequila bottle lay open, dripping onto the carpet from the bedside table. Sam had totally forgotten what had just happened in the living room. His eyes were streaked with red blood vessels, their green colour muddied. I picked up the cash on the table.

"Well, this is a wonderful surprise." I righted the liquor bottle. Sam was beaming with pride, impervious to my sarcasm. "You let us think you left every cent you had in the beach bag with the towels and stuff. Just curious . . . did you try using your card when buying a drink by the pool earlier, or did you put that on my tab?"

Sam looked as if I'd just punched him in the stomach. He jumped up and moved to the door. I caught his hand. "Okay. I'm sorry. I told everyone I'd let them know at the end how much they owed me, so I shouldn't expect anything different from you," I said, forcing a smile.

"I'm sorry too. I wasn't trying to deceive you," Sam said. "Money is my Achilles heel—you know that." He blinked and twisted his watch again.

"It makes you act like a jerk," I said and walked into the bathroom.

"Let me run you a hot bath," Sam said. "Then I'll go watch sports in the living room and let you nap in peace."

My smile was genuine that time, and I nodded. I needed some quiet time, alone. A minute after I'd submerged myself in the bubbly scented water, someone knocked at the bathroom door.

"What do you want?" I shouted.

"It's me," Rachel said.

"It'll have to wait."

There was another knock, more forceful than the last one.

"Okay, okay, let me turn off the tap so I can hear you, Rachel."

She wanted my okay to charge a new outfit to the room.

"Okay but don't go crazy; just one," I said.

Shit, we all needed stuff for tonight and for travelling on that boat for the next two days. I don't know why I hadn't thought of that.

"Hey Rach. Go on ahead. I'll meet you in the clothing store downstairs," I called.Pulling the plug, I realized I had to rush before I could relax. Some holiday.

In the store, I found a light-coloured linen top with loose drawstring pants. "Rachel, do you think this'll get me through dinner tonight and the sailing trip?" I didn't want to buy more than what was absolutely necessary.

"Honestly?"

"Yes. I wouldn't be asking if I didn't want an honest response. What are you thinking?"

She put the outfits she'd been holding down on a chair. "I think the linen outfit is practical. It's great for tonight, and for night time on the yacht, but —" She took the hanger with the pants from me and held them up. "But this'll be too warm for daytime," she said. "You need shorts, something sexy and less practical."

"Joan?" Rachel said. "You know my friend Frieda would advise against giving me carte blanche," she said and winked, "but since you're forcing me to accept your generosity, can I get shorts too and something for Neil as well?" She already held a man's button-down shirt. "Maybe you should do the same for Sam." Rachel's thick eyebrows moved strangely. There was a list of questions etched in the lines of her forehead.

I thought for a second. "Okay. Buy what you want, but it's not a gift, Rachel. You're running a tab with me," I said. Her smile unnerved me.

I hesitated, knowing Sam had money upstairs but it wasn't my place to tell Rachel that. I settled on a pair of identical Bermuda shorts; beige and white jeans with navy polo shirts for Sam and me.

"That is so Sam," Rachel said, admiring my choice. "And he'll like the idea of matching outfits, too."

I wanted to have time for a nap before the eight o'clock dinner we'd planned, so I left her to amass her totally impractical choices.

# CHAPTER 30

## *SAM*

Jesus, what was wrong with me? Carla was probably right—I was a loser. Her last words haunted me. "Grow up, Sam. You're bad-boy persona has lost its charm." I squeezed the last bit of the toothpaste onto the little plastic brush the hotel had provided in the typical square cardboard box. I walked naked into the bedroom and threw it on the bed. Not all the staff spoke English so I'd take the empty toothpaste with me later to explain what I needed replaced. The bathroom had become white and foggy. Getting in the shower hurt my burnt skin. It was sensitive to both the heat and the force of the water. Wow, it really hurt. I changed the temperature to cool and stepped out refreshed. Within seconds Joan's face appeared in the mirror as I bent over the sink with the disposable razor in one hand.

"Hey, lovely lady, you're back," I said.

She wiped the lather from around my mouth and kissed me. She sat on the edge of the tub and watched me finish up shaving. I folded my towel carefully over the towel bar. "Come, I've got something to show you," she said.

"No, Joan. Thanks, but . . . Joan, I want to explain. I don't think—"

"Do me a favour. Don't think, don't talk," she said.

The outfit was unexpected and tailored to my tastes. But I was annoyed to feel indebted again.

"Look, tomorrow on the boat, we're going to dress the same. Cute, huh?" She held up her own navy polo shirt and pair of khaki Bermudas." She'd been spending money like it was water. "You okay?"

I smiled, nodded and tried to think of something appropriate to say. I dug my hands into the pockets of the terry robe I wore.

"Well, you could say thank you." Joan laughed. She took off her clothes and climbed under the sheets. "We still have time for a quick nap before dinner. Want to join me?"

I cuddled in next to her. My arm fell around her waist. I couldn't help comparing her to Carla. Carla's back was so much fuller, her shoulders so much broader, her hair so much thicker and darker. I hugged Joan and rolled to the other side. I stared at the blue pastel wall. Was this par for the course after losing someone ? I grabbed the cash off the bureau when I realized sleep wasn't happening.

I knocked my head repeatedly against the elevator wall. Fuck Carla for wanting more than I could provide. Our money problems had ruined us. I blamed her shopping, and she blamed my gambling. What I needed a woman with her own money.

A young girl, dark and full figured, folded shirts in the hotel shop. She liked the way a pair of white jeans hugged my butt, so I bought them along with a button-down, long-sleeved shirt. I paid cash and went next door to the jewellery store.

When the salesman turned over the price tag of the thing that had caught my eye in the window last night, I paused. I strode confidently back to the salesgirl to return the shirt. The navy polo Joan had bought me would be enough. This other purchase was more important.

When I entered the living room, I noticed they'd ordered a bottle of red. "Joan, turn around," I said. Her honey-coloured hair was arranged on top of her head, and she wore a gold belt over a new light-coloured linen outfit. "You look amazing."

"Why, thank you," she said, kissing me on the cheek.

"I'll just be a minute changing," I said and carried my shopping bag straight past the others through to the master bedroom. My wrist had a tan mark but no watch. Damn it.

Downstairs, the formal steak house in the hotel looked expensive and not at all special. Neil said he'd prefer more authentic stuff, so we walked to a recommended Mexican café close by. The casual decor and atmosphere felt right. The music was loud and made me want to tap my feet. Neil and Rachel were playing with their silverware, using them like drumsticks. The waitress, a cute girl with long black hair, suggested we try their margaritas and start with a plate of nachos.

After the nachos, Rachel ordered a pitcher of sangria.

"None for me, thanks," I said. I pulled out my Purell and passed it around.

"Sam, what's wrong with you?" Rachel asked. I told her I didn't feel like drinking; I'd had too much at the casino in the afternoon. A trio of musicians surrounded our table. I waved them away. I looked at Joan to see if I'd done the right thing.

She leaned over. "Good move. Thanks."

The Spanish music set a casual mood. Rachel and Neil used their fingers to dig into our nachos platter. I swallowed and screwed up my face without intending to. Joan saw me but I think she felt the same. "Rachel, Neil, hold up." I asked Neil to wait while I filled a side plate for me and one for Joan. For the rest of the night the two of them teased us.

We took turns describing what kind of yacht we expected to see on the dock tomorrow. I slipped my loafers off. Soon Joan's bare feet tapped lightly on top of mine, and I shivered with excitement thinking of skin-on-skin contact. I grinned at her, my confidence about the night ahead growing.

"Salsa?" Joan asked me, taking my hand. Her hips moved and knocked my arm.

There was a small dance floor, but no one else was on it. I hated dancing. I had confidence in myself about many things, but swinging my hips was not one of them.

"I will," Neil said, standing. "No, sorry." He held his hands around his rib cage. "Some other time ... if I'm lucky." He resumed his seat.

"Then I will." Rachel jumped up. The girls kicked off their sandals. They slid forward and back, hips swaying, like real pros. More Latin rhythms followed, and then a jazzy Duke Ellington tune I recognized. Neil knew the words too and we both sang along loudly.

Joan called, "Enough!" after about four dances. She gulped down a full glass of water as soon as she reached the table. I could see her skin glowing with a thin layer of sweat.

Rachel poured herself a large tumbler of sangria, polishing off the pitcher.

"Rachel, that string of seed pearls is just gorgeous. Are they new?" Joan said.

Her hand flew to her neck. She was beaming as she glanced over at Neil and squeezed his hand. It was clear who had bought her the gift.

I waited for everyone to express the right amount of admiration for the necklace Neil had given her. In my back pocket was the silk pouch holding my surprise. It seemed as good as moment as any. "I happen to have a little momento for you too," I said, hoping Joan responded with at least as much enthusiasm as Rachel had.

"I love it," she said. She struggled to open the clasp of the necklace under her hair. I jumped up behind her to help. Her fingers felt the shell-shaped silver charm that hung from the slim chain. I let out the breath I'd been holding.

"I've got another surprise," I said. The others looked at me. There was no turning back now. "I found my credit card in the pocket of my swim trunks. I don't guarantee it'll be accepted, but I'll try putting tonight's meal on it."

Joan put her hand on top of my bouncing knee while we waited for the waitress to return. I exhaled loudly when she carried it back, smiling.

"Good for you for taking that risk. That took guts," Neil said as he patted my shoulder.

I shrugged his hand off, pissed at him. Condescending prick. He had it too easy.

Everyone thanked me for taking care of the meal, and my face felt hot. "I'm off to find a drugstore so I can stock up on Gravol and sun block for tomorrow."

"I'm going to head to the registration counter to clear the bill," I heard Joan say. "See you back in the room, Sam."

Rachel was turning off the living room lights when I entered our suite. "I'm going to go lie down with Neil." She nodded toward the closed bedroom door. "He's feeling better, but he's not himself yet— too sore all over." She turned around with her hand on the bedroom door handle. "Say good night to Joan. Tell her I arranged for a wake-up call for us at five thirty."

"Thanks. And Rachel," I said, "go easy on him. Remember, he's got broken ribs."

"Yeah, I don't expect *him* to do any weight bearing," she said, teasing.

I winked at Rachel and shook my head. The other bedroom door was open I walked in and called "Joan?" She came out of the washroom, holding a frothy toothbrush. "Any surprises with the bill?" I asked.

"None," she said. Joan took the fashion magazine she'd bought somewhere into the bedroom and left the washroom to me.

It felt like we were an old married couple. When I'd washed up and gotten close to the bed I noticed what she'd done. "You've stolen all my pillows." I chuckled. I sat down on my side of the bed and wrestled some pillows from behind her. "Maybe on the trip to Miami you'll take a little time to figure out what each of us owes you. No one wants to feel—"

Joan repeated she wasn't worried. "Remember the bill itemizes all room charges." She marvelled at some of the new fashions. "Fur is back in style," she said with raised brows. She read each page of her magazine as if it had to be studied. Occasionally, she underlined something of interest.

"What needs underlining?" I asked, curious.

"A book title, because the review was excellent. Don't you ever do that?"

"I guess I'm smarter. I can remember book titles." She knew I was teasing. I lifted the covers on my side and crawled over to her. "It's going to be a long trip in a small space for two full days isn't it?" That sounded like a complaint. I backpedalled unsuccessfully. "No more talking. I just want to lose myself in the smell of your hair. You must be the most generous, thoughtful person I've ever met," I whispered into her ear. "How'd I get so lucky to end up with you?"

Joan reached over to turn off the lamp. She shimmied back so we connected, her behind fitting into the curve my body made. I was afraid she'd pull away, my erection frightening her. I put one hand on her shoulder, and she moved to lie flat on her back, close to me. My fingers brushed against her skin, tracing the soft downy hairs that led below her navel to the rim of her black lace bikini bottoms. "I know you bought these in place of underwear, but it looks strange to see you in bed in a bathing suit."

"They didn't sell underwear in that store, and I didn't want to go outside the hotel." She looked stiff and stared at the ceiling.

"What is it?" I asked.

She didn't reply, which wasn't a good sign. Undeterred, I bent my head and kissed her softness. My mouth soon felt the heat through the fabric. Her pubis bone rose, but almost simultaneously a hand flew up and pushed my head away. I raised myself onto my elbows, but her eyes had shifted to the wall on her side. Her short nails dug into my scalp as she pulled my hair back.

"Hey. Stop that," I said, sitting up.

"I'm sorry. I'm not sure I want to."

"Fuck." I threw off the covers and marched into the bathroom to grab the terry robe I'd left there earlier.

I returned to sit on her side of the bed. A lone tear made its way to the side of her mouth, and she licked it away. "It feels like a betrayal of sorts even though I know Joe would want me to go on living and be happy." She sniffled and reached for a box of tissues, avoiding my eyes.

Oh God. Not that. My erection was going soft.

Joan struggled to compose herself, breathing loudly. She sat with her back against the rattan headboard. "I know this isn't fair to you," she began. "I'll try, but promise me you won't be upset if I change my mind, all right? Come back to bed. I want to."

I moved to my side and sat down along the side of the bed. She placed one hand on my back and held it there. Come, go, come, go — was I hearing this straight? Was she kidding? My erection disappeared. I got up and punched the wall. The noise and the hole in the plaster took us both by surprise.

I whirled around. I ran a hand through my hair and rubbed the back of my neck. "It just shows how poorly the place was built . . . nothing but drywall and flimsy cardboard." I inhaled deeply. "Fuck it." I left the door open when I stomped into the kitchenette in the main room. In the fridge I found a mini bottle of vodka and poured myself a fresh drink. Joan came and touched my arm.

"Come on, we've got to be up before six," she said, "and now there's only four hours left to sleep. I'm not going to freak out over the wall. I've put you through enough for one night." Back in bed, Joan told me she'd seen her stepson Ian punch a wall once and the same thing happened. Great. Good to know.

She stretched one arm across my body. I pushed it away. The hole in the wall had changed what the argument, if you could call it that, was about, but I was no less pissed by her on-again, off-again interest in sex. Joan rambled on with her thoughts about sex at our stage in life, widowhood, guilt, and love. I grabbed my pillow and covered my head with it. Finally, she got the message and shut up. We both were asleep before either of us thought of anything else to argue about.

# CHAPTER 31

## JOAN

## Friday, February 7, 2003

## Day 7, Cozumel

A series of rapid knocks woke us. Rachel called through the closed bedroom door. "It's half past five. Rise and shine," she said.

"Good morning." I hopped out of bed, determined to pretend last night never happened.

He rolled over and groaned. "It's too early."

I pulled apart the blackout curtains, but with minimal dawn light, it made no difference to the light entering our room. Sam held his head to prevent his skull from blowing apart. He must have had a pounding headache.

"I'm guessing you've got one hell of a hangover."

"Sam opened on eye to look at me. "Joan," he said, pausing, "How badly did I frighten you off with my outburst last night?"

I headed into the shower. Even in four-star hotels, the water temperature can be weird. I stood under the freezing shower, waiting for the temperature to change. I didn't get out until the room was steamy and my muscles had relaxed again.

"Any hot water left for me? You'll see what I did for packing our belongings; you just need to find ties." He moved from the sink into the shower exchanging places with me. In passing he lightly kissed my wet shoulder. "Will you call the front desk and ask for large elastics to be sent up?" Sam said.

On the bed were two white plastic laundry bags which Sam had taken from the closet. He was right. We had to improvise, just till we received our luggage in Miami.

Downstairs, we piled into a cab. "Marina, *por favor*," Neil said to the cabbie. He squished in beside me and passed me a piece of hotel stationery. "Give me your contact information so I can get the money to you when I get home." I squeezed his hand and complied.

He dropped my hand and pointed. "We're here. That was fast."

The captain was a broad-shouldered woman wearing beige Bermuda shorts and a forest-green polo shirt. I smiled; the captain, Sam and I, looked like we were all in uniform while no one else was. The other crew members wore tee shirts and short-shorts or cut- off jeans like Rachel and Neil but they also wore name tags. They stood in a straight line, waiting for us at the end of the pier. The captain introduced herself and led us on board. The deck of the *LiAm* had a beautiful, oiled wood surface. The boat's furnishings and fittings were either pure white or shiny brass. It oozed class, luxury, and simplicity. The noise coming from below deck alerted us to the presence of other people on board, working in the kitchen or elsewhere.

"Stations," the captain said. Over our heads she called, "I want to be closing in on Havanah by dinnertime. Untie us." Her gaze shifted from the crew to us. "Let's have a pleasant safe trip." She climbed an outdoor ladder and disappeared above us to the navigation deck, which was off limits for us. There was a flurry of activity. The inboard motor started; white threads and big bubbles bounced alongside our boat as the water parted and a trail of foam appeared in its wake.

Minutes later, a young man joined us at the stern. "I'm Billy."

I made the introductions. Billy stayed on deck with us, pointing out landmarks in Cozumel until we couldn't see land anymore. "Tomorrow night, Mr. Chew will meet us at the Miami Yacht Club. He'll have your passports and suitcases."

"That's our Li," Rachel said with a questionable hint of pride in her tone.

"Can I show you around a bit?" Billy provided brief explanations of the obvious. "When we get below, you'll find notes Mr. Chew wrote to Miss Joan." I raised my eyes, anxious to see the messages but manners held me in place. "There are two heads, two dining areas, and two galleys, on this deck and below deck, but sleeping quarters are on the lower level only. Breakfast is prepared in the upper kitchen to avoid disturbing anyone's sleep and served in the bow." Billy adjusted his Ray-Bans farther up his nose. "So are we all set here?" He nodded and disappeared.

"Anyone know why we're motoring and not hoisting these sails?" Sam asked, looking officious in his navy baseball cap.

"I guess we'll find out later," I said.

Billy reappeared. "One more thing. Dinner is served under the canvas roof at the stern, where our activity supplies—like fishing gear and shuffleboard discs—."

I saw Rachel nudge Neil.

"Breakfast and lunch are served at the bow, where the second kitchen is. You'll also find towels, outdoor showers, and lounge chairs there." He used both hands to point ahead and behind him with a turn of the wrists. He looked like a flight stewardess showing passengers the exit doors. "Breakfast will be served at eight o'clock. Everyone set your watches now. It's exactly 7:15 a.m."

As promised, there were two sealed envelopes. It was déjà vu for me as I recalled the envelopes awaiting me the first day I'd come aboard the *Liberty*.

Sam stood over my shoulder as I opened the first one, addressed to all of us. It informed us of the distance we had to travel, which explained why the *Liberty* would be arriving in Miami approximately twelve hours before us on Saturday.

"Holy shit," Neil said. "That means we're sleeping on this boat tonight and staying put all day tomorrow as well."

"Come on, Neil,' Rachel said. "Did you think we'd travel from Mexico to Miami more quickly than the *Liberty* would travel the lesser distance from Nassau to Miami? Even I knew it would take longer." She shoved him, and he gasped. "This is a very special treat, and I'm going to enjoy every second of it." As an afterthought, she added, "Oh sorry, Neil. I keep forgetting about your sore ribs because you look so great."

"Thanks, but I'm still sore," he said.

Like Rachel, I was excited too. At least I would be as soon as we began sailing in the calm open waters.

"Hold on, you two. Can I read the rest of Li's letter?" Sam said. He took it out of my hand. "Li writes:

> *'I've allowed Royal Caribbean to take an imprint of my personal credit card as collateral against any suit that may befall the company, should I lose your passports and you sue them.'"*

Sam paused and said, "That was smart. Better him than me." He laughed and continued reading:

> "*'I trust you will arrive in a timely fashion so my wife Amy and I can continue our holiday. We had planned to stay on in Miami, so this is less of an inconvenience than you might imagine. Although this is a longer journey than is common, we have provided a number of first-run movies for your entertainment and ample refreshments. Amy and I send our best wishes for a pleasant experience sailing aboard the LiAm.*
> *Sincerely,*
> *Master Li Chew'"*

"I'm impressed," Neil said. "It's a good thing this happened when we were with Joan and not just on our own, eh Rach?"

Rachel took a long time responding. She swallowed a few times. "Let's go find that cooler Billy told us about," she said.

"Go ahead," I said. I'll catch up." I tore open the other envelope once I was alone. It was from Amy. In it was an invitation to join her and Li on the next part of their trip, their two weeks at the yoga retreat in Miami Beach. I was already aware of their intention to go there and had planned to google it. One line was written in capital letters: that she didn't want to be alone with Li, that she'd become afraid of him. She described an incident where he had humiliated her. He'd thrown a crystal wineglass against a wall. I thought of that hole in the bedroom wall of the Cozumel hotel suite. Maybe Amy had done something to provoke Li, just as I had last night when Sam reacted so vehemently.

> *"If you've gotten close to that young man with the red hair, then by all means, ask him along. There'll be no cost to either of you. We own the property, and I need a friend as well as a buffer between Li and me."*

I folded the letter and put it in my laundry bag-cum-suitcase. I felt sorry for Amy and wanted to help her. So far, this hadn't been the relaxing trip I had wanted, so maybe a yoga retreat would give me a little peace before I returned home. Even being caught between Li and Amy seemed tolerable, and would delay Sylvia telling me how to reorganize my life the moment I got back. On the one hand, I wanted to run to Sam and surprise him by inviting him to stay with me for at least one of the weeks. On the other hand, I wasn't sure I was ready for anyone, and I didn't want to have to work at a relationship. No one from home was worried about me or would mind if I extended my vacation. The single item on my calendar was a project I had set for myself: house hunting. No urgency there. I made up my mind.

# CHAPTER 32

# RACHEL

Li knew I was on the boat. Joan had to have provided details about each of us in order for him to have gotten our passports and luggage etc. Perhaps this was his way of fulfilling his promise to see me again before the end of our cruise. I dug into my fresh croissant with gusto, before I remembered those nachos from last night. My linen napkin held up to my lips, I coughed and spat out the pastry. Me, Rachel Gordon, on a private yacht, eating off bone china with sterling cutlery, a warm breeze blowing a white tablecloth against my bare legs . . . it was a little much to wrap my head around. I wished I could take a selfie and send it to Frieda.

Sam understood. "I'm Robin Leach, and this is *Lifestyles of the Rich and Famous*." He laughed. "Incredible, isn't it?"

"Yup, I could get used to this," I said.

Neil chuckled. "I wouldn't bother if I were you." He laughed and pulled on his sweatshirt. The morning air was cool.

Joan spread her towel over a chaise and moved it to face the sun. She had found a magazine and sat back in her pants and long-sleeved top.

"Shit, I've got goose bumps." I chanced a look at her to see if Joan was giving me one of her I-told-you-so looks, but she was engrossed in her magazine. I waved Billy over and asked for a few extra towels or a light blanket to cover my legs until it warmed up.

"I'll be a minute. They're stored in the berths," he said.

In the meantime, I warmed my hands on my steaming coffee mug. The mainsail was hoisted, but the jib was furled. I knew too little about cruising yachts, so I didn't want to ask why. I listened carefully and felt proud of myself for detecting the sound of a motor. Not that I cared, but around Joan I often felt inadequate. I laughed. This was my idea of carefree.

"What's so funny?" Sam asked.

"Nothing much." I looked up. "Thank you, Billy," I said and gathered the blanket to my chest.

A thin staff member holding brochures appeared. I'd never seen such long black lashes or such violet-coloured eyes. I peered more closely. He was wearing thick black mascara.

"You've got the most gorgeous violet eyes. Can I call you Violet?" I asked.

"Rachel, that's rude," Joan said.

"No, no, no," he said. "Violet it is."

Violet told us he performed many duties on board, primarily as a beautician: manicures, pedicures, hairstyling, waxing, and massage. Joan and I glanced at our watches.

Neil commented that he'd like to do something more physical, and Violet told him they had skeet shooting off the stern and free weights there as well. Apparently, Billy was the one who handled those activities.

"Amazing." Sam jumped up and knocked over his hot coffee. "Shit shit, shit . . . ow," he said, bending over and fanning his thigh.

Neil went to find Billy and get ice.

I wondered what it was Sam had found amazing.

"You burned yourself, huh? You okay?" Joan asked. She held her head in her hands, a worried look on her face.

"He's fine, Joan. The coffee wasn't even that hot. Right, Sam?" I was eager to choose a polish and get a manicure.

"Sam —you okay?" Joanie repeated. He nodded but only after a cloth filled with ice chips had been applied to his burn would she look at me.

I hit her arm playfully. "Come on Joan, I'm a mess. Hard to say which treatment is my biggest priority.  How about you?"

"Lucky for us, we've got two full days here, so we can spread the treatments out," she said.

Violet went over to the breakfast table, where the guys were still lingering over their coffees. They put their *Miami Herald* newspapers down, and Violet said, "In case you haven't guessed, I'm multi-talented." He battled his eyes, and I now wondered if the lashes were false as well as mascaraed. "I'm the resident barber, massage therapist, and a competent chess player." He looked at Neil. "You could use a full back wax, but I have a feeling our extensive list of films will suit you best." Violet pointed to the steps leading to the bunk level. "There're kept in a case inside the trunk down below— the trunk that serves as a coffee table . . . so you may need to move a thing or two." He slicked his hair back behind one ear, where I noticed a large diamond stud earring.

Neil seemed especially keen on checking out the film titles. "Will let you know what I find," he said as he disappeared below deck.

Two hours later, we reassembled for lunch. "Nice tans," Sam said. "See? I was sensible today. I had a sports pedicure in the shade this morning." Was he waiting for someone to say, "Good boy"?

Our meal of cold gazpacho and shrimp salad tasted wonderful. Billy opened a crisp Pinot Grigio, and we all too quickly finished the bottle.

We watched, mesmerized as a squall moved across the flat sea in ripples of darker blue. It seemed to pick up speed the closer it got to our ship. The boat bobbed gently at first. Then it rose higher and fell on the next wave. Another motorized yacht cut the wave, creating more bumps and potholes. I wasn't sure my lunch was going to stay down. I braced the edge of the glass table. Joan's hands clutched her stomach. I looked at her. She was pure white.

"Are you going to be sick?" I asked.

She shot out of her chair and held a hand over her mouth. That was answer enough. She swallowed, repeatedly.

"Sam, where's the Gravol you bought?" she asked when she could talk.

He stood, took her arm, and led her to their double berth below.

I drank my water. Turning to Neil, I asked if he felt all right.

"I'm fine. Personally, I think when you're sea sick, you're better off staying where you can keep the horizon in sight. But maybe she just needs to sleep till we hit calmer waters. It may rain," he said, looking up.

"No, that was just a squall, a gust of wind and some clouds that'll pass—not a sign of anything sinister," Billy said. "Sun showers are the norm in the Caribbean." I knew sun showers didn't involve dark clouds, but he was obviously a more experienced sailor, as well as the one more familiar with weather patterns in the Caribbean.

The sun reappeared. My blanket had long since been stowed. "Where's Violet?" I asked Billy. "Will you tell him I'd like to see his polish colours? I'm ready for my manicure."

Neil told me he was going to see how Sam and Joan were. It was clear Neil wasn't my kind of man. Who was it who said, "Nice guys finish last?" Probably some woman who'd been too dumb to grab a good deal when the opportunity had presented itself. I decided not to follow that train of thought to its logical conclusion. After my manicure, I admired how my cherry-red nails coordinated perfectly with my new bikini and congratulated myself that I hadn't gained an ounce on this trip so far.

Sam returned, more charming than ever. "Let's face it—Neil's got a TV and enough DVDs to keep him amused for the rest of the trip. Joan's sick as a dog and has taken enough Gravol to put her into a deep sleep. So it's just you and me, Rach." Sam sat on the side of my sun cot, picked up the lotion, and dropped the strap from my shoulder.

I turned my head, and his lips found mine.

"Want to try that one out?" Sam said pointing to the big double chaise. "It reminds me of an ad for a South Beach hotel —saw it in a magazine left on  the plane we came down on last week."

I nodded, knowing exactly which advertisement he was referring to.

"New bathing suit," he said. "Very nice. Come closer." Sam extended his hand. His finger connected with my skin and made small circles around my hip bone. "You know, some men are breast men, and some are leg men, but me, I go for the hip bones." I could barely stand still. He watched my face for a reaction. I had new goose bumps, unrelated to the temperature. With his free hand, Sam pulled the string at the back of my bikini top. At first I resisted, making a feeble attempt to hold it up with the pressure of my arms, but I couldn't help the burning desire that was building inside me.

It was fast and furious. He was alternately tender and rough. His fingers fine tuned my pinky interior and plucked my sweet spot before a thick, sticky wetness moistened my bikini bottoms and made me peel them off,  Not caring who might hear I screamed. "Now, take me now."  He was so big it hurt for one brief second and I held my breath till he softened. The staff disappeared. No one interrupted us. I hopped up as soon as I knew we were both done.

Sam pulled a towel around his waist. I strode naked to the freshwater shower at the prow. "Christ, Rachel. How can you do that?"

I thought of Kate Winslet and Leonardo DiCaprio leaning into the wind together in *Titanic*; the shower was positioned equivalent to where they'd stood. Having an outdoor shower there was ingenious. I moved my hands up to my hair and let the water rain down on me, washing away his smell and my sweat. It was a glorious feeling, standing naked, exposed and sexually satisfied.

A while later I went downstairs to see how Neil was doing. He was changing the DVD.

"Leave that. Come outside with me." I took his hand and pulled, but he resisted. "You like?" I asked, twirling in my new bikini.

"I was about to watch *Mission Impossible*," he said. "Stay here with me." I shook my head. I found a hair tie for my damp hair and shoved all the loose strands under the hat I grabbed off the coffee table.

"You may not need to work on your tan, but I do." I laughed at my joke, and Neil kissed my hand before sending me on my way like a child.

Back on deck, Sam said, "You're back. I'm so glad. I thought you'd finished with me." I made a face that said I wasn't falling for that poor-me routine. We had each other's numbers, and any pretense at something more was ridiculous. We got real, and he asked me about New York and what I did—all the types of things people generally spoke about before having sex. He was sitting at the table where he'd been working on a crossword before lunch when Violet reappeared. "Violet, could you get us a couple of Coronas, please?" He winked at Violet who just shook his pretty head.

Sam and I clinked glasses and downed our beers.

I spread a plush towel on one side of the double chaise. The sky was cloudless. The different shades of blue were infinite in number. The temperature was warm and comfortable, definitely not as hot as Mexico. I lay on my stomach.

"Sam, give me a hand, won't you?" He took hold of the strings of my top and then reconsidered, letting them fall back to my sides. I raised myself up enough to look for and find the suntan oil, which I passed to him.

He cocked his head to the side and paused." I see dimples," he said, touching the tiny indentations just above my bum. His hands felt good on my skin. His thumbs were on my shoulder blades, but his fingers, extended along my sides, were making me quiver.

I laid my cheek on the towel. His breath warmed my neck. "Shouldn't we be worried about Joan?" he said.

"Never mind her. It's Neil I'd be worried about, if I were you. If we're going for a second round, the bell has already rung." I turned over and shielded my eyes. "Maybe we shouldn't push our luck?"

"Yeah, I need a shower and a nap. It was a nice afternoon, Rach. Thanks." Sam's sudden departure confirmed what I already knew. At least we both knew the game we were playing.

# CHAPTER 33

## Joan

## Saturday, February 8, 2003

## Day 8, aboard the LiAm

"Did you notice the yoga mats laid out for us at the stern when you came upstairs?" I asked Sam. I raised my eyebrows, challenging him to join me and do yoga today. I'd had a light dinner and a great sleep. A few minutes later when Rachel and Neil arrived at the breakfast buffet Saturday morning, I asked them the same question.

"Someone's feeling better," Rachel said.

"I'll participate only if everyone else does," Sam said. He opened his mouth in shock when Neil and Rachel agreed it would be fun.

Sam and I took our yoga much more seriously than did the others, but it didn't matter. I led, calling out the asanas, but gave up after a while. Rachel told Neil she thought her back was burning. She excused herself, ostensibly to find her suntan oil, but didn't return.

"Let's see who can hold a plank the longest. Neil, time us. Aloud," Sam said. It was a good excuse for Neil to stop, and he seemed more than ready.

"Get into plank on the count of three," Neil said. "One, two, three."

Sweat rolled down my nose and onto the mat. I saw it drip from my underarms. My arms quivered. I collapsed.

"Well, thank God." Sam patted my back a few times. "I thought you had me. I wouldn't have been able to hold it much longer." I sensed him beside me; he sat up and crossed his legs, took several deep breaths while I lay on my back, doing the same. "You're stronger than you look Joan," he said, with another pat for good measure. Sam got up and walked away. Neil threw me a towel, and I wiped my chest with it. I didn't think Sam was going to return, but he did, holding plastic tumblers of ice water. After a sip, he helped me up, and all three of us moved into the shade.

When Billy had stowed the mats, he offered fishing as an option, but neither Neil nor Sam had the inclination. They begged off, saying they needed to stay out of the sun. At the bow we hung out around the breakfast table for the next few hours. Sam and I played chess while Rachel and Neil read. Every few minutes, I heard her ask him about a question about a crossword in a *People* magazine she'd found.

"I can't tell you the year of that movie. Ask me when George Foreman won his heavyweight boxing championship and who he defeated—that I can tell you." He was doing a poor job of masking his frustration.

"Jesus, Neil, you're more clueless than me. Were you living under a rock through the '90s and the millennium?" Neil threw his own magazine down and stomped away. There were weights in the box with the mats at the other end of the yacht.

Suddenly Sam said, "You threw that game. Why did you bother? Why not just say you'd had enough chess?" He tossed his plastic cup into the sink, and it rattled around like a roulette ball on a circling wheel.

Rachel and I exchanged looks and I said, "Sorry, but this is my last afternoon to get sun before I return to the cold. If you have cabin fever, you'd best find a better way to deal with it than picking a fight with me. I've a low tolerance level for bad behaviour." I put my hands on my hips. "I'm used to finishing things I start—that's just me. But the game was taking too long . . . not my fault." I picked up the suntan oil and joined Rachel on the chaise.

"Want to lie  with us, just for fun?" Rachel said, and I saw her wink at Sam, who jerked his head toward us. "Sam, don't be a stick in the mud. Go spot Neil, before he hurts himself," she said. I looked around for my hat and found it under the cot. When I stood up, I saw an exchange between Sam and Rachel. Something strange was going on but I didn't want to be drawn into it. As I tied my hair back in a very high ponytail, she added, "Neil shouldn't be doing those free weights without a spotter."

When Sam got up to go, so did Rachel. She said, "Violet can't do both of us at once, so I'll head back there and ask him to do my pedicure now, all right?"

I nodded. Neil, Sam, and Rachel were all having fun in the stern, which was the designated activities area. I was glad to stay put at the bow and do nothing, not even talk. Talking constantly gave me a headache.. But if I started dating, I'd have to do it all the time. I'd rather become a hermit, I thought. Had I become anti-social?

Lunch was another delicious meal: salade niçoise, prepared with fresh tuna and cracker bread. Because there was that wonderful large canvas roof and beautifully presented tray of finger foods including cheeses, breads, nuts, fresh and dried fruits, we were inclined to sit through the rain shower, talking and picking at the food long past the point of hunger.

"Billy, more wine, por favor?" Rachel said. I could only shake my head. Eventually I called Violet over to ask if he could bring the supplies from the activity area and give me a manicure at the bow.

"Wow, you're getting ballsy. We were told all services and activities were restricted to the stern," Rachel teased.

Eventually, Neil convinced us to join him and watch a movie.

Rachel twirled her wild hair. "Do you think I should get a wash and blow-dry? I want to look decent when we dock." I thought it was a great idea and hoped there'd be time for me too.

Sam tugged on my hand as the credits rolled. He narrowed his eyes once he'd pulled me through the bedroom door. I leaned against it, and he held both my hands above my head. "Joan," he began in a sultry voice, "I want it to be good like it was on the ship. Can you handle that?" His smile was weird and I got a creepy feeling, but then I remembered this was just Sam and I was probably just feeling nervous. His green eyes bore into mine, searching for a clear signal. "I'll take my cue from you—just be straight with me."

Naked in bed, we rolled toward one another. In no time, I had worked up a sweat. My insides clenched. First I was panting, then

I held my breath, waiting for the release, the internal flood as the dike opened up. I felt Sam's explosion, heard his sigh of satisfaction. His weight rose above me and plopped down at my side. "Ah, that was great," he said. Sam shimmied to sit up against the back wall. "Joan, I don't need to warn you. You've seen it this week—I can be an ass." He smiled his charming smile, the one that begged me to ignore the faults I didn't yet see and forgive the ones I did.

He had no idea he was no longer playing me, that he was the one being used. "What are you thinking?" I said, smiling innocently. I looked down at my folded hands atop the white waffle bedspread.

"You're as much a movie fanatic as me. Do you remember the one—the title escapes me—where Jack Nicholson says to Helen Hunt, "You make me want to be a better man'?"

I smiled. "Yeah . . ." I waited for him to continue. I knew he was trying to con me. Sex at fifty was different from sex at forty. Who knew to expect growing pains after fifty? The round port window let a lot of sun in. I faced away from it. With eyes squeezed shut, I gave some thought to what I really wanted. I was only ready for something or someone now and then. And if anyone didn't approve, that would be their problem, not mine. Where did this feeling of confidence come from?

"I'm glad," I said, in response to his earlier question lest he think I hadn't been listening. I rolled over again. Sam's lack of originality and references to all things Hollywood were wearing thin.

"I'm so happy you're happy," Sam said. A broad smile stayed on my face as I fell asleep in spite of the sunlight.

About an hour later, Sam and I were awakened by Billy. "Cocktails are being served up on deck." He knocked twice more. "You two up?"

We found Neil and Rachel snuggled up close against the rail at the stern. The dinner table was set beautifully and romantically. Candles were everywhere. The frothy wide wake trailed behind the yacht like a bridal dress train. A platter on the bar held pickles wrapped in prosciutto, stuffed mushrooms, and canapés with oysters. Violet carried a tray with our drinks and showed off his nail lacquer, a good match for his eyes.

The dinner meal was superb, as our chef had outdone himself. But this meal was a noisy affair. Sharp loud screeches and grinding sounds interrupted our conversation constantly. It signalled the flurry of activity going around the boat which made us aware of the pressure the crew felt to make our arrival deadline. We heard ropes scraped against the gunwale, latches dropped here and there, and cranks tightened all over the ship. Then we saw the luffing of the sails followed by the tacking and turned to the voices of all the calls shouted by one crew member to another. Our captain joined us for coffee and dessert and to apologize for all the noise.

"Oh, don't be silly; we've had a good time guessing which noise was associated with which boat part," Rachel said. She left the table and began hopping on one foot. Sam jumped up and caught her arm. "Sor...ry... I'm a little tipsy tonight."

The captain now wore long khaki slacks. She finished her black coffee and looked around the table at the rest of us. "We must make good time. If anyone feels unwell, it'd be best they go below deck; don't want to stop to pick up a man overboard, if you know what I mean." She looked at Rachel and then at Sam for some reason. I hope you enjoyed your stay. Mr. Chew invested a lot of time in making these preparations," she said before returning to the bridge.

"Funny, she sounded resentful about that, didn't she?" I said, leaning over to Rachel. We lingered around the dinner table with our special coffees and biscotti. It became too cold and we went below deck. When we heard the crew members shouting to one another, we grabbed our belongings and headed up the ladder. The moon dangled over the calm water as the lights of the marina came into view over the port side. The starlight was like a ribbon dressing up the night, reminding us of how wonderful the gift of this trip home had been. Sam had been right to wonder why we were being treated so well. Why would Li or Amy, who I'd only known a few days, extend themselves so much? I shivered. What catch could there possibly be?

Rachel and I hopped up and down when Li's figure became clear. We waved with enthusiasm, but his arms remained at his side. In no time we were docked. Ironically, Rachel and I were more reserved in the physical welcome we extended to Li than Sam and Neil, who slapped his back and pumped his arm vigourously. Two cars sat nearby. One was a white Dade County cab, ostensibly to take Neil, Rachel, and maybe Sam to the airport. The other was a black limo.

"Right on time," Li said.

Neil wrapped me in one of his big bear hugs. He looked like a sailor as he swung the two small white duffels over his shoulder, stepped onto the pier and offered Rachel a hand. She ignored it and turned to Li.

"Li?" Rachel said, totally sobered, the lilt in her voice questioning.

But all he said was "Have a safe trip." Li looked away.

I felt sorry for her. I hugged Rachel, her frizz out of control once again and engulfing my head. "I'll phone you," I promised. She stretched out her arm, and Neil came back to assist her in stepping onto the dock.

Touching Li's arm, Sam stumbled over his expression of gratitude. He hinted about a repayment plan.

"That's out of the question," Li said." Please don't embarrass me by talking about expenses." Sam wiped a tear from his face. I looked away, embarrassed for him.

"Why you left these phones I'll never understand," Li said. "I thought you and Sam might both be coming with me, so I kept your phones separate. Neil's and Rachel's are packed in their luggage."

"Actually no, that's not going to work out," I said. I ignored the confused look on Sam's face.

"But thanks for the offer," Sam said, saving me from having to explain what he'd gleaned rather quickly.

I passed my phone to Sam. "Give me your contact info before you go." I went to the bow and waved to Rachel and Neil. "Stay in touch, you hear?"

"You'll see me, probably before you see anyone else." Neil called back. I shook my head, acknowledging the reminder yesterday that his father lived in a Toronto retirement residence close to Sylvia. It seemed so long since we'd had that first dinner table conversation in the Rembrandt Dining Room on the *Liberty*, and I'd forgotten.

The cab driver honked. Neil opened the door for Rachel, who got in, and he walked around the car. Sam, Li, and I waved from the *LiAm*.

Another car pulled up. A long tanned leg emerged first. Then a tall busty woman with long dark hair emerged. She was a Penelope Cruz look-alike, and from Sam's descriptions, I knew it had to be Carla.

Rachel must have guessed too because she stepped out of the cab, her eyes wide and her mouth hanging open.

Carla glanced at Rachel. Then she scanned the pier and the various yachts moored there. The door on the other side of the second cab opened next. Another surprise popped out, the cutest red-headed toddler.

This time it was Sam's jaw that dropped. He seemed to crumple like a marionette whose puppeteer had thrown down the strings. "Oh no," he said in disbelief. With one stride he glided from the yacht onto the pier.

The little boy sank to his knees and crawled behind the full black-and-white polka dot skirt his mother wore. Carla's black V-necked top was partly covered by a small purse hanging off her arm. She picked him up. He covered his mouth and spoke into her ear before he wobbled back up to lean on the wall. She epitomized the sophisticated model, not the contemptible floozie Sam had led me to imagine. In spite of myself, I liked her.

My head swung to Sam, who walked toward her, paused, and then walked the rest of the way. He covered his mouth, just as the young boy had, when he talked to Carla.

I looked down at my freshly manicured nails and scraped the polish off my thumb. I turned to see Neil's reaction, but the cab had pulled away without any of us noticing. Li's hand pushed my shoulders down, and I realized I'd been holding them tensed up near my ears.

Carla switched to Spanish, talking to the child. Sam edged back against the whitewash wall and stood in that familiar cowboy pose. He bent to talk to the child.

I found myself waiting for Sam to say or do something. "I'll be in touch," he called to me.

The youngster plopped on the ground and moved toward Sam.

Li crossed from the yacht to the pier in a flash. "Sam, give me Joan's phone." I saw Li hold open the car door for Carla and the little boy.

I stepped onto the pier, holding my plastic bag of belongings. Sam had left his bag on board. He hesitated at the trunk of the big dark car, unsure whether the right move was to sit in the front with the driver or be a family and sit in the back with his beautiful ex-wife and child. I smiled when Sam reached for the handle of the back-seat door and waved from the rear window.

# CHAPTER 34

## *JOAN*

The drive to Boca Raton took two hours. I saw nothing of interest in the dim light outside. Without preamble, Li listed the details he'd handled to resolve all my problems. I interrupted him to ask where Amy was.

"Well, that's what I wanted to talk to you about." He offered me a drink from the bar alongside the door at the rear of the limo.

"Just a water bottle, thanks. So tell me how Amy is. Not sick, I hope."

"She's excited that you're coming to the yoga retreat. You'll love it there." He was trying to sound casual, using speech patterns that seemed unnatural to him. "Although we made our best effort and hired Chinese developers and staff, the peace and serenity in our Florida property doesn't come close to replicating what you'd find in an Asian health retreat. Sadly, I'd say it's American visitors who make it impossible." I smiled, understanding more than he knew.

"But you didn't come alone to convince me to go to the retreat. I'd already decided to join you."

"Yes, it's the weeks following our yoga experience that I need to consult with you about." He turned to face me. His long fingers traced a crease in his pant leg. "I've made a reservation for an extended visit for Amy at Sherwood Hills Recovery Resort in Utah."

"You've lost me," I said. "I'll assume this is a drug and alcohol treatment kind of place but how does it concern me? That's a private issue between you, Amy and your doctor."

"To be clear, Amy doesn't yet know about the treatment centre," Li said. "But I want to confirm what I assume you've guessed. Amy is an alcoholic who needs treatment." He rubbed his chin, covering his mouth with one hand.

I tried to control the shaking of my hand. I thought back to Amy's letter and her worry that Li wanted to get rid of her. "You can't railroad her and abandon her like an underage child. I was in that bar with you, one night, Li. I'm not a doctor." I raised my voice without meaning to yell at him. "You're being impossible" I was almost screaming I was so mad. His body physically pulled back away from me. The driver loosened his collar but kept his eyes straight ahead.

Li patted my leg. "You're too intelligent for this outrage, Joan. Do you think a renowned centre would accept a client without their consent and commitment to treatment ?"

His expression was humourless. "And that's where you come in," he said.

I put as much distance between us as the sedan's back seat allowed. I shook my head, thinking of the time I'd seen Amy's personality changed by overindulging in alcohol. People on holidays often let themselves go. I'd seen it with Mike on the ship too, and with Susan and Sam and many others whose names I would never know.

But it was different with Amy; I sensed it was a serious problem. I turned to Li. "What is it you think I can do?"

Li's fingertips rested on the top of his knees. "Amy's situation is grave. We've tried other avenues under the care of her physician. She told her therapist that she blames me for her drinking. Apparently, it gives her satisfaction to see how it impacts on me." He wiped his nose with a handkerchief and stuffed it in his pants pocket. "But Amy wants me to feel guilty, and this I will not do." He rubbed his hand over his mouth and covered his lips while covering his chin. He sat very still.

"Again, what does this have to do with me?" I said.

"I've decided to leave Amy . . . when she is well." Li faced me.

My mouth opened. It became dry. I closed it."What a sport," I said, narrowing my eyes and sucking on my cheeks. Something in my mouth tasted bitter. I broke from Li's gaze and looked out at the dark night. Amy was aware that Li was a cold man and maybe she would find greater happiness with someone else. This could end well, and she would be much better off. I took a big breath, and my chest rose. Yes, I could help my friend by not abandoning her. Without a friend's support, she would see Li's plan as I had initially—that he was getting rid of her, not that she had an opportunity to get rid of him. Of course, this would only work if I could convince her of the necessity of treatment, that it would give her hope for a better life after Li.

In some small way, Amy's situation reminded me of my own. I felt as if I now had a better outlook on the after-Joe chapter of my life.

"Do not judge, Joan. I'm not leaving because of her addiction." He turned to look out the window. "Actually, right now, it is why I am staying." He still wasn't using contractions regularly, but I was more accustomed to his speech pattern now.

I stared out the front window, allowing myself to be mesmerized by the red taillights ahead, which seemed to flash on and off through the highway construction we now traversed. Cars sped up and slowed down at irregular intervals. The rocking sensation was the same as on the ship.

I sat back and crossed one leg over the other, shifting my weight so I faced the window, away from the lights and away from Li. I closed my eyes and pictured Amy, small and so in need of a friend.

My brain tried to sift through a sea of questions. If it weren't for Amy, I could have been stuck in Cozumel for ages, or maybe Li had formulated his plan when my desperate situation presented itself. Maybe it wasn't Amy at all but Li who'd wanted to get me home. I looked at him. Did Amy suspect his plan? And if I questioned his fidelity, she must too. I looked around at the interior of this luxurious car and considered the expense and time he'd spent in helping me and the others. I shifted, recrossed my legs, and yawned.

"You are tired. I understand, but we must conclude this conversation before we see Amy in Boca tonight."

"Li, why do I feel you're making me an offer I can't refuse?" I lacked the energy or inclination to make a better *Godfather* joke even after I noted his confused expression.

He smiled. "Joan, you are a smart woman," he began. "I did not get you out of your fix at great personal expense and inconvenience because my wife wanted me to." He faced front. "No, I did it because Amy and I both need you to help her." A more sensitive man might have shown some emotion, but not Li Chew. "Amy admitted to me that she wished she'd had more self-control in front of you. That's what gave me the idea."

What a manipulative, conniving man. So he would have asked this of me even if I hadn't been stranded in Cozumel. For him, my misfortune was a stroke of good luck.

Li cleared his throat. "Joan, I believe you can convince Amy to go to this rehab clinic. Ever since our night in the bar together, she's been obsessed with seeing you and showing you she can drink moderately. But she can't. She either doesn't touch alcohol or she drinks until she passes out." He twisted his wristwatch and pulled his starched cuffs down to his wrists. "All I'm asking of you is to spend time with her and to see for yourself. Only then will you make the recommendation to get treatment if you think it makes sense."

I shivered. "Could we turn down the air conditioning, please?" I asked. What had I done with all my time since Joe died? I'd retreated into my own private world, sleeping, watching nonsense on television, making obligatory visits to take Sylvia to lunch once in a blue moon. It might make me feel good to be of help, to feel useful, needed even. It might matter to Amy.

Li's voice penetrated my thoughts. "My wife's behaviour taunts me. She won't give up alcohol. It's how she gets my attention, how—"

"Jesus, Li, listen to yourself; if you wanted to help Amy, why didn't you to get her to a doctor before this?" I exhaled, exasperated.

"Simple," Li said, "she'll only see doctors she chooses and I mistrust." He paused; "Because she pays for their services and the reverse is true for a doctor of my choice." Li breathed quietly through his mouth. It sounded like a soft wind moving among the leaves of a willow tree.

"I get it; it's become a trust issue, as much as anything," I said. I leaned my elbow on the back seat's arm rest.

"I told you, I want to leave her. And soon." Li cleared his throat and said my name. I didn't move. He reached out a hand.

I flung it away. "I don't like feeling used," I said. I rubbed my eyes and asked for a tissue to blow my nose. "You want me to convince Amy to go, for her own good—and for yours as well." I was getting the feeling he was feeling defeated and in need of help. I was seeing a different vulnerable side of him.

"Yes," he said simply.

"Do you think I'm so spineless that I'll do your bidding simply because I owe you? Maybe I'll just pay you back and not feel beholden. I'm quite capable of doing that, you know." I was huffing and I forced myself to breathe slower.

"Yes, I researched you. Probably around the same time you googled me. But it's your help, not your money, I want." He looked up to the roof, through the glass panel. There were no stars. "Do it for Amy, not for me." After a pause, he asked, "Agreed?"

"I'll let you know after I've spent some time with Amy at the retreat. If I decide against this proposal, I'll liquidate some stocks till I'm in a position to repay you in full. That's the most I can agree to."

He nodded and looked out the window, away from me. He brushed his hands together to signal our business was concluded. He pulled a pillow out from below the seat and leaned against the window.

I sat back. The swaying of the car was making me sleepy. I yawned again, louder this time.

"If you want, you can recline the seat on your side. Go ahead and try to sleep," Li said.

My eyes closed, but my brain was figuring out a plan. I would definitely stay with Amy and hope to convince her that beating her addiction would allow her freedom from Li as well as from alcohol. But Li didn't need to know that yet. There was something honourable and cleansing in taking control of one's future, as I well knew, and maybe I could help Amy do just that.

# CHAPTER 35

## *JOAN*

## *Friday, February 1, 2008*

## *Montreal, Canada*

At noon, I was seated in Le Montrealais Bistrot-Bar, more commonly known as the Fairmount Bistro-Bar. Hans stood at the entryway. He scrutinized the faces of the diners but didn't recognize me.

Although the long ponytail was gone and he now wore a businessman's suit, I recognized him and was surprised when he didn't return my smile. Soon after Joe's diagnosis, we'd toured Belgium. When we met Hans, Joe thought it was a chance encounter. He didn't know I'd arranged it. We were tourists indulging in waffles and lattes in a crowded outdoor café in Brussels. A skinny stranger with long blond hair approached and asked if he could share the table. Joe questioned him about his occupation which led to a debate about suicide, death, dying, heaven, and hell. It was Joe who'd asked for Hans's business card. At that time there was some support for Death with Dignity on our side of the pond but legalization of assisted suicide had only come to the state of Oregon, which had a residency requirement.

"God does work in mysterious ways," Joe said when Hans left.

"Really, Joe?" I said, mocking him. "But I'm glad for you. I know it's what you want." I wasn't really sure what I thought at that point. I threw parts of my unfinished waffle to the pigeons which clustered around our table causing all the tables nearby me to scowl and cluck at me. "Je m' excuse. Pardon. Pardon." I said, trying to look very sad and apologetic.

We paid our bill and left to roam around the central square in Brussels, otherwise known as La Grande Place.

"Do you think there's a God?" Joe asked. He didn't look at me.

"Well, if there is, he's a devil," I said. I touched the top of his spotted hand. "We're here by a fluke, our lives are meaningless, and our only options are choosing how to live and die."

"Joanie! And they call me depressing." He laughed.

I looked up and realized I'd kept Hans waiting too long. I stood up and waved him over. "Nice to see you again. Please sit, Hans."

"It's Mrs. Sax, isn't it?"

"Joan is just fine. Thank you for coming." I passed him the wine list. "And have a look at the menu. You have time for lunch? Oui?"

We ordered a charcuterie tray and two glasses of Sauvignon Blanc. He placed a small envelope, bulky because of its bubble-wrapped lining, on the table. I slid it onto my lap and into my purse without opening it.

His hair was stylishly short now, and his suit seemed tailored in the typical European fashion. My hand moved to my dry, brittle hair. The grey roots were beacons advertising the fact that I'd stopped caring. Ever since Esther had died, I'd been looking forward to this meeting.

I recalled Joe had done all the talking last time. Hans sipped his water while I folded and refolded my napkin on top of the table. What a socially inept pair we made. As soon as the waiter brought our food, Hans dug in. He stabbed a piece of cold chorizo and gulped it down without chewing. He drank a full glass of wine and asked for a second.

"Are you by chance ill?" he said, coughing that familiar smoker's cough.

I shifted in my chair. "No, but this is my insurance policy," I said, patting the purse hanging from my chair back. I cleared my throat.

"*Pas de problem,*" he said. "However, I need your assurance these medications won't be used by anyone else other than yourself." He gazed at me and I nodded. "Physician-assisted suicide is available in many places. However, without a doctor at hand, things can go wrong. I must know my instructions are clear." He picked out a sliver of cork from his wineglass and clucked rudely.

"Yes, I know that, Hans. I remember the last time we had this conversation. It was a traumatic experience for me, too graphic and too cloak-and-dagger. Sweden's laws have relaxed since then. Other countries will follow, I'm sure. They have to —"

He waved his hands, as if to block out the sound of my voice, and we sipped our wine. He held a slice of cold meat up to his lips and pulled it off the fork with his teeth. "A wonderful sampling." He smacked his lips. "Is this the famous Quebec Oka?" he asked. Eventually only bread crumbs and grease spots lay on the meat and cheese tray.

I drained my wineglass and let my gaze drift to the falling snow. Hans's voice droned on, but I'd stopped listening. My foot tapped, and I glanced at my watch. I heard him mention guilt-ridden customers and wondered if he knew that applied to me at one time. Whether I was clinically depressed or just worried about turning into Alice and falling into a dark, scary rabbit hole where nothing is familiar, I wasn't sure. As Rachel had once said, "You've got to get busy living or get busy dying."

Last I heard, Rachel had relocated to Hong Kong. And Amy, who'd been unsuccessful in her latest suicide attempt, had ended up a vegetable. Sam and I were no longer in touch either, but that was a long, sad story I kept locked up. Hans mentioned Alzheimer's and regained my attention.

"What did you say?" I asked.

"I said I have many clients in the early stages of Alzheimer's who want their permanent sleep meds before they forget where they've put them." He laughed a distasteful laugh.

I shoved my plate into the centre of the table. "I'm sorry, but I have another appointment. Thank you for coming." I placed a thick envelope on the table and excused myself.

The weather had turned frigid, and the snow fell heavily. I took a deep breath and felt the cold burn inside my chest. I didn't think of myself as lonely, although this was my seventh winter without Joe. There just weren't many people whose company I enjoyed besides the two women I'd met in the riding association of the Liberal

Party. We were trying to force our federal politicians to deal with assisted suicide for people with several conditions, not just to obtain legislation for the terminally ill. Specifically  our subcommittee worked with the mentally ill and their families. Organization for people with Alzheimer's needed advocates to speak up for them. I pulled at my running nose and stared into space. Sadly, we hadn't made much progress. It was my friend, Sally, who had pointed out we were like those women who went before us and drafted a proposal about when to act with regard to abortions, and before that, women's suffrage.

I picked up my pace, aware that I was enjoying the sound of the crunch under my feet and the brisk air. I saw something in the window of a boutique and wondered if I ought to buy Sylvia a gift. No, she was still the bitter, hard-to-please individual who wouldn't be happy no matter how hard I tried. I had to admit, I sometimes identified with her cynicism. Sylvia seemed determined to outlive us all. And with all her faculties intact. It just wasn't fair.

I traversed St. Catherine to arrive at the museum. Montrealers were a different breed from Torontonians. The well-dressed shoppers were as interesting to study as the shop windows. As it happened, Montreal was the one Canadian city Joe and I had never been to together. I stood in line at the ATM. Was that Sam Hoffman? No, thank God.

I'd seen him once right after our Royal Caribbean cruise. He'd called and said he wanted to come to Toronto and explain about Carla. "I've got a better idea," I said. "Meet me in Montreal, and we'll have a romantic weekend in the old city." What a disaster that had been. He talked about Carla over French onion soup. It was our first breakfast on the *Liberty* all over again. I pulled a string of melted mozzarella from the side of my mouth, splattering soup all over the front of a silk blouse and staining it forever. He'd been so absorbed, he hadn't noticed.

"Carla and I are over for good this time. I'm done talking about her. But she did show up and present me with a son, so we've got to get along for his sake."

"What's his name?" I asked. It was embarrassing that he knew so little about his own son. We shopped and saw a movie premiere that evening.

Sam beamed, impressed with his abilities when he ordered our late dinner in French. "I can do that in Spanish too, I'll have you know."

I couldn't help rolling my eyes and looking to see if anyone nearby had overheard. He loved the movie, while I hated it. Every comment he made hit me as superficial and shallow. None of the film's characters seemed authentic to me, and one spoke with a false French accent, but Sam hadn't noticed. All he could comment on, to explain why he enjoyed it so much, was the scenery. I'd been so bored that if I'd been there with anyone else, I would have insisted we leave.

I ignored the "Stop" sign because I was inclined to yield. Rachel used to tell me I was too serious, that life wasn't meant to be taken so seriously. So here I was, not taking myself or this situation so seriously. What was the worst that could happen? Even with all the drama, I remembered the cruise as a happy time, my first foray into the world of being a young widow.

In the hotel room, I removed my makeup with care. I felt my heart racing, and I pulled on the brush in my attempt to smooth my hair. The butterflies I felt in my stomach gave me a thrill because I hadn't had sex with anyone since the cruise and that was over five months ago. I opened the body lotion provided by the hotel and slopped it over my hands, shoulders, arms and inner thighs.

He played me like an instrument, his touch light and sensual. I heard a crescendo when I came.

"Yes! Yes, Rachel!" he called.

I turned to ice. At first I tried to make a joke, not wanting a confrontation, but it couldn't be avoided. I jumped up, ran to the bathroom, and splashed cold water on my face. That Sam and

Rachel had been intimate was a shock. I packed up and left the room. The Fairmont provided another suite but I remember not sleeping much that night, recalling Sam's comment, the way he'd defended himself.

"Joan, calm down, it's not like you were emotionally mature enough for a long term relationship then anyways," Sam had said.

In front of the Museum of Modern Art where I now waited, a Chihuly glass sculpture stood. It'd been purchased in 2005, three years ago, and was still the most expensive piece of art outside a public building in Canada. I saw Neil approaching the orange-and-yellow octopus-like sea creature. I ran around the front. His arms engulfed me before my feet even closed the space between us. While hugging him back, I rubbed my hand back and forth over what was now a grey, almost white, buzz cut.

It had all started when I'd taken him up on an invitation to lunch with his father once and liked the old man's residence so much, I moved Sylvia in soon after. Neil and I took the two of them, my mom Sylvia and his dad Chuck, out to lunch at least once a month. If she weren't literally blind, she might not have thought we made such a perfect couple. The last time I'd seen Neil was the day of his father's funeral. We began keeping up by phone after his monthly visits ended.

I waved and rushed into his outstretched arms.

"Princess, you look wonderful." His large hands rubbing my back filled me with a sense of security and love—though we never spoke of love. Love is what I'd had with Joe. Lust is what I'd had with Sam. This was different: no longer platonic, better than contented, but defying definition.

The exhibit was inspirational. Such creativity, colours, and grandeur. Wandering among the beautiful creations of mere mortals made me think life had a purpose. Galleries of all kinds filled me with light as well as awe. But today, I held my breath, worried that Neil's lumbering form might knock a fragile piece and bring it crashing down. I felt relieved when we exited without incident.

"Want to go over to Mountain Street for a café au lait and pastry?" I'd developed a sweet tooth and could not resist the pain au chocolat of these French bakeries. Although it was a steep street and precarious to manoeuvre in the best of weather, Mountain Street had an old-world charm I loved.

"So who were you meeting this morning?" Neil asked, as we treaded carefully through the snow.

I stumbled and grabbed hold of a freezing iron railing. The adrenalin rushed to my head, and my eyes widened in the cold air. I blinked repeatedly. A pain shot up my leg from the ankle. My eyes teared up, and I swore at the ice that hid under the fresh snow. One hand touched down on the sidewalk, and I lowered myself to sit on the curb.

"No, Joanie. No, you can't sit here. We'll get you back to the hotel and get some ice on that." Neil positioned himself behind me and used both hands under my arms to pull me up. "Lean here while I hail a cab." I started patting my pockets, searching for my gloves, but my balance wasn't any good. I wobbled. "Don't move!" Neil yelled. "Sorry, I just don't want you falling," he said more softly.

Neil was a gentle lover. He hugged me and cuddled after. "It's only nine. Do you mind if I turn on the sports channel?" I smiled, turned on the bedside lamp, and found my book. He acted as if he didn't mind the too-many-to-count interruptions when I shared ideas or special descriptions or plot twists from whatever novel I was reading. Loving this way was a developmental stage we all progressed through like childhood, adolescence, adulthood and old age, but without labels. Only the young who documented everything, tagged everything and posted everything needed to label the stages of love.

Neil's dark skin was barely wrinkled. His head rested against me, and I rubbed his light grey buzz cut, enjoying the feel of the bristles as if I were running my fingers through the short pile of a carpet. He reached for the remote to turn off the television.

Once my light was off, he turned toward me. I leaned in to kiss his skin, which smelled of his special body lotion, one that I still hadn't gotten used to. It went on oily and soaked in eventually. I thought it was a bodybuilder thing when I'd first seen it and laughed, insulting him. That seemed so long ago.

Neil snuggled closer, his dark eyes still closed. "I hope it's all good, whatever you're thinking."

I kissed him on the lips.

He inched up, resting on one elbow. "I want you to check your calendar in the morning, tell me when you can next visit the farm in Colorado. Maybe March? April?" he said. "I don't like waiting so long between visits."

To describe his property as spacious would be an understatement. Neil loved space—space filled with nothing except natural fibres and wood, which was why the interior of his glass and wood bungalow was so beautiful. He also enjoyed cooking and eating at home. I understood why he preferred living there, but I still had family in Toronto.

"Will you think less of me if I admit that, at this age, I like eating more than sex?" He laughed.

"I might feel the same, but I'm not admitting it," I said.

His large hand cupped my face and kissed me. His voice was muffled, but I heard him say, "Good night, Princess."

I lay in the dark thinking about how much we'd grown together, how much we shared in our tastes and interests. I'd never imagined we'd end up this close. It began when I'd rented his summer cottage, that first time. I took it for a week with the kids and their significant others. After the first week when they left, Neil joined me and we had the place to ourselves. He taught me to chop wood for the cold August nights. I liked the outdoors less than I had when I was younger. There was a lunar eclipse one night and I recall saying I'd like to see it if I was awake but he'd never get me to agree to sleeping outside on the hard ground.

"Okay, Princess," he'd said, and thus my nickname was born. His cottage was on a lake in Ontario but totally hidden from the road and the water. It was less than two hours from my midtown home. The drapes were slightly parted and I watched the shadows dance across the ceiling behind the chandelier as I recalled so many good times. My eyes closed, although sleep was nowhere near.

The tossing and turning had started. I hated these nights. I couldn't sleep and I became so tired, I felt sick the closer we got to dawn. I wanted sleeping pills so badly, I could barely stand it. It was four o'clock.

"Why aren't you sleeping? Is anything wrong?" Neil asked. He turned toward me, placing one hand on my shoulder.

I leaned forward, kissed the side of his face, and rubbed his shoulder. "Nothing's wrong. Go back to sleep."

"Is your ankle bothering you?"

"Not really, but I'm going to take another Tylenol. I'll be right back." I got out of bed, found my purse, and padded into the bathroom. I took the two bottles Hans had brought me and added them to my toiletry kit.

I was leaning against the washroom door, wondering if it was safe to leave them in there, when I felt Neil pushing against the door.

"What are you doing?" he asked. I couldn't hold him off. The door flew in, and I moved out of the way, not sure how I'd explain myself. With one hand I held firmly to the edge of the sink; with the other, I clutched my toiletry bag to my chest and stared in the mirror at Neil's angry face.

"Flush them down the toilet," he said.

I didn't ask how he knew. "No," I replied, feeling nothing but defiant and defensive.

"You've been obsessed with this ever since I first met you. It's not healthy."

My back was to him, but our confrontation continued through the mirror. Neil couldn't understand.

"Don't you see? I want to go out before I've deteriorated and lost the ability to control my destiny."

"But not now. You can't deny you had a great day today; we had a great day" He put his hands on my shoulders and tightened his grip. "Say you'll consider talking it over with . . . I don't know who . . . someone?"

"Come on, Neil. You know if I told a psychiatrist the truth, something awful would happen. That's the Catch-22. I have to lie every time I see a therapist and am faced with that mental health questionnaire, the one that digs to find just how depressed a person you are. I'd never admit to considering suicide. Some people, even educated people, think only crazies take their own lives." I turned around to face him and exhaled loudly.

"When did you get these?" he asked, taking my toiletry bag out of my hands and picking out the two bottles with foreign labels on them.

I hugged him and buried myself in his warmth. "I got them today. They allow me feel like I have options, that's all." I couldn't look him in the face.

Neil passed me some tissues. "Can't you trust me to take care of you?" His strong hands gripped my shoulders. "Don't you know I love you?"

I swallowed. It was the first time Neil had used the L word. I didn't know how to react.

"I know you've stopped feeling guilty for supporting Joe's plan. But you still have bad feelings because at the end he made his decision without you. Tell me how that's any different that what you're considering doing?" Neil ran a hand over his head. He'd confronted the elephant in the room. The tears welled in his eyes, and he stomped back to bed. I followed. We sat side by side. "It's crazy. For no rational reason, you're assuming you're going to die like Esther. Joe was actually sick when he took his life." Neil reached forward to move the hair off my face.

"Those pills . . . those pills . . . are my insurance policy," I mumbled. "I wasn't going to do it now. I don't want to wait too long... to get anywhere near as bad as Esther got."

"Then let me hold them for you. Do you understand how much—" He lifted my chin and kissed me, spreading my lips with his warmth. "Joanie, I want you in my life. Life is about handling change as well as about making choices. That's it." Neil turned the lamp on and licked his lips. "It's a slippery slope. What if you never get Alzheimer's, or what if there's a cure next year and what if—"

I put a finger against his mouth. "Do you know anything about dementia? Have you read the studies?" I said. The words came out mixed with mucus and tears. I pulled at my dripping nose. I had such terrible genes.

He pulled me into his chest. "Say you'll marry me. I want to grow old with you." The words drifted down the side of my head and into my ears. He held my head firmly in his large hands, letting me think before looking at him and responding.

"For better or worse?" I said. I pulled back, wanting to hold his gaze while I answered. I heard Neil breathing through his mouth, then a silence, a held breath.

"I know what I'm getting into. Say you'll marry me," Neil repeated. His big white grin dried up my tears.

"Of. . . of course I will." We hugged, sitting there, face to face on the side of the bed.

"Wow. Big day tomorrow. Gotta get a ring. And call the family." Neil rubbed his brush cut. It seemed a new habit we both picked up. I looked at my long wine coloured nails and couldn't remember when I'd broken that bad habit. Nice to think life involves constant change and change is always good. "Better get some rest, you. You're going to be a bride." Neil was gushing with enthusiasm which warmed my heart and if he'd been white, I was sure I would've seen him blush tonight.

I lay on my back and rested my head on one bent arm. I should have been thinking about the wedding and all the rest of it but my mind wandered in a different direction. I was happy not to be a young idealistic bride. I was experienced and cynical. Had I been younger I would have had a hard decision to make; whether to bring children into today's world. I recently read a nonfiction book which listed frightening statistics about the States. If the literacy rate in the U.S is only 7% how low must it be in Kenya? The overpopulation problem seems to be getting worse in spite of China's attempt to impose  the one child per family rule. Everyone's seen news footage of starving children with distended bellies and refugees trying to escape countries where terrorists have taken over from legitimate governments. Nuclear and biological warfare are the stuff of nightmares and horror films but their existence necessitates crazy spending on research  just to be prepared for those who are ahead of us. There are more megalomaniacs allowed to address the United Nations than ever before and dictators are popping up more frequently than groundhogs. I rolled over and sighed.

Neil turned toward me. "Think wedding." He kissed my shoulder and put his head back on the pillow.

I smiled and continued ruminating: So many problems. Sadly the only people smart enough for the job are too smart to want the job. I picked up my head, rolled on my side, and punched my pillow before stuffing it comfortably under my head. The world is a mess, and ironically, each successive generation thinks they're doing everything better while making everything worse.

"Don't tell me—you're thinking about the state of the world so when someone asks tomorrow if you had a good sleep, you can give them the speech?"

"Nope: I'm thinking the reason I want to marry you is that when we watch the news or have dinner we talk about things that matter even if we disagree about the particulars.'"

"Okay, but switch it up; think about where you want the wedding. Night Princess."

# CHAPTER 36

## JOAN

### Sunday, August 29, 2010

### Toronto, Canada

Neil answered the door while I was out cutting flowers from our terrace garden. I heard Ian's voice and rushed across the flagstone floors of our penthouse condo. I loved these visits with Ian and Jordy, the newest addition to our family. Ian wore a baby sling that allowed him to carry the baby facing him, pressed up close to his body. I watched Neil undo the straps and pull Jordy into his arms. Little Jordy grabbed the wire-framed glasses perched atop Neil's bald dome. It had taken some time, but eventually our friends and family became comfortable with our living arrangements. They were even happier when we recently tied the knot. Ian was our biggest supporter.

I took the glasses out of Jordy's hands and kissed his fingers.

Ian hung up his coat. "Where were you Sunday?" he asked Neil over his shoulder. "You're supposed to be my gym buddy. I was expecting to go for lox and bagels later, like usual and you let me down."

"What are you, a girl?" Neil teased.

Ian shrugged and shook his head. He laughed and bounced Jordy over his shoulder.

"Come in, come in, can you stay for dinner?" I said.

I kissed Ian's cold cheek, took the baby from Neil, and carried him into the family room. I erupted into a string of nonsense words. "Jordy, Jordy, Jordy, Joe. Jordy, Jordy, Jordy Joe, Sweet as sugar and good as gold, Jordy, Jordy, Jordy Joe," I sang as I rocked him in my arms. "Oh, my!" I cooed and made a loud sound as I kissed his middle. "Oh, my little Jordy." I snuggled into his short neck and inhaled his baby powder scent. "How come I love you, like I do, do, do? How come I love you, like I do, oh yeah!" I stood Jordy up, forcing him to put some weight on his short stocky legs, and bounced him up and down on my legs.

"Are you going to talk to me or should I leave?" Ian said, teasing.

"Somehow you were able to get the afternoon off. Say you'll stay for dinner."

The baby stood for a bit before his knees gave out and he collapsed on my lap, giggling. His full cheeks puffed out and made his large dark eyes shrink to slits. I said, "Each time I see him, I see a stronger resemblance to his grandpa than the time before. This hair . . . it's so straight and so white."

A silence fell like a blanket over the room. Even Jordy was still.

Neil cleared his throat and offered to get Ian a drink. I got up to follow Neil into the kitchen, but Ian stopped me with a hand in the air.

"I think I always knew but couldn't understand why you and Dad weren't honest with Rebecca and me," Ian said. "Wouldn't Dad have loved this little boy? You both knew he planned his exit. It still makes me mad sometimes."

"Of course Dad would have adored his namesake, but he wasn't given the luxury of time," I said cautiously. I shifted in the big wing chair and drew my legs up under me. I knew we'd have this conversation one day. "But Ian, you were young . . . there wasn't time . . . there were legal issues. And you'd already expressed such disappointment about your dad rejecting chemo."

Neil returned with a tray, carrying three cans of cola and shot glasses with ice. "From my perspective, it was a hard decision your dad made, and he didn't want anyone trying to talk him out of it or feeling guilty later because they'd tried and couldn't talk him out of it. Don't you understand, Ian?" Neil sat on the big sofa on the other side of Ian.

My hand moved to pat Ian's knee, to reassure him there was no malice in our motives, but the knee bounced more wildly and his voice rose.

"But after . . ." Ian said. "But there was lots of time after. I was hurt you didn't treat me as an equal." He shook his head. "Actually, I've come to think I'd do what Dad did too, so yes, I do understand. But I guess I was hurt he confided in you and not me too."

Little Jordy fussed. Ian picked him up and cocked his head knowingly. He dug into the large diaper bag and pulled out his supplies. After spreading the plastic-backed sheet on the loveseat, he quickly changed the baby's diaper.

Ian went into the kitchen to dispose of the dirty diaper. "I guess the line I grew up hearing from you, 'Life's about making choices,' bears out from beginning to end," he said. The sun was going down and the pinkish-grey sky was picturesque.

"About dinner, we were going to barbeque." I said. "Your Uncle Phil is joining us."

Ian smirked and questioned me with his eyes. "Dad never trusted him—hated him, in fact—and now you're having him over for dinner? I don't understand."

"Come on, Ian." I sipped from the can and took some roasted almonds and cranberries from the bowl on the coffee table. "People change. One of those choices we get is choosing to forgive." I smoothed the silk blouse I was wearing, waiting for him to comment further.

With the baby held firmly against his body with one arm, Ian poured his drink into a glass and added ice. "You do surprise me, Joan. First you get a job volunteering at the art gallery, then you join another book club, and now you're entertaining relatives you don't even like." He said he had to warm a bottle he'd brought, so we all moved into the kitchen.

I carried the dish of nuts and cranberries to the kitchen island. Neil hopped on a stool and opened a beer. "Want one?" he asked.

"No, this is fine," Ian said.

I took the baby, who had fallen asleep over Ian's shoulder, and transferred him to my own shoulder without waking him. But he jerked and began crying at the buzz of the microwave. Before you knew it, he was howling. That kid not only had Joe's hair but also his lungs and ability to project his voice. I followed Ian out the French doors leading to our expansive rooftop terrace.

Ian positioned Jordy on his lap, threw a flannel sheet over one shoulder, and held the bottle to the baby's lips. It was impressive to see Ian's confidence and ease in handling the baby; he remembered to stop halfway and burp him, then resettle him with a bib in place to finish the rest of the bottle. After the final burp, Ian asked me to get the baby's Roots cardigan from the diaper bag. Finally, as if he'd just completed a marathon, Ian slumped forward, brushing his own thick dark curls off his forehead.

"Your dad would be so proud to see what a capable young father you've turned out to be." I was very appreciative of Ian's efforts to dress Jordy in things I'd bought him, whenever he came to visit. Joe would have gotten such a kick out of that too. There was so much he was missing. Neil sensed the shift in my mood and was holding my hand as we looked across our balcony at the beautiful skyline with its iconic the CN tower. I crossed my arms in front of me and rubbed away the goose bumps.

"Want me to get you a sweater?" Ian asked. "It's starting to feel like the end of summer, isn't it?" he said.

I felt glad that he said what I wanted to hear. My shivering signalled the end of August, nothing more.

"Shit, I'm sorry." He hit his forehead. "I remember why I dropped by today. I came to say congratulations. Saturday's *Star* had the results of a photo contest, and you won second prize. Not too shabby!"

I looked at Neil, who was beaming. "I entered her photos in it. She didn't even know until after I'd done it."

"Thanks," I said. "It was a total shock when I won and saw my name in print! Can you imagine?" I sat back and wrapped my shawl closer around me, gazing up at Neil. "I'm getting myself very busy, busier than I want to be, I sometimes think. The photography is still just a hobby, but I've started volunteering at the AGO every other month." I nodded at Ian's smiling but surprised expression. "I'm loving that. I enjoy taking students on a tour and explaining things to them."

"Really, Joan? You've given up lobbying for assisted suicide in Canada? I never thought I'd see the day," Ian said.

"No, I'll never give that up. I've been a member of Dying with Dignity Canada for years now and their meetings keep me up to date on developments. Those rights are as basic as the right to abortion or gay marriage or gender equality, in my opinion" I saw Ian roll his eyes and look to Neil. I pulled a tissue out of my pocket and blew my nose. "If you've got time to kill, we could discuss something new; what do you, as a conservative, think of adoption by gays?"

"Stop, Joanie." Neil brought me a blanket to put across my lap. "She's just teasing," he said to Ian. "But Joanie has been writing speeches for Dying with Dignity. It shows, huh?" He patted me on the back. I shrugged and tried to push his hand away, making an angry snort, although the sound effect was unintentional.

"But, in all seriousness, if I'd been Esther, I would have wished to die instead of existing with no quality of life in a home where I did little more than breathe. And eventually, she forgot how to breathe. I can't imagine a worse death." I swallowed. "Remember that when and if my turn comes," I said, looking from Ian to Neil in turn. I refilled the nut bowl and offered it around. Ian opened the fridge and grabbed a beer from it.

"You must realize that Esther couldn't choose for herself. There's a difference. There won't be any laws that circumvent that issue," said Ian.

"Not so. A person could have had a living will to express their wishes."

"It's never going to happen, Joan." Ian seemed to be speaking to Jordy. "Our laws will never allow for mercy killings whether they're doctor assisted or not."

Okay . . . enough, we've heard it all before," Neil interjected, wiping his forehead.

It was pointless to argue. Privately, I acknowledged that my work with doctor-assisted suicide research wouldn't bring change in my lifetime. However what we were doing was important. We were laying the groundwork for the future. Talking about it made my heart pump faster and filled me with energy. But time wasn't on my side. That was why I realized I needed something else which Hans provided. I finished my drink and swallowed a burp.

"What's wrong?" Neil said, aware of my every move.

"Nothing , silly," I said and moved to plant a kiss on his cheek.

Ian, as always, strove to avoid any lengthy discussion about the topic I had such strong feelings about. "Anyway," he said, walking to the closet, "you have all these new pastimes and a social life to boot. You've come a long way baby, as the old cigarette ad used to say."

"Oh, no, Ian," I said, a hand on the edge of the closet door. "This means you're not staying for dinner." It was a statement, not a question.

"When you and Shelley work out your issues, the four of us can have dinner together. It wouldn't be so hard if you could just meet her halfway."

"Don't you know how stubborn this one is?" Neil said, placing a big arm around my shoulder.

I took the baby from Ian while he put on his wind breaker. "I am not." I said, moving away from Neil. "I love Shelley. She's just strong like I am. I can't even remember who was wrong this time." I looked at Neil who'd been bugging me all week to call her and apologize for being pig headed. "How about you and Shelley come for dinner next Saturday, then? Tell her I'm sorry."

Ian made a face over the baby's head.

Neil squeezed me close and kissed the top of my head. "Never mind, I'll call her myself," I said. We walked Ian and the baby to the elevator, the one that opened to both penthouses on our floor. When the door closed, I breathed a sigh of relief. I loved our frequent visits with Ian but I had a lot to do before our company arrived for dinner.

# EPILOGUE

## *Friday, October 19, 2018*
## *Thornhill, Canada*

The fall colours lift my spirits each and every year. Yellow leaves, red leaves, orange leaves, and piles of decomposing brown ones blanket the front lawn of the pretty low rise we moved into. Neil, in his wrinkled khakis and flannel shirt lies sprawled on the sofa with his book held close to his face. I open the closet door in the hall. He hears me and puts the book down.

"What are you looking for?" Neil asks. He walks toward me and waits, hovering over my shoulder as I riffle through the coats.

"The rake. Those leaves need raking," I answer.

He turns me to face him. His kiss is soft, and there's patience in the voice that calls my name.

"Joanie, remember Anna? She's the building superintendent. She does the raking."

I nod. I don't know where I've heard that name before. "Anna? I think I had a friend named Anna once. She was Chinese," I say.

"No, you're thinking of Amy. We met her on a boat trip." Neil goes everywhere with me, but I don't remember being on a boat with him. Sometimes he follows me from room to room inside our apartment too. I wander into the bedroom and close the door. It made a whining sound.

It creaks open, and he sees me on the floor kneeling. "Is everything okay?" he asks.

When I nod, he returns to the TV room. I pull out the top drawer from my bedside table and it falls onto the carpet. Clunk. "Oh my."

Neil's back. "What was that?" he asks before seeing me on the floor, with the top drawer beside me and a pile of stuff scattered around me. "Oh I see," he says. "I'll be back: going to get some oil to fix that squeaking hinge." He leaves.

I spread around the contents: my address book, paper clips, hand lotion, elastic bands, business cards for coffee shops, hairdressers, nail polish salons and shoe repair places, pens and sharpeners, but not pencils. I smile at that. "What good are pencils without sharpeners?" my mother used to say. There are my readers, my first digital camera, a slew of four-by-six old photographs, a kitschy Eiffel tower key chain, my wedding photo with Joe, fridge magnets collected while travelling, and a photo from my honeymoon with Neil. Some of this I should throw out.

Neil returns with a yellow-and-black tin. "Can I help you find something?" he asks, bending down. His knees creak, and I see his facial muscles contort as one knee touches the hard surface.

"I'm missing my engagement ring," I tell him. "I remember putting it in a little blue box inside this drawer but it's not here." My hands start rolling over one another as if my brain knows what I'm about to say before I do. "I take off my ring every night before I apply my hand cream."

"I know, Princess." He kisses my hands. "That's why your hands are so soft." Neil rubs his thumb over the back of my hand. "You still use the hand cream, just like you remember, but you lost that ring a long time ago."

"I did not. You're lying. You stole it." I throw his hand down and lean on the bed to help me get off the floor.

He takes hold of my arm. "I don't want any help from you!" I yell.

Neil walks out, leaving me shaking on the side of the bed. I start to cry. It's scary living with a man who steals from you.

My first husband Joe was the trustworthy one. Neil tells me Joe died, but I could have sworn he visited me just last week. If he'd died, even if we were divorced, surely I would have gone to his funeral. Sylvia tells me Neil loves me, has been my husband for over ten years now and takes good care of me. I believe her but why don't I remember that? She gets upset when I ask her.

I rearrange the contents of the open side table drawer. There are a few stacks of papers with elastic bands. I notice my ring is missing and want to remember to ask Neil about it later. I don't see the blue box it came in either. Sticking out from under the bed is a large manila envelope. Did it come from the drawer? It says, "insurance policy," in big bold letters. I open it, curious. Inside is a note: *"Give this to Neil if you want to know where your policy is."* And it's signed by me. I recognize my own writing.

"Neil, sweetheart," I call, walking into the living room. I smile. I feel good that I know exactly who I am talking to. But my hand is shaking badly. I place the letter and envelope in his outstretched palm. "Do you know what this is about? You look after our insurance, don't you?"

Neil has something in his eyes. He rubs them. His face collapses upon itself like he's about to sneeze and he covers his nose but he doesn't sneeze. It's dripping into his mouth. Instead he grabs the bridge of his nose. "Yes, Joanie, I know. You don't have to worry. I'll take care of it."


THE END